Death
on the
Page

Also available by Essie Lang

Trouble on the Books

Death
on the
Page
A CASTLE BOOKSHOP
MYSTERY

Essie Lang

CROOKED
LANE

NEW YORK

Copyright © 2020 by Linda Wiken

Published in the United States by Crooked Lane Books, an imprint of The Quick Brown Fox & Company LLC.

Crooked Lane Books and its logo are trademarks of The Quick Brown Fox & Company LLC.

Library of Congress Catalog-in-Publication data available upon request.

ISBN (hardcover): 978-1-64385-294-2
ISBN (ebook): 978-1-64385-315-4

Cover illustration by Teresa Fasolino
Book design by Jennifer Canzone

Printed in the United States.

www.crookedlanebooks.com

Crooked Lane Books
34 West 27th St., 10th Floor
New York, NY 10001

First Edition: March 2020

10 9 8 7 6 5 4 3 2 1

Chapter One

"Did you just say that Savannah Page is staying overnight *here*, in the castle?" Shelby Cox found that information hard to process, knowing how protective the Alexandria Bay Heritage Society was of Blye Castle.

"I did indeed say that. She'll be staying overnight in the guest suite after doing her Saturday signing," Edie answered, some amusement in her voice. As a member of the Heritage Society board, Edie Cox had been in on the decision to allow someone to actually spend the night in Blye Castle. She'd expected a surprised reaction from her niece once the news got out, and she wasn't disappointed.

"I can't even begin to imagine what that will entail," Shelby continued. "What about security? And what if she damages something, like one of the antiques? And where will she stay? What is the guest suite, anyway?"

"This isn't so new a thought for the board. We've actually discussed the idea of having a guest suite to rent on weekends over the past couple of years. We just never followed through on it before, and what better time than when a best-selling author comes to visit? One of the larger bedrooms that's right next to a bathroom has been prepared, renaming it and the bathroom as the guest suite. That was its original purpose." Edie waved her right hand toward the ceiling, which Shelby took to mean upstairs. "If this is successful, the board may make it a permanent feature."

"So, it sounds like the board obviously wants to compete with Singer Castle."

"The word *compete* hasn't been used, but we know the guest suite is definitely a big attraction at Singer, and I'd imagine, if handled properly, it could be here also."

"That sounds like a complex project. I'm glad I'm not involved in it."

Edie grunted as she reached for the top shelf and turned a book face-out. Shelby smiled. It wasn't often that she and her aunt, the co-owners of Bayside Books, got to work together. At least, not until winter set in, when they would close down the secondary castle location. During the tourist season, Shelby was in charge of the store in historic Blye Castle on Blye Island in the Thousand Islands, while Edie ran the main store in Alexandria Bay, New York.

But this was a special occasion coming up, the thirty-fifth anniversary for the store, and both locations were going all out over the weekend with displays, specials, and a book signing at each shop—tomorrow on the mainland and Saturday at the castle. It was also a celebration of Edie's tenacity. She'd run the store for the past thirty or so years entirely on her own, adding the second location when Blye Castle was opened to the public by the Heritage Society.

Shelby's arrival in Alexandria Bay seven months earlier had come at a welcome time, as Edie had needed a helping hand in running the bookstores while she mended from a knee replacement, but now Shelby had made the decision to make it a permanent move.

"You and me both, Shelby."

"Well, having Savannah Page agree to do signings of her new book, *Lies and Death: The A. R. Smith Story*, at both stores is a great start for the anniversary celebrations," Shelby agreed. "Even if it is true crime," she couldn't resist adding.

"What do you mean by that?"

"Well, when I think of a book launch, I think of fiction."

"Ah, you still have some things to learn about being a bookseller," Edie replied with a smile. "Her previous books have sold well in the store, so why not celebrate this new one? Customers love the hoopla."

"That makes sense. I'm looking forward to meeting her."

"As am I." Edie's smile was wide as she walked back to the counter. She still favored her right knee and, on occasion, had been known to admit that almost four months of physiotherapy might not have been enough.

"But what's with the castle sleepover?" Shelby couldn't let it go. "Is she doing research or just wanting to hide out?"

"You'll have to ask her when she arrives in town on Friday, although in her letter to the board, she did say she was researching a book about Joe Cabana. At least, that's what I heard." Edie got a glint in her eye. "Maybe she was hoping to run into his ghost."

Shelby put down the box of books she was holding, feeling a bit unsettled. Although Joe Cabana had been murdered on the island decades before, the more recent death in the spring still bothered her. She jumped slightly as the door to the bookstore flew open.

Taylor Fortune leaned against the doorframe and breathed deeply and slowly for a few seconds before waddling over to the desk.

"What on earth are you doing here?" Edie asked, hands on her hips.

Taylor gave her a small wave and eased herself onto the stool behind the cash register, her right hand rubbing her extended belly. "I begged Shelby to let me come in for a couple of hours. I was going stir-crazy at home, and I promised to sit on this stool until it's time to go home." She folded her hands in a prayerful mode as she said in a pleading voice, "Please, ma'am . . . more time in the store."

Shelby burst out laughing. "You sound even more desperate than when you called last night."

Taylor explained to Edie, "My mother-in-law arrived a few days ago. I didn't expect her until after the baby is born, but she wants to help set up the nursery and do some shopping. Can you imagine? She doesn't think we can get the nursery ready?"

She looked from Edie to Shelby, but neither commented.

"Maybe she just wants to share in the prebirth excitement?" Shelby guessed, never having been in the situation herself.

"Be that as it may, and as well-meaning as she might be, I don't think I can take it. You don't know what she's like. She's only been here a few days, but she takes over and doesn't let up. Chuck, my big, strong police officer husband, is back to being a little kid in her presence. He's no help in battling for me. I'm on my own with her. So, I told her I was working here in the store for a couple of hours each day until the baby comes. I hope you don't mind." Taylor ran her hand through her short blonde hair.

Shelby shook her head. "I don't mind at all, but I wonder what your doctor will say. He did want you to take it easy, didn't he? Has that changed? Are you sure he's okay with this? And what about the boat ride over here to the island? Doesn't that make you the least bit nauseous?"

"It never has before. I have great sea legs, you know. And the doctor will call it stress relief. After all, he has warned me to keep my anxiety level low. I can't with her around."

"Does Chuck know how she affects you?" Edie asked, walking over and placing a hand on her shoulder.

Taylor shrugged. "I guess part of him knows, but like I said, mother, child. It's hard to get out from under that woman's thumb."

"Well, as long as your doctor approves, you're welcome here whenever you need the excuse to get out of the house," Shelby said. "We want you to stay healthy and safe."

"Thanks, Shelby. I'm going to be all right, really. I've passed the critical months that gave me so much trouble when I miscarried last time. And I'm feeling great. I really am."

"Aside from a major case of mother-in-law-itis," Edie volunteered.

Taylor started to laugh until it turned into hiccups. Shelby quickly brought her a glass of water, and Edie rubbed her back.

"Okay, we stay away from hot topics and jokes," Edie said. "Let's discuss our upcoming author signings instead. We were just talking about Savannah Page and her overnighter here in the castle."

"Seriously?" Taylor gasped between hiccups. Her look of bewilderment made her look even younger than she usually did, almost like a kid in high school rather than a mother-to-be in her midthirties. Of course, it was mainly because of the youthful pixie cut framing her heart-shaped face.

"Serious enough," Shelby jumped in, bringing her up-to-date.

"Oh, wow. She's brave."

"Why do you say that? You don't believe in the ghost stories, do you? You've never mentioned them before."

Taylor quickly shook her head. "But just think about it. It's a big castle, which can be sort of scary on its own. At night, by herself? Would they really allow that?"

"The board has hired someone to work as a butler to stay the night and attend to her whims, so she won't be alone," Edie answered.

"Even so, from what you both have said about the board members and how they coddle the castle, I'm surprised it's happening. Does she at least have a friend staying with her?"

"I understand her fiancé is traveling with her," Edie said, "but it sounds like she's doing it solo. We'll find out soon enough. She arrives early tomorrow afternoon and will do her signing in the main bookstore at four PM. Then we'll take her, and I guess her fiancé, out to dinner. I've made reservations at Absinthe & Aurum. You and Chuck are more than welcome to join us, Taylor. It would be easy to add two more."

"That would probably mean bringing my mother-in-law along, and believe me, you don't want that. Thanks anyway. It would have been nice to escape."

Edie gave Taylor's arm a pat. "All right. Now, you just settle yourself on that stool, or better yet, take a chair with a back on it. And we'll start hanging these anniversary sale banners." She glanced at Shelby and then over at the door. "I'd hoped Matthew might have time to help us, but I guess we're on our own."

Shelby shoved a comfortable chair over to Taylor and then set up a folding step stool on one side of the bay window. She was about to stand on it when the door swung open.

"Matthew," Edie cried out. "Great timing. I'm not that keen on Shelby doing the climbing."

"Oh, but it's okay if I fall and break my neck?" Matthew Kessler replied, a smile on his still-tanned face. As the castle caretaker, and in fact, the person in charge of the entire island, he spent a lot of time outdoors with his beloved gardens.

"That's not what I meant, and you know it."

"Well, don't say it's because I'm a woman and not capable of it," Shelby said, enjoying making her aunt squirm a bit. It was all in good fun, and Taylor soon joined in.

"I can understand you not letting me do it, Edie," Taylor said with a chuckle, "but I do think Shelby is quite capable."

"Thank you," Shelby said with a nod of her head.

"You're welcome."

Edie threw her hands in the air. "All right. I get it. You two are welcome to arm-wrestle for the honor if you'd like." She looked pointedly from Shelby to Matthew.

"No, thanks," Shelby answered first. "I'd hate for Matthew to think he showed up in vain."

"Always a pleasure, Shelby," he crooned, although his eyes were on Edie, who blushed.

He climbed up and secured one side of the banner, then moved around to attach the other.

"What's the scoop on our author staying overnight in the castle?" Shelby asked as he finished.

He folded the step stool and placed it in the back room before answering.

"I probably know as much as the rumor mill does. Apparently she asked, or maybe it was her publisher, and the board, in their great wisdom"—he glanced quickly at Edie—"decided it would be good publicity. Isn't that right, Edie?"

Edie nodded. "There wasn't a lot of discussion. We also had the vacant board position to discuss. I felt the decision about opening a guest suite had already been made before it was presented at the board. But all the boxes were ticked—insurance, supplies, extra staff—so it was a go. Security was my big concern, but our valiant leader felt that having a butler on hand overnight would be sufficient. And, of course, you'll be on the island, Matthew."

"As always. My only concern is the security, but I wasn't consulted."

Edie made a clucking sound in her mouth. "You are truly underappreciated. I really would have thought you'd have been in on the initial talks."

He shrugged. "I know my place, and right now, it's in the gardens. I'm still pulling out some of the wilted late-blooming summer flowers. Ladies," he said with a salute from his nonexistent cap.

Shelby looked around the store and smiled. She knew it would be a weekend to remember.

Chapter Two

F riday dawned sunny and warm, perfect weather for a September morning. Shelby got up early so she could enjoy a coffee on the upper deck of her rented houseboat before rushing off to the bookstore.

There were three ways to get to the upper deck: from the outside by a ladder at the side and by stairs at the back, and from the inside via a door in the former wheelhouse that had been converted into a bedroom when the houseboat was taken out of river circulation. That part of the deck was small and sported a wrought-iron bistro table with two chairs, positioned for an unhindered view of the river and nearby islands. The front deck was larger, allowing for two Adirondack chairs, a larger table, and a portable grill. Shelby thought of that as her entertaining deck.

She settled onto one of the soft, tufted chair cushions she'd bought for the iron chairs shortly after moving in. In a few minutes, J.T., the itinerant cat of somewhat questionable heritage who had adopted her a few months earlier, jumped onto her lap, which wasn't unusual. He had the look of a Maine coon but the coloring of an orange tabby. Whatever. It worked. She'd named him after her favorite singer, Justin Timberlake, for no reason other than that she'd heard one of his songs on the radio while she was trying to come up with a name.

She pulled back her long, curly dark hair and gave it a twist, tucking it behind her head as she leaned back. She smiled as the sun warmed her face.

She heard a car horn in the distance and checked her watch. She'd been out there for half an hour and, she suspected, had dozed. She pushed out of the chair suddenly, sending J.T. scrambling, and they both made their way back inside.

After a quick shower and a bowl of granola, she called J.T. and placed his dish on the floor. She took a bowl of dry food with her into the bedroom and left it in a corner, knowing J.T. could find it and self-feed, which would tide him over until she got home after dinner at the restaurant. Taking a bit more care than usual in choosing a not-too-clingy tunic top and leggings, she finally deemed herself ready to go and locked up, making sure J.T. was still inside.

She made her usual stop at Chocomania, her favorite shop in the Bay, since it combined coffee and chocolates, on her way to the dock. She greeted the owner, her good friend Erica Bryant, with a quick hug.

"Good to see you," Erica said, placing a single dark chocolate truffle on a piece of wax paper. "For you. Tell me what you think."

Shelby bit into it and closed her eyes in pleasure. "Amazing," she said, once she'd swallowed every bit of it. "Caramel and something with a bit of heat. Chili powder?"

"Cayenne, but close enough. You don't need any more for the bookstore right now, do you?"

"Maybe after this weekend. But I'll stop by for some personal stock after work tomorrow."

"Sounds good, and tonight's the author dinner, right?" Erica pushed some stray hair back into the scarf she wore to keep it off her face. "I'm almost ready to cut this mop off." Although her auburn hair was short on the sides and top, the draping bangs were long and often seemed to have a mind of their own.

Shelby knew a cut wouldn't happen—at least she hoped not. She so wished her own curly dark hair looked as good as her friend's. Maybe she was the one who should get a cut, but she couldn't picture herself with short hair. Not with these curls, anyway.

"Tonight is the dinner, and it's at your brother's restaurant," Shelby said, then asked casually, "How's he doing these days?"

Erica eyed her before answering. "If you mean, how is his on-again, off-again relationship going, I'm pretty sure they're in *on* mode. Please tell me that was just an idle question."

"Definitely. He's a nice guy, but there were no sparks when we went out on that one date. It's just that I haven't been to his restaurant in a few months, so I was wondering."

"I should think that's all you're doing, what with your knock-out Coast Guard agent around." Erica wiggled her eyebrows.

Shelby smiled, letting her thoughts wander to Zack Griffin for a moment. "I haven't seen as much of him these days, actually. He seems to be working all hours."

"Ah, the river never sleeps."

"Very sage, Erica."

They both laughed. Shelby took a quick look around the shop, noting that only one of the eight round tables was in use. The light sand-colored walls displayed various delicious-looking paintings and photos of chocolates and truffles. Among them were also some photos of chocolate-loving kids—the one with twin preschoolers holding melted chocolates in their hands was Shelby's favorite. The kids were local, and their mom was a high school friend of Erica's, but Shelby hadn't yet met them. Erica had planned some group picnics over the summer, but they both had been canceled at the last minute, one because of the weather, the other because of sick kids. *One day*, she hoped.

Shelby finally left, latte in hand. She made it to the shuttle in plenty of time and stood in the short lineup until they were allowed on board. Terry's Boat Lines, not one of the regular tourist boat lines servicing the islands, used one of its smaller boats as a shuttle to get castle staff on-site a good hour before the regular shuttles started running.

She could see across the river to Heart Island and the spectacular Boldt Castle. It was much larger and more impressive by far than Blye Castle, but she wasn't complaining. In the months since she'd started working at Blye, she'd come to love the three-hundred-square-foot room the store rented at the front right corner of the castle, the one she thought of as hers. Which was true in a way, because, as Shelby had been surprised to learn, she was actually a co-owner of the two bookstores, thanks to her mom.

The summer had gone by much too quickly, and in another few weeks, when the tourist season officially ended and all three of the destination castles closed until the spring, they'd be moving most of the castle stock to the main store for the winter. Shelby had never gone through a winter in Alexandria Bay and was wondering just how the bookstore would manage when the small town rolled up the tourist carpet. But her aunt Edie had been going strong all these years, and Shelby was determined to work hard to help her achieve more milestones for the bookstore in the future.

Just then, one of the crew members appeared at the side of the shuttle and signaled them to board. Shelby decided to spend the short twelve-minute trip at the railing, letting the roiling wake mesmerize her. In fact, she was surprised when the shuttle docked at Blye Island.

She didn't have any help in the store for the day, unless Taylor popped in. That was okay, but she had asked that Cody Tucker help at the castle on Saturday rather than working in the main store. He was their longtime part-timer who this year was available only on the weekends he came home from college. She knew they should have hired another part-timer by now, especially with Taylor unavailable, but it just never seemed to get done. What still amazed Shelby was the amount of paperwork involved in running the stores. It seemed to suck up all the extra hours. She really should task Edie with hiring; reading résumés would be a good way to keep her at home to do some more recuperating.

Shelby doubted it would be overly busy, as there were no school or day camp tours these days. Mainly just seniors or the odd tour bus with foreigners on board, eager to see the legendary charms of the castle. She'd found she enjoyed meeting the inquisitive, gesturing customers, knowing they were there to enjoy and, hopefully, to shop. She unlocked the store and got the coffeemaker in the back room going, then gave the shelves a quick dusting.

*　*　*

By midafternoon, Shelby felt in desperate need of a break. It had been busier than she'd thought, with a steady morning of shoppers, much to her delight. She'd also heard that several of them were planning to attend the signing later at the main store. That's what Shelby and Edie had been hoping for—a couple of successful sales events, bringing in enough profit to help carry them over the slower winter months.

She locked up an hour early so she could help out at the main store during the signing. She had just locked the door behind her when she heard the whistle from the tour boat approaching the island and hurried to the dock. During the short crossing, she busied herself with a mental checklist of everything she needed to bring to the island for the next day's signing. It wasn't a long list, but she had yet to host an event with total confidence.

Shelby had to almost elbow her way into Bayside Books. Her eyes were drawn to Trudy Bryant, who looked like she was frantically trying to juggle the cash register and the long line of customers. Shelby took a look around the space, wondering why Edie wasn't right there beside Trudy, helping to ring up sales. Maybe she was unpacking more books in the back room.

The featured author, Savannah Page, looking exactly like the photo on her book jacket, sat at the signing table. Her shoulder-length dark hair had red highlights that danced in the sunlight streaming through the window. It framed a full face that looked determined but friendly. Shelby felt instantly that this was someone she'd like to get to know better, and she looked forward to dinner after the signing. A tall, bearded young man, whom Shelby had never seen, was opening Savannah's books to the title page for her to sign. Her fiancé, maybe?

Shelby threaded her way to the back room.

Edie was nowhere to be seen. There was no way she'd leave Trudy on her own at such a busy time. This wasn't right.

This wasn't like Edie.

Chapter Three

Shelby rushed over to the counter, ready to help Trudy bag the purchases.

"Where's Aunt Edie?" she asked under her breath.

"I have no idea. She said she was going home for a late lunch. That was about two hours ago. I haven't heard from her since then. I called a couple of times, but there was no answer, and I'm getting worried."

Shelby was about to ask why Trudy hadn't called her to come over immediately but realized that would sound accusatory. And besides, she couldn't have just locked up the other location any earlier. She tried not to give in to a feeling of panic.

"Who's the man with our author?" she asked instead.

"That's her fiancé, Liam Kennelly. He's traveling with her and has been a dear, stepping in to help. I knew it would be busy, but this is crazy." Trudy took a moment to push the lock of shoulder-length gray hair that had fallen across her face back into place.

Shelby allowed herself a moment of satisfaction, thinking about the number of sales, but then focused on Edie. "I'm going over to Edie's to see what's up. I'll keep you posted. But first, I'm going to call Cody and see if he can come in. He should be back in town by this time of day."

Trudy nodded, not taking her eyes off the lineup.

Cody answered on the third ring and agreed immediately to come help out. Shelby felt relieved. She'd been worried when he started college that they'd really miss him, but so far, he'd come home most weekends and was usually available to work. Of course, he'd moved away only a couple of weeks earlier. Who knew what weekend routines he'd establish once he felt more settled in at the college. She just hoped he'd come back to Alexandria Bay more often than not.

She reached Edie's house on Catherine Avenue almost out of breath. Her anxiety had increased with each step. She hoped Edie was all right. It was so unlike her to abandon the store, and even though Trudy didn't seem exceedingly worried, Shelby could tell she was trying to downplay her concern. Besides being Edie's right-hand woman in the store, Trudy was her longtime best friend.

Shelby stood at the front door and took a few deep breaths before opening it. As usual, Edie hadn't locked it.

"Aunt Edie. Where are you? Is everything okay?" Shelby paused, waiting for an answer that didn't come. Hopefully Edie hadn't fallen on her way home or going back to the store. Her knee wasn't one hundred percent healed yet, and anything could happen. Shelby couldn't think of one scenario that didn't involve a bad outcome. Unless Edie had lain down for a quick nap and just kept on sleeping.

Shelby checked the bedroom on the main floor that Edie used these days, then walked through to the kitchen. No Edie. She called out again and looked out the back window. An empty glass and plate rested on the small round plastic table beside two unoccupied chairs. Edie had been there at one point, anyway. Shelby rushed out the back door and down the steps. Edie was lying on her stomach to the left of the sidewalk, beside the flower garden.

"Aunt Edie, I'm here. Are you all right?" she called out as she hurried over. Shelby knelt beside her and Edie groaned, her face turned toward the flowers.

"Damn cat from next door. It went scooting, and I tripped over it. Help me sit up."

"Not before I know you're okay. Did you hit your head?"

"No, but I twisted my right knee. It's quite painful. I'll need to have you help me stand up."

Shelby helped Edie roll over onto her back, with much groaning, and hiked up the long, multicolored skirt her aunt so favored. She saw that the knee, Edie's new knee, looked about twice the size it should. "You can't stand on that. I'm calling an ambulance. It needs to be taken care of."

"No, I don't want to be a bother," Edie said, pushing herself up on an elbow and trying to downplay the groans. "And besides, I've got to get back to the store. Trudy will be swamped."

"I insist we call an ambulance. And Cody is helping Trudy, so stop worrying about that. Oh no, I left my purse and my phone on the kitchen counter. Do not move an inch."

Shelby took the stairs a couple at a time, snatched her smartphone out of her purse, and ran back outside. On the way she dialed 911 and blurted out what had happened. She grabbed a cushion from one of the outdoor chairs and eased it under Edie's head. She debated about getting some of the pain medication she knew Edie kept in the kitchen cupboard but decided to leave that to the EMTs.

She held Edie's hand, stroking it, while they waited. Edie had stopped objecting and was leaning back against the pillow, eyes closed. When Shelby heard the ambulance pull up in front of the house, she breathed a sigh of relief. She called out, and two first responders were soon tending to Edie. After many long minutes of taking blood pressure and other readings, they helped her onto the gurney and wheeled her to the ambulance.

Shelby told Edie she'd see them at the hospital, but Edie insisted she go back to the store and help take care of the author.

"There won't be much to see at the hospital, and I'll probably be enjoying my meds anyway. We have an author to take care of along with a dinner to host, and I'm counting on you to take over. Again."

Shelby squeezed her hand. "All right. I'll call Matthew, though."

That brought a smile to Edie's face, which promptly turned to a grimace of pain.

Chapter Four

All the way back to the store, Shelby struggled with the feeling that she should have gone with her aunt. But when she walked into the store and saw the crowd and a touch of mayhem, she knew this was where she was needed right now. Cody had shown up, and she smiled her thanks at him as she made her way to the cash register.

Trudy raised her eyebrows in a question, and Shelby told her she'd explain when it quieted down a bit. Finally, the majority of purchases had been made and the fans had persuaded Savannah to do a short reading.

"Is that all right with y'all?" she asked Trudy as she stood up.

"Absolutely. Do you want a space cleared over by the bay window?"

"No, this will do just fine. Y'all can hear me, right?" Savannah looked comfortable in front of the small audience. Since Shelby had last seen her, she'd pulled her hair back and secured it at the nape of her neck with a colorful green scarf that matched the tones in her long-knit top. Shelby admired both her style and her ability to wear such a clingy outfit with such confidence. She wished she could pull off something like that.

The crowd tried to get closer to Savannah as she moved around the desk to perch on the corner of it. Her fiancé had wandered to the back of the room, apparently used to the routine. For having so many people in such a small space, Shelby was surprised at how quiet it had gotten. The customers were listening to every word brought to life by Savannah's southern drawl. Shelby briefly wondered if that was how her own mama had sounded. Shelby knew her mother had come from the South, but until recently, that was about all the information she'd had about Merrily Cox.

The spell took a few moments to break after Savannah's final words. Then everyone applauded and the noise swelled once again.

Shelby looked around the store at the happy faces and noticed a woman in a brown coat and beige fedora at the back, moving toward Savannah. In one of her hands she held a letter-sized manila envelope, and she had a look of determination on her face, or what Shelby could see of it with the brim of the hat tipped so far down. She just hoped it wasn't an aspiring author wanting Savannah to read her manuscript. That could be awkward.

"So, where's Edie?" Trudy whispered to Shelby.

"She fell in the garden and hurt her knee, her recovering knee. I called an ambulance and she's gone to the hospital."

"Oh my gosh. I thought she was still mad at me and wouldn't answer the phone or come back until the signing. And then when she didn't turn up . . ."

"What would she be mad about?"

"Oh, we had a silly argument. I think the pressure of the last couple of weeks has gotten to her, what with the anniversary celebrations and the signings. She still doesn't have all her energy back, although she'll deny it if you bring it up, which is what I did, and she got mad."

Shelby sat down on the stool. "I had no idea. I'm sure I could have done more around here if she'd told me."

"That's never going to happen. She won't tell you a darned thing unless she's at her wit's end, believe me. I should go to the hospital when we close up, and then it's bridge night. I hate to leave the dinner on your shoulders, but will you be okay?"

"Sure thing. I did call Matthew, so he's on his way there also."

"That's good. I'll head over as soon as I lock up."

"Thanks, Trudy." Shelby glanced at Savannah, who was sitting down behind the table and taking a sip of water. "I guess we can get going soon now that most of the customers have left, and let Cody close. Why don't you go now?"

Trudy had just dashed out when the mystery woman slapped the envelope on the desk in front of Savannah. "Do you remember me?" she demanded in a loud voice. The woman glanced around the room at the surprised faces, a tight smile on her face. Her black hair peeked out from under the hat, the curls ending above the collar of her coat. She seemed to tower above the other customers.

Savannah looked puzzled, as did the several remaining customers.

"You do look familiar, but I'm afraid I can't quite place you," Savannah said. "I meet so many people at signings and my other events."

"I'm sure you do, but I'll never get to do that, not since you stole my story." She placed her hands on her hips, and although she faced the other direction, Shelby would have bet the woman's expression was menacing.

Savannah's jaw dropped, and it took her a few seconds to recover. "You must be mistaken. I have no idea what you're talking about."

"Oh, don't you? I suppose you also don't happen to remember the writers' festival in Albany last spring? The one where we had coffee after our panel and I ran my idea by you? The one about Joe Cabana, the mobster who died on Blye Island? I know you have a contract for that story, my story, and you're here to do research. My research. My story."

Savannah stood abruptly, knocking her chair against the bookcase. "I'm sorry. You've gotten this all wrong. It's my own idea that I'm working on. I would never need to steal someone else's. I have quite a creative mind, you know." With hands on hips, they looked like they were in a stalemate.

The other woman must have felt that too. "My name is Jenna Dunlop, since you seem to have forgotten it, and I warn you, you'd better remember it. I won't let this go." She shook her finger at Savannah. "And neither will Joe Cabana. There's a curse attached to him, so you'd better watch your step."

She turned and marched to the door, turning back before opening it. "You can read all about it on Twitter, also."

All eyes remained on the door as it banged shut behind her. Savannah slowly sat back down while Liam put his hands on her shoulders.

"That's ridiculous," he said to those remaining in the store. "Savannah would never resort to that. The woman is delusional."

Shelby looked from Liam's determined expression to Savannah's stunned one, then turned to the few remaining customers, who looked like they'd actually been enjoying the entertainment. "Well, that's one for the books, as they say. I want to thank you all again for coming out today. Cody is happy to ring up your purchases," she said, pointing at him as he slipped behind the counter.

Shelby felt someone touch her elbow, and she jumped.

"Why, Felicity. How nice of you to stop in," Shelby said, trying to calm her breathing. She was pleased to see the owner of the art gallery from next door. "Are you a fan of the author or the genre?"

"Both, actually. I was quite pleased when Edie told me about this event."

Shelby assumed that Felicity was a few years younger than Edie, looking very much the glam art gallery owner type, which might explain why they weren't close friends but rather business acquaintances. It always looked like Felicity had just stepped out of a hair stylist's chair, and her black hair never showed any telltale gray. Shelby wondered if there was someone in Felicity's life these days or if she was still processing what had happened in the spring.

Felicity looked at Savannah and then back at Shelby. "That was quite the performance. That Jenna Dunlop should have gone into theatre rather than writing, although from what I hear she's working full time at the Brew House—you know, that pub around the corner. What an awful experience for Savannah Page."

Shelby followed her gaze. Savannah seemed to be just fine, although Shelby could imagine how embarrassed she felt. Shelby felt dreadful for her.

But . . . what if it was true?

Chapter Five

"That meal was absolutely delish—and filling," Savannah said with a broad smile. "Thank you so much, Shelby. I want you to know that I've enjoyed this afternoon more than most signings. I'm just sorry we weren't able to meet your aunt to also thank her. She and I have been carrying on a delightful email exchange."

Shelby marveled at how Savannah had been able to keep up the cheery dialogue throughout the meal. In fact, she hadn't mentioned the verbal encounter with Jenna Dunlop at all. Shelby had realized she should follow the woman's lead and do the same. She did notice, though, that Savannah kept glancing at the door and had been startled when their food arrived. She looked exhausted whenever she stopped talking, and Shelby hoped she'd be able to get a good night's sleep before the next day's signing and her overnight stay in the castle. Who knew how restful that would be?

"Oh, I know Edie's very upset about missing this too. She loves being in the bookstore and meeting authors in particular.

I doubt she'll be able to get around tomorrow, and she definitely won't be able to come over to the island, but we'll see." Shelby sat lost in thought for a few seconds, worried about what was happening at the hospital.

"Well, please give her my best."

"I will, and I know I speak for her, too, when I say we were really delighted you included Bayside Books in your book tour and allowed us to do a launch. How did you start writing true crime?"

"I really didn't know what I wanted to write when I first started out. I just knew I wanted to give it a try, and then someone in my online writing group suggested a mystery. But when I got into doing all the research about murder methods, I got hooked on finding out more. True crime just seemed a good fit at that point. Does that sound a bit weird?"

Shelby smiled. "Nothing in the publishing world sounds weird to me. And that was obviously the right choice for you."

"It was, but I'm starting to feel like I want a challenge these days, to try something a bit different. I thought that writing about a cold case would do it. And when I heard about Blye Castle and the unsolved murder of Joe Cabana, it just clicked." Savannah took another sip of her wine. "I really like Alexandria Bay. It has a homey feel about it. Have you lived here all your life?"

"No, my dad and I moved away to Boston when I was three. It was just the two of us. I moved back only a few months ago, and it does feel homey but also sort of strange. What about you two? How long have you been engaged?" She looked from

Savannah to Liam, hoping her abrupt change of subject didn't seem odd to them. She didn't want to get any further into the reason her dad had moved her away, and she found it so easy to talk to Savannah that she was worried she might do just that.

"Six months, two weeks, and some hours," Liam answered. "Not that I'm counting."

Savannah laughed and reached for his hand. "We met at a writers' event, and after I signed my book for him, Liam swept me off my feet. Didn't you, babe?"

"Yes, I'll take credit for that. And, not to change the topic, but I also want to thank you for tonight, Shelby. I'm actually surprised to find such an amazing menu in such a small town. And this place looks trendy. Again, not what I'd expected."

Shelby glanced around at what had started life as a mansion in the early 1900s. She guessed that some interior walls had been removed to give the layout an open and spacious feel. The earthy colors blended well with the stone fireplace that anchored one side of the room, right next to the massive dark oak staircase leading to what she imagined were offices and possibly more seating areas. She'd never asked. What had caught her attention the first time she'd been there was the wide wraparound porch that, in summer, offered another delightful eating area. She'd reserved a table for that night next to the large picture window in the front, which allowed a view of both the tiny white lights twinkling under the roof all year round and, in the distance, the larger lights of the harbor.

"The owner, Drew Bryant is Trudy's son, from the bookstore. He's a trained chef."

"Really? How nice for Trudy," Savannah said with a laugh. "I love the name of the restaurant, Absinthe & Aurum. It's very memorable, as is the food. Now, if I could just get Liam cooking."

He smiled. "Once you start doing all the housework, babe."

Shelby laughed. She'd enjoyed the last two hours chatting with the couple.

"Well, we really are delighted you're here, and I'm so looking forward to the signing at the castle tomorrow," Shelby said. "As you may have noticed, we have many enthusiastic and avid readers in town, and tomorrow we'll add the tourists to that customer base."

"We're both looking forward to seeing the castle, also," Liam answered.

"Do you mind if I ask why you want to sleep in the castle?" Shelby asked, looking at Savannah.

Savannah glanced quickly at Liam before answering. "It's for research, but also, partly, because I'm fascinated by it," Savannah admitted, crossing her arms on the table and leaning toward Shelby. "The castle, the island—they're romantic, and yet, so mysterious. Don't you feel that way, spending all that time there?"

Shelby nodded. "I do. I totally understand. I remember when I asked my aunt why she wanted a bookstore on the island, she said it was because of the romance of it."

"Exactly. She's right. I feel the same way even though I've never been there. It would have been the perfect spot to spend the weekend with Liam, but I need to stay focused on the research. Especially if Joe Cabana is wandering around."

She winked at Shelby, who glanced at Liam, but his face didn't give away a thing.

"Why Joe Cabana?"

Savannah smiled and tucked a few strands of hair behind her ears. "I'm fascinated by his story, especially about all the rum running during Prohibition. It's history, although it also seems so current, what with all the news items I've been reading about the smuggling going on these days on the river. Just like the old days. And then there are all the stories about his connections to the Mafia and, finally, his murder. From what I've read, it wasn't a mob hit. Maybe something to do with love?" She paused and leaned forward, lowering her voice. "And also, what if those stories about Joe Cabana's ghost are true? I'm open to that. Maybe he'll speak to me and I can add a proper ending to his story."

She grinned, but Shelby couldn't tell how seriously she took the whole idea about the ghost. Savannah didn't mention the curse, either. Of course, the first Shelby had heard about it was when Jenna Dunlop had mentioned one earlier. Maybe Savannah would find out about it in her research. Or maybe Shelby should ask her aunt.

"So, is it his ghost or the illegal activities that first caught your attention?" Shelby asked.

"Oh, definitely the smuggling part of it. I was intrigued when I read about the current-day smuggling ring that was broken up by the Coast Guard recently. In fact, I have an appointment on Monday morning with someone over at their station, but I'm hoping I won't be handed the standard line. You wouldn't happen to have any contacts, would you?"

She looked so hopeful, Shelby almost blurted out Zack's name, but she knew it would be best to ask him first. "I do know someone, and I'll ask him for you." She glanced at her watch. "I'm sorry, I don't mean to rush, but I'm anxious to get over to the hospital before it gets too late and see how my aunt is doing." Edie had already arranged with Drew for the store to be billed for the meal.

"Of course," Savannah said, reaching across the table and giving Shelby's hand a squeeze. "Please give her our best wishes, and thanks again for everything." She looked at Liam. "I think we'll just hang around for another drink before heading back to the hotel, shall we?"

Shelby stood, resisting the urge to ask at least one question about the incident at the store. *Not the time.* "Please do. Enjoy the rest of the evening. I'll see you at one thirty tomorrow afternoon. We'll start the signing at two and go for two hours. You're all right catching the boat on your own?"

Liam stretched his arms out to the sides and leaned back in his chair, grinning. "I have been known to take various modes of transportation on my own. I can even handle a skiff or a small motorboat if need be."

Savannah hit him lightly on his upper arm. "Don't mind him. We'll be there. Don't worry about us. I'm really looking forward to it all. It'll be quite the adventure."

Chapter Six

The next morning, Shelby got up early after a restless night and took her time getting ready to go in to the store. She felt like she'd barely slept and wondered if she could hide away in the back room at the store later for a short nap. *Not going to happen.* For one thing, she didn't have a chair in there. Something to think about? Probably not.

She wasn't sure why she felt unsettled. After all, Edie was in good hands. Matthew's. And she was prepared for the book signing. What could go wrong? Maybe that was it. She couldn't think of anything, but she didn't want to jinx the day.

As she fed J.T., she thought about how much she had enjoyed the dinner the night before. Usually, she felt on edge when in a new social situation, but with Savannah and Liam, she had been relaxed.

She sat at the kitchen counter, coffee in hand, watching the cat scarf down his food for a few minutes, then heated a croissant in the microwave and took it and her coffee to the upper deck. J.T. was right on her heels, and as soon as she sat, he leaped onto her lap. Like he'd been doing this for years. That brought a smile to Shelby's lips. A nice change from the worry lines she was certain had been etched into her face the previous night, after what had happened to Edie. Incidents like that drove home how fond she'd grown of her aunt, even though part of her still struggled with the fact that both her father and aunt had deceived her about what had happened to her mom for so many years. She gave her head a shake, as she always did these days when the disturbing thoughts returned. She was grateful for what she had now.

However, she was a bit hesitant about the coming of the winter months and the fact that her home, the houseboat she rented, would be pulled out of the water and berthed on land. She'd have to move, giving up the somewhat exotic lifestyle she'd been enjoying for several months. Shelby's contingency plan was to move into Edie's house, the Cox family home since the mid-1920s. When she'd first moved to town, she'd been hesitant to give up her independence even for a few months. But now that she had made the decision to stay, she was sure a few months in the house would work out just fine.

Shelby had to admit it would give her the chance to ask some more questions about her mom and dad. What better way than to be in the same house as Edie for hours on end?

She had stopped by the hospital after dinner the night before to check on Edie. The fact that her aunt had refused to stay overnight had created a whole new batch of problems in Shelby's mind, but she had been assured by both Edie and Matthew that everything would work out just fine. In fact, Edie had insisted the injury wasn't all that serious. While Shelby highly doubted that, she knew when to back off and exit gracefully. Matthew had said he'd take care of Edie. She wanted to find him and have a talk about Edie as soon as they both got to the island in the morning.

Pushing worries about Edie to the side momentarily were other concerns about what had happened the afternoon before in the store. She still couldn't believe that woman had actually made a scene, but she had seen and heard the encounter herself. She also realized that Savannah could easily have canceled the second signing. Shelby thought that was what she might have done in the same position. She was grateful that hadn't happened and was determined to make sure the day's event went smoothly and happily. Although she had a small fear the woman might show up again. Maybe she should mention it to Matthew and he could keep an eye out for her.

No wonder she hadn't slept well.

She quickly checked her smartphone and looked for Jenna Dunlop on Twitter. If the woman had followed through on her threat, Shelby wanted to be prepared. However, she couldn't find an account in that name, nor was there any hint of a scandal on Savannah's Twitter feed.

Shelby glanced around the bay one more time, her eyes resting on several ducks floating away from her houseboat. She hated to leave such a tranquil spot, but on the other hand, she also loved being at the bookstore. She left J.T. on the chair, wondering if he would follow her inside and spend the day cooped up or decide it was a day for wandering.

She finished getting ready, grabbed her bags, and was just about to pull the door shut as she left when J.T. dashed inside. She'd made the right choice in leaving out some extra dry food.

She decided to go directly to the shuttle and save her usual visit with Erica for the end of the day. She looked forward to that part of her routine, but today she couldn't shake the apprehension that had plagued her overnight, and it wasn't something she wanted to share. She was certain it wouldn't take long for news about the bookstore confrontation to spread around town. She just hoped it didn't bring out gossipers who'd want to bombard Savannah with questions.

The boat ride over to the island seemed choppier than usual, although there was lots of sun and not much of a wind. As she stepped onto the dock, she spotted Matthew at the bottom of the stairs. He was still there once she'd climbed them.

"I thought we should have a talk about Edie," he said, and turned to lead the way up the path to the castle.

Uh-oh. That feeling had definitely returned. She'd planned to phone Edie from the store, not wanting to wake her if she was having a late-morning lie-in, but maybe she should have done so anyway. She unlocked the door and stepped inside, glad that Cody wasn't due in for another hour.

"What's up, Matthew? How is Aunt Edie this morning?" Shelby asked as she dropped her bags behind the counter.

"She's assured me that she'll be just fine and the whole thing happened because of that cat, so it could have happened to anyone, and not to fuss over her."

Shelby chuckled. Her aunt sounded in fine form.

Matthew grinned and continued, "But I don't think she should be working in the store on her own or even walking there."

"I agree, and I'm sure we can work something out with Trudy. But when she does come back to the store, I could drive over in the mornings to drop her off before catching the shuttle. It's overnight that I'm most concerned about."

He leaned against the counter and pushed his ball cap back, leaving his hair in disarray. The look suited him, Shelby thought. Sort of intellectual, like her dad had often looked when he emerged from his study.

"She'll probably be all right," Matthew said. "There's no reason for her to go upstairs in the house. It's just getting her up the front steps and making sure she doesn't go out back on her own."

Shelby groaned. "Easier said than done."

"I agree, but I think this really shook her up. The surgery had been expected, but this came from out of nowhere. Maybe she'll be a bit more sensible in the future. There's no way she wants to be housebound again and back to using a walker."

"I'm sure she doesn't, but she also seems to think she's superwoman."

"That kind of runs in the family." He peered at her as if he was looking over the frames of nonexistent glasses.

Shelby chose to ignore that. "Do you have any suggestions?" She knew what she was hoping he'd say, that he'd stay over until she got better, but she was also prepared to volunteer if necessary.

He nodded. "I know you've got the cat to look after, so I could move in until she's back on her feet. It's slowing down on the island now, and as long as I get back here early in the mornings, it should be all right. I've got my own boat, as you know. Of course, I have to be here tonight for our overnight guest."

Shelby tried to keep the smile from her face. "That would be great of you, Matthew. I know she'd appreciate it, and I certainly do, too. I could stay with her tonight."

"I'm sure Trudy would be happy to do it also, if you give her a call." He pulled his cap back down over his forehead. "Okay, it's settled. Now I just have to convince Edie." He winked and walked to the door. "By the way, that author sent over some flowers first thing this morning."

She didn't envy Matthew having to tell Edie of their new plans. But now she had a bookstore to run and a book signing to prepare for. And some flowers to enjoy. She found the bouquet of cut flowers, a variety of fall colors and varieties, in a green crystal vase, perched at the end of the counter. They certainly added a cheery note to the place. She wondered, yet again, about the encounter the day before and fervently hoped Jenna Dunlop didn't reappear that day.

By one PM, Shelby wished she'd taken a break instead of opting to work right through her lunch hour. Although Cody had arrived on time, it had turned out to be a busy day, with lots of late-summer tourists. Shelby imagined many were anxious to get a final visit in to the castle before it closed for the winter. She bet it was like that at the other two tourist destinations in the Thousand Islands, Boldt Castle and Singer Castle, as well.

The bookstore door opened, and Shelby glanced up in anticipation. She hoped it wasn't Savannah Page, because she planned to be at the dock to greet her, but the author could just as easily come early.

Chrissie Halstead, who handled PR and, temporarily, volunteers for the Heritage Society board of directors, entered and rushed over to the counter.

"Do you have any idea what's happening out there in the main hall?" She pointed to the door.

"Uh, not really. I've been busy in here. What's happening?"

"It's crowded, that's what, and I have them lined up and waiting for your signing to begin. I wonder if it had anything to do with that confrontation in your store yesterday?"

"You heard about that?"

"This is a small town, Shelby, and the news is all over. You shouldn't be surprised. You know, they do say even negative publicity is good. But back to my concern. I'm worried about all these customers clogging the main entrance. They keep drifting towards it, and I can't spare a volunteer to stand and keep an eye on them." She glanced at the Fitbit on her wrist and gave it a tap. "Is your author here? Maybe you could start earlier to ease the congestion?"

Shelby was caught off guard. Never in her wildest dreams had she anticipated a crowd large enough to throw the ever-confident Chrissie into a spin. "Well, I would, but our author hasn't arrived yet. I'm expecting her on the one o'clock boat. In fact, I was just about to go down to meet her."

"Well, maybe you should consider bringing her inside through the French doors in the conservatory and slipping around the edge of the crowd. By the time they realize it's her, she'll be tucked inside. Then I'll tell the crowd you're just getting her settled and it won't be much longer. Okay?"

"Sure. That sounds reasonable. There's a really big crowd?"

Chrissie smiled. "There is. I've been doing a lot of promoting on social media, and it's paying off." She looked around the store. "Will you need help? Can you handle this?"

"Cody is on his lunch break but will be back any minute, so we should be just fine. Thanks anyway."

"Well, I'll stick my head back in now and then, and if you need help, I'll be happy to do whatever. By the way, I love what you're doing to your hair these days. Ciao." Chrissie gave a small wave and headed back into the hall.

My hair? Shelby hadn't changed the style or the color since she had arrived in Alexandria Bay. It was still long and curly and brown, although she did tend to wear it pulled back more often these days.

She could hear the voices growing louder outside the door. A crowd . . . wow. She hoped they could handle it. She appreciated Chrissie's offer of help. Not so long ago, she hadn't been too sure they would even be friends. Not after Shelby had pegged Chrissie's fiancé as a possible murder suspect in his aunt Loreena's death.

She was glad all of that was behind them. She didn't like to have conflict in her life.

Cody returned, pulling the door shut behind him and turning to Shelby with a huge smile on his face. "It's bedlam out there. We're going to clean up today."

Shelby laughed. "So Chrissie has been telling me. She also wants us to start the signing as soon as Savannah arrives. I'll slip out and wait at the dock. The boat should be in any minute. By the way, you're looking especially awesome today. It couldn't be because of a certain visiting author, could it?"

Cody's cheeks turned red, and Shelby bit back a smile. "Red looks great on you, by the way." She meant his bow tie rather than his cheeks, which had deepened in color.

She hurried down to the dock, feeling her excitement mounting, and arrived just as the tour boat was pulling in. She waited until she spotted Savannah and Liam, gave them a wave to attract their attention, and after quick hugs, led them to the castle and the door Chrissie had suggested.

"There's quite a crowd lined up in the main hall already, so we'll just try to skirt them this way," Shelby explained, holding the French door open for them.

"I'm so pleased to hear that," Savannah squeaked, and Shelby took a quick look at her. She hoped it was excitement she had heard in Savannah's voice. The author's smile, however, didn't seem quite as vibrant as it had the day before. Shelby hoped everything was okay. Maybe Savannah was concerned that Jenna Dunlop would turn up again. Or perhaps, like Shelby, she hadn't slept very well. She certainly looked polished and ready to meet her public, though. The stylish red pantsuit she was wearing hugged her curves, and the white-and-black polka-dot blouse added to the glam appeal.

Liam walked with his hands in the pockets of his windbreaker, watching where he was stepping, seemingly paying little attention to the others around him.

"Here we go. Keep close," Shelby said, and led them into the bookstore, but not before a couple of alert fans tried to pin Savannah into giving them an autograph right there and then.

Cody rushed over to meet them. "I'm delighted to see you again, Ms. Page."

Savannah laughed, delighted. "Please, I thought I asked you to call me Savannah. And it's nice seeing you again, Cody."

His face lit up, and he ushered Savannah to the table. "May I get you some water or coffee?"

"Water would be perfect, thank you." She looked at Liam, who was scanning the store. "This is delightful, Shelby. As nice as, if not even more charming than, the one in Alexandria Bay, but don't tell your aunt I said that." She winked.

Shelby grinned. "She'd be pleased, believe me. Now, do you need anything else?"

Liam came over to stand behind Savannah's chair once again. "I think we're all set," he answered, and pulled a pen out of his jacket pocket, handing it to Savannah. She put her hand on his, but he quickly pulled away.

Something's not quite right, Shelby thought.

"If you don't mind, we'll open the doors right away," she said. "They're worried about it getting too crowded in the hall. I'm afraid we'll have to bring them inside in batches; we're such a small space."

"That sounds reasonable." Savannah pulled an extra pen out of her purse and placed it on the desk. "Liam will open the books to the title page again, if that's okay with you."

"Thanks, Liam." Shelby smiled at Liam, who glanced toward the door as if preparing himself.

Savannah took a sip of the water Cody had set on the desk and also looked at the door, biting her bottom lip. Shelby hesitated, wondering if Savannah needed a minute to calm her nerves, which seemed odd, because she'd been so calm the day before.

Oh well, they had to get started. Shelby nodded again at Cody, this time to open the door.

The first two customers almost tripped over their own feet in their rush to get inside.

By the time four thirty rolled around, Shelby was exhausted. She looked from Savannah to Liam to Cody, and they all appeared to be in the same shape. They'd had new customers arriving even after the signing had officially ended, but Savannah had agreed to continue. Now Cody had put the *Closed* sign on the door. They all needed a breather. It also left them just enough time to put everything back in order and deal with the cash before closing. Shelby let out a sigh of relief that nothing had happened: no woman in a brown coat, no accusations, no distractions at all.

"I can't thank you enough, Savannah. That was another terrific signing. A major success."

"It was, wasn't it?"

Savannah smiled, looking relieved. Shelby had never really thought about how exhausting a signing must be for the author. Having to be "on" for that long. Shelby had never been a big talker, and she could in no way think of how she'd do in such a situation.

"I loved that," Savannah continued. "And such an enthusiastic group of fans. I really hadn't expected this much happening in Alexandria Bay. And, of course, it's such a treat to be signing in the castle. Thank you so much for having me. Both days have really been a lot of fun. I hope we can do it all again when my next book comes out. Maybe do a launch here, since the books will be set in the castle. We'll keep in touch."

Shelby beamed. Nice praise for Bayside Books, and a super idea as well. She could just imagine the crowds for that, although she wasn't quite sure what the Heritage Society would think. Oh well, plenty of time to think about that later.

"So, what are your plans now? Back to the mainland before settling into the suite tonight?"

"Yes. We're having a quick bite at Riley's, as recommended yesterday by Trudy. And then I'll just grab my overnight bag. The board has arranged a ride back over here with Terry's Boats, I think it's called."

Shelby nodded.

"Anyway, I'm supposed to meet him at the dock at seven. I want to be over here before it's dark. Liam is doing"—she looked at him—"what exactly?"

He shrugged. "I'd planned on a walk around town, since we really haven't had a chance to do that, and then early to bed with a book. Not one of yours, I might point out." He grinned. He seemed to be back to the easygoing guy from the night before.

Savannah chuckled. "He's read them all, or so he says. Anyway, thanks again. I hope we'll see you sometime tomorrow before we leave. Will you be in the store?"

"Tomorrow, yes. Maybe I'll see you before you head back to the mainland in the morning."

"Sounds great. Thanks again." She gave Shelby a quick hug and then hugged Cody, too.

He was still smiling twenty minutes later as they waited for the final boat of the evening.

Chapter Seven

Sunday morning openings at the bookstore usually left Shelby with a feeling of anticipation. It could be the make or break day of the week. If sales had been lower than usual, a busy Sunday could change the week's totals, even though they were open shorter hours. Or vice versa. Of course, it wasn't etched in stone; it was just a little game she liked to play. But this morning was different. Yesterday's sales had been amazing, and she had been smiling since doing the tally the night before. She now felt confident that Bayside Books would be in good shape for the slow winter season.

She quickly sorted the cash float into the till, put the coffee pot on, and did a quick survey of the room, knowing it would all be okay. Even though both she and Cody had been exhausted after the signing, they'd done a thorough tidying before closing the night before.

She was all set. She looked out the door into the hall, wondering if Savannah had lingered and might stop by before leaving. There was no sign of Savannah, but the uniformed security, all two of them, looked like they were on a mission. She walked over to Jim Nesbitt, the supervisor of the security staff, and asked what was going on.

He looked surprised by her presence and then guarded. "We're doing a quick search of the castle before we open."

"Why?" That wasn't usual procedure.

"Sorry, I don't have time to talk. I'm really busy," he answered, and walked off at a good clip.

Shelby's curiosity was aroused, and when she spotted one of the younger security staff, she hurried over to him. "What's going on?"

He looked at her and then over at his supervisor, who was headed into the music room. "I don't know if I should be telling you this, but we're looking for Miss Page, the woman who stayed in the guest suite last night."

"What do you mean, you're looking for her? Hasn't she already left the island?" Shelby glanced at her watch.

"It doesn't look like it. All her stuff's still up there in the room, but nobody's seen her." His radio crackled. "Uh-oh, gotta go."

He rushed off, leaving Shelby to worry.

She wondered if Matthew would know more about what was going on. She went to the front door and looked out, eventually spotting him to the left of the doorway, pushing aside some of the bushes that edged the castle, apparently searching behind them.

"Matthew, what's happening?" she asked as she reached him.

He glanced up and frowned. "That author is missing, and we're searching for her."

"Oh my gosh, can I help?" She felt her pulse racing as the worst of her fears, ones she hadn't even realized she had, pushed forward.

He stood up and rubbed his lower back. "Security seems to have it under control. Nesbitt has assigned us to sections, so I'd say just go back inside the bookstore and wait it out."

Not going to happen. "Well, let me help you anyway. There's a lot of bushes along here to check out." She emphasized that by sweeping her arm along the abundance of greenery.

He thought a moment. "Yeah. Okay. I've already done the back. You can start over there at the front corner and work your way across. I'll catch up when I'm finished here. If you have something long-sleeved, it would be best to put it on."

She looked at the sleeves of his shirt—covered right down to his wrists. She did have a sweater she kept at the store for emergencies.

"I'll be right back. I need to get my sweater."

She ran inside and had her hand on the doorknob when she heard voices calling out. She couldn't make out what they were saying, but she followed them up to the second floor and into the room known as Mrs. Blye's sewing room. One of the interior doors stood open, and she could hear several voices. They sounded distant, and she couldn't figure out where they were. She'd thought this was simply closet space. Where were the voices coming from, anyway?

She found the same young security guard, now upstairs in the hallway, and asked what was happening.

"They've found something, down one of the secret passages," he said before hurrying off.

She'd heard rumors that the castle had several secret passages but had never seen them and had assumed they were no longer in use, if they had ever existed to start with. Obviously, she had been wrong. Had someone broken into the castle?

Just then, Nesbitt came rushing out of the sewing room and almost bumped into her.

"What are you doing here? Please go back downstairs and wait in the bookstore."

"What's happened? What have you found? Please tell me."

He paused a moment, as if considering, but shook his head. "Please go now."

He grabbed her arm and spun her around, pointing her to the stairs. She decided it was best to do as he said and walked quickly back downstairs, looking for someone to talk to.

She spotted Matthew coming in the front entrance. "What have you heard?"

Matthew placed a hand on each of her arms and took a deep breath. "I was told they found her body at the bottom of the stairs, in one of the secret passages."

Chapter Eight

Shelby paced the bookstore, trying to keep calm although her pulse raced and her mind seemed stuck on what Matthew had said. She pulled books off the shelves and, after dusting them, reshelved them all. Anything to keep busy while waiting. All she'd been told initially was that the castle would be closed for the day and no one was to leave until the police okayed it.

But what about Savannah? How could that have happened? And what about Liam? Had he been told? He'd be devastated. What could she do?

The waiting was stressful. She debated about calling Edie and telling her but decided she didn't need those details while recuperating. Besides, Shelby didn't have much to tell. She'd go to see Edie once she could get back to the mainland and break the news in person.

She almost dropped the two books she had just pulled off the shelves when Tekla Stone, the Alexandria Bay police chief, walked into the store.

"A bit jumpy, are we?" Stone asked, not unkindly.

"You could say that." Shelby stuck the books back on the shelf.

"A cup of coffee would probably help us both."

Shelby nodded and got them each a full mug from the back room. Shelby couldn't taste the coffee she was drinking, feeling her anxiety level rise as she waited for Chief Stone to start the questioning. She had nothing to hide, but the chief always affected her like that.

"That was much needed. Thank you, Shelby," Stone said, putting her mug down on the side table. She was standing beside the counter and looked every bit the part of a no-nonsense police officer. Even though she only came up to Shelby's nose, that didn't make her any less intimidating. Her stocky build filled her blue uniform and her official hat had been pushed back from her forehead, allowing gray curls to escape.

Stone motioned over to the two wicker chairs, a favorite place for customers to relax while thumbing through books. She waited until Shelby sat in one and then took the other. Between them was a narrow, glass-topped wicker table with sunlight playing on the pattern. The bay windows behind them let plenty of light flood into the small bookstore. The pale-green color on the walls also helped to brighten the compact space. Melon Green, it was called. It was one of the things Shelby enjoyed most about their space in the castle.

"Now, what can you tell me about Savannah Page?" Chief Stone pulled a small black notebook out of her jacket pocket.

"I can tell you about the time we spent together during the signings she did for the store the past two days, one in each location, but that's about it. And we went out to dinner Friday night. Edie probably knows more because she's the one who's been in correspondence with her for the past few months. And she probably has a bio on her author website. Has her body really been found? And in a secret passage? I wasn't really sure there were such things in the castle. It sounds too much like a fairy tale. I've never seen them."

She bit her bottom lip to stop herself from rambling. She was really nervous.

"Well, that answers one of my questions. I was sort of surprised to hear they were never mentioned in the castle brochures. There's no one here from the Heritage board, and those I've talked to didn't have an answer. I would think they'd be a really interesting part of the history of this place. Do you know why they weren't listed?"

Shelby shook her head. "Like I said, I didn't know they were real, although I'd heard rumors."

"Rumors? From who?"

"I can't remember. It was shortly after I started working in here. Maybe one of the volunteers mentioned it. Or maybe even Aunt Edie. I'm sorry I don't remember more."

"That's okay." Stone looked longingly at the empty coffee cup before continuing. "Tell me about the time you spent with Ms. Page."

Shelby tried to provide as many details as she could about the two signings and the dinner, wondering how it could help.

"Oh, and there was an incident at the main bookstore that you should know about. A local resident, Jenna Dunlop, made a scene, accusing Savannah of stealing her idea. Savannah denied it, of course, but it was really upsetting."

"What happened?" Stone paused in her writing, her attention now laser-focused.

"Well, Jenna said her piece and then stormed out of the store. I'd been worried she'd show up here at the castle yesterday for the second signing, but she didn't."

"Do you know anything more about this idea?"

"Not really. She said they'd met at a book festival or something and Jenna had told Savannah about a plot she wanted to start working on. And now, apparently, that's the new book Savannah is here to research. It is, or it was, to be set in the castle. Anyway, this Jenna was loud and made a big commotion."

Stone sat back and seemed to be considering the information Shelby had given her. "Tell me about her."

"Well, she looked to be in her forties and had curly black hair. And from what Felicity said, she's a bartender at the Brew House."

"Okay, I'll track her down. Thanks. That's awfully poor timing for her, unless it's not."

"I just thought of something. Has Savannah's fiancé been notified? Liam Kennelly. He'll be devastated."

"Nobody mentioned a fiancé. He wasn't staying here with her?"

"No, it was just Savannah. I understand that's how she wanted it. She was doing research for her book, you know."

"Yes, something about connecting with Joe Cabana's ghost." Stone made a derisive sound. "Where did this Liam stay, in that case?"

"They had a room at the Skyliner Hotel. I'd imagine that's where he was. He must be so worried."

"I'll get Lieutenant Fortune on it right away. Mind if I use your phone?" Stone asked as she stood.

Shelby nodded and pointed to the counter. She found it hard to make out what the chief was saying on the call, though she'd meant not to eavesdrop on the conversation in the first place.

Finally, Chief Stone turned back to her. "One more thing: did Ms. Page say anything about her laptop? Do you know if she brought it over here with her?"

"She didn't say, but she's a writer who was doing research, so she must have had it with her? Why? Is it missing? Or, you know, she could have been using paper and a pen."

"You could be right. It doesn't look like anything is missing from her room. It just seems to me that every writer would have a laptop with them. Even I use one all the time, except for writing out tickets, that is." Stone paused, then added, "I'm arranging for the shuttle to be here in an hour to take those of you who have been interviewed back to town. I'm not sure if you'll be able to come back tomorrow, so better check first."

Before Stone had reached the door, Shelby called out, "How did she die? Did she trip and fall down the steps?"

Stone turned and looked at her, waiting a few seconds before answering. "It could have been an accident. She either went

54

exploring or maybe even sleepwalking and fell down the stairs. They're awfully steep, you know. But then, there are still a few unanswered questions."

Like, where is that laptop?

Tekla let the pause drag out a few seconds before adding, "Like, how did she fall backward?"

* * *

Shelby was at Edie's and had just finished explaining everything she'd found out, which wasn't much.

Edie sat silent for a few minutes, then said, "You know where the whisky is kept. I'll have some, too, please."

Shelby poured them each a small glass and sat back down at the kitchen table across from Edie.

"To Savannah," Edie said, and downed her drink.

Shelby took a sip and set hers aside. She felt a shiver as she thought about the dead author. "It's quite a shock. I liked her and enjoyed talking to her at dinner, and she was really pleased with both the signings. She'd even sent over some flowers to the castle on Saturday morning." Shelby took another sip and then finished the glass.

"She and her fiancé sent me a beautiful bouquet of flowers, too. Wasn't that thoughtful of them? I'm sorry I didn't get to meet her."

Shelby nodded. "You would have liked her, and Liam. I wonder how he's doing."

"Poorly, I'd imagine."

"I can't get my head around the fact that she's dead. And how did she get into the secret passage? Did someone tell her about them? They must have. How long have I been working at the castle and never known where they are?"

"She was doing research. She'd want to know details like that for her book, especially if it was about a ghost," Edie said.

"I suppose. But she was alone in the castle aside from the butler they hired. I guess the police must have thoroughly questioned him. I'd imagine the board thoroughly vetted him before hiring him."

Edie nodded. "Frank White. He's Oscar Munro's brother-in-law, so we took him at face value. I'm not sure if you've met Oscar, but he owns the leather shop and he used to be a member of the board. He sang Frank's praises, of course."

"What does Frank do when he's not a butler?"

"He's recently retired but used to work at the Skyliner Hotel. And now that he's retired, he spends a lot of time as a volunteer at the soup kitchen, so I'm told. I guess they felt those were close enough work experiences to hire him as a butler."

"They? Weren't you part of that process?"

"I was, up to a point. They took the vote at last month's meeting. Remember, Trudy was ill and I couldn't get away from the store?"

Shelby nodded. "Do you know which room he stayed in at the castle? Nobody has said anything about that."

Edie thought for a moment. "They were putting him in the nanny's bedroom, next door to the nursery."

"So, although he was on the opposite side of the open staircase, he was still on the same floor. You'd think he would have heard something. Savannah must have screamed when she fell."

"Maybe he did. You don't know what he told the police."

"Yet. You know, the Skyliner is the same hotel Savannah and Liam were staying in. That's a coincidence, isn't it?"

"That sounds like reaching, Shelby. It is one of our nicer hotels, after all. Where are you going with this?"

Shelby shrugged. She wasn't quite sure herself. "What about the cleaning staff? They usually start right after the castle closes. I've seen them getting ready some nights."

"As far as I know, they'd been canceled for Saturday and were supposed to get there to clean and tidy the guest suite in particular before the castle opened on Sunday."

"I didn't notice them there, but I guess they've been questioned. I wonder if they saw anything."

Edie shrugged. "You know, those steps are very steep and narrow."

"You've seen them?" That surprised Shelby.

"I have. But I didn't dare use them. They're all made of uneven stones and looked, to me anyway, to be quite narrow. Plus, I'm sure it's all damp and uninviting down there."

"Where do they lead? Are there tunnels under the castle?"

Edie held out her glass, and Shelby brought the bottle over to the table, pouring another half a glass.

"There's a huge wine cellar down there at the end of one of the tunnels, I hear, although I think it's been empty for decades. And there are some other passages on ground level that lead from the kitchen to the dining hall so that, in those days, the servants wouldn't interrupt the swanky dinners. There's even a small painting in one of the dining rooms where the eyes move. The maids would slide the eyes to the side so they could see what course the guests were on."

"That's like at Singer Castle," Shelby interrupted. "Very cool. Do any of the underground tunnels lead outside?"

"I'm not sure. What are you thinking, anyway?"

"I'm just wondering. I mean, the chief did question how Savannah fell backward. How would she know that's what happened, anyway?"

"Tekla is a very experienced police officer. If she said that, she must be basing it on something."

"Think about it, though. How could Savannah have fallen backward? It's not as if she'd easily lose her balance, like an older person might."

"Easy there," Edie warned with a smile.

"Hmm, I'm sure you wouldn't either, Aunt Edie," Shelby added quickly. "I suppose she could have gotten dizzy looking down the steps and then turned away quickly, stumbling. But wouldn't she step backward toward the door before turning away from the stairs? I think I would."

"What are you suggesting? Something more sinister? Another murder at the castle?"

Shelby shrugged. "It's possible, but maybe not probable. Since Frank White was the only person in the castle with her, he'd be the most likely suspect. If not, someone would have had to get there from the mainland. But how would he enter the castle? Now, if the underground passage exits outside the castle, that would be a way in."

Edie sighed. "I think you're being quite fanciful now and blowing this all out of proportion." She reached for the whiskey bottle and refilled her glass. She held it up to Shelby, who shook her head. "I'd really hate to think it was murder."

Another murder? It seemed unlikely. Or did it?

Chapter Nine

S helby finished washing her supper dishes and stuck a dark-roast coffee pod in her Keurig. When her coffee was ready, she headed outdoors. She planned to drink it while enjoying the view from the upper deck again. Living on a houseboat certainly had its perks and this was one of them, something she knew she'd miss when winter came. But Shelby had already put a deposit down for the houseboat once it was back in the water. She only hoped the winter would pass quickly, especially since she wasn't one for outdoor sports.

She'd just settled into one of the two Adirondack chairs, pulling a pashmina over her shoulders, when she heard foot-steps along the dock. She walked over to the railing, leaned over, and smiled. Her favorite guy, Zack Griffin, had almost reached the houseboat.

"Ahoy," she called out.

He looked up, grinned, and saluted. "Sunbathing at this hour?"

"I wish. Would you like some coffee?"

"Nope. I'm okay, thanks," he said, stepping onto the deck and climbing up the ladder. He seldom used the stairs at the back—or stern, as he liked to remind her—of the boat.

She liked watching his powerful arms, but she had to admit she enjoyed watching all of him in action. She felt herself blush at that thought and retreated to her chair.

He climbed over the railing rather than swinging open the gate. He looked at her a moment and then walked over, tilted her chin with his right hand, and kissed her.

Her mind, as usual, questioned if this was really happening, but her heart knew it was.

"Are you all right? I heard about what happened at the castle. That must have been upsetting."

She nodded. "I'm shocked that there's been another death on the island but also stunned because I knew her. And I liked her. She'd just done two signings for the bookstores, and we'd had dinner together on Friday night. It just doesn't seem possible that now she's gone."

Zack squeezed her shoulders. "I know it's hard. Tell me what I can do to help."

"This helps. But I'm not the one who's really hurting. I can't imagine what her fiancé is going through."

Zack lowered his six-foot frame into the chair across from her. "I heard that she'd been staying at the castle alone overnight. I find it hard to believe the board would go along with that."

"From what Chrissie Halstead told Edie, it's great PR. Well, that part sure backfired. But I heard they were considering having the guest suite available for rentals, just like at Singer Castle."

He stretched and leaned back. Shelby could see how tired he was, even though those fabulous blue eyes, the ones that always looked like they were smiling, were alert. His sandy-colored hair looked tousled, like he'd just gotten out of a motorboat. She wondered if that was the case but didn't ask. She hadn't seen him since the previous Sunday night. It must have been a busy week for him.

"That would involve a lot of security hassles, I'd think, but I'm sure they'll attach a large price tag to it." He closed his eyes for a few seconds and then looked at her.

"Hmm. This may put a stop to it. What have you heard from your local law enforcement buddies?"

"Buddies? You mean Chief Stone?" he asked. "I've already told you how she thinks of me."

"A pain in the backside rather than a Coast Guard Investigative Service agent?" Shelby chuckled.

"That would be it. I probably know little more than you do, especially since you were there. I'd expect the State Police were there, too."

"Yes, I guess so, but I haven't talked to any of them yet. Only the chief questioned me. I'd just arrived at the store when they were searching for Savannah." Shelby felt a sliver of a chill run down her spine. "They could tell she'd been in bed at some point and, for some reason, had gotten up and gone wandering. Do you think she was searching for Joe Cabana's ghost? I wonder if she heard something and thought that's what it was."

"Did she seriously believe in that stuff?"

Shelby shrugged. "She said she had an open mind, but I think she was hoping for a connection of some sort. Maybe not a sighting but a feeling of what it was like in the castle in those days. Apparently she was interested in writing the story because of the recent smuggling reports."

Zack almost did a double take. "What?"

"Yeah, that's what she said. She'd read that the Coast Guard had broken up the smuggling ring, and then she started thinking about smuggling during the days of Prohibition, and that led to Joe Cabana's story."

He shook his head. "Well, at least we can remove the smugglers from the suspect list this time."

Shelby took a sip of coffee to cover the flush in her cheeks. She'd been the one pushing that theory when Loreena Swan's body had been found in the Grotto earlier in the spring. It had turned out she was way off base, in relation to the murder, anyway. However, there had been smuggling going on, and the Grotto had been used as a hideaway when boats were evading Coast Guard patrols. That had all transpired just a few months ago, and now this was happening.

"Savannah had an appointment tomorrow with someone in the Coast Guard office so that she could ask some questions about it. Maybe you can find out who it was and pass on the information?"

Zack nodded. "I'd like to know who that is myself."

"What is it about Blye Island? It looks so peaceful and romantic, with this gorgeous castle and grounds. It's not a place you would expect there to be so much death."

Zack reached out and grabbed her hand. "It's not the place, it's the people. Now, there is one thing I wanted to talk to you about, Shelby." He sounded serious, and she turned to face him.

"No getting involved. No asking questions, coming up with theories, or in any way investigating, understood? You're smart, you're tenacious, and I don't want anything to happen to you. Got it?"

She was about to argue with him, but fortunately, her brain kicked in. "Of course not. I'll try not to. I learned my lesson last time. I know it's none of my business."

Zack stared at her, and she tried not to squirm. She really would try hard not to get involved. But Savannah Page had come to Alexandria Bay to do two events for the bookstore. Shelby did admit to herself that the real reason Savannah had come was to stay in the castle, but she was also happy the author had agreed to do the events. And she'd been so friendly. Shelby had really enjoyed the dinner with Savannah and Liam.

What was it about Blye Island? Was it cursed?

Chapter Ten

Shelby sat at her kitchen counter, her breakfast dishes pushed to one side, with a pen and paper in front of her. It was her usual Monday morning dilemma. Namely, what to do on her day off. She knew that housework had to make it on that list at some point. She didn't entertain much, mainly just her aunt or Zack for a light meal, and then she'd scramble to get the place all tidy. But she knew that, at least once a month, a thorough cleaning was necessary, especially with J.T. leaving deposits of fur on various pieces of furniture and accumulating in corners. It was a tough sell, though, as a leisure-day activity.

She acknowledged she wasn't getting very far with any of it. Her thoughts kept turning to Zack, wondering what he was doing at that moment, wondering if he was wondering about her, and at the same time thinking she was behaving like a silly schoolgirl. They had been dating since spring, and although she tried not to get too far ahead of herself, she had to admit her feelings for him were growing. The problem was, when she let her mind wander to a future with Zack, her dad's words of warning ran through her mind: *Be wary of love. Don't jump into a serious commitment.*

Of course, she really was getting ahead of herself. They were still in the early stages. She just had to relax, not overthink things, and enjoy. Part of her knew that; the other part still heard her dad. She shook her head. *Enough for now.*

She turned a critical eye to her living space. Much smaller than her previous apartment in Lenox, but somehow it felt more spacious. Maybe it was the large windows that let in lots of light and gave spectacular views of the water. Or maybe it was the fact that the amount of furniture perfectly fit the space. She hadn't brought any with her, thinking it would be only a temporary move to Alexandria Bay. Instead, she'd sublet her apartment to another editor at the publishing house where she had been working. The idea had been that Shelby would give her plenty of notice before she returned home. When she'd decided to stay on, she'd taken a week off and gone back to pack up her personal items, bringing them back to the Bay. Of course, many of those boxes were now stored at Edie's house. She'd been lucky that her friend had bought the furniture and would stay until the end of the lease.

Shelby decided to do the cleaning first and then make a much-needed food run to the General Store on Market Street. She started writing a to-do list for the day. After a few moments of thought, she added the name *Liam*, knowing this was skulking at the back of her mind. She really should stop by and see how he was holding up, if he was even still in town. She had no way of knowing if he'd already left, but she felt she owed him a visit.

Without giving it much thought, Shelby dialed the police station and was pleased when Chief Stone answered. She realized, too late, that she hadn't given much thought to what she wanted to say.

"Hi, Chief Stone. It's Shelby. I was just wondering if it was okay to go over to the store today, or is the castle still off-limits?" That sounded reasonable, although she had no plans to follow through.

"Yes, it is accessible today. I'm surprised you weren't notified. Anyway, everything is back on track."

"Well, not really everything, right? Have you determined how Savannah Page died?" She crossed her fingers that she'd get an answer.

Stone didn't answer for a few seconds. "It is against my better judgment to tell you, but I know you'll find out soon enough. Ms. Page was murdered."

"How can you be sure?"

"I do know what I'm doing, Shelby. And the coroner agrees. From the way the body landed and the bruising on it, it appears she was pushed and fell backward. Now, that is all I'm saying about this. I have to get back to work. You take care, Shelby."

Shelby shivered as she hung up. *Take care? Murder?* Of course, she'd wondered if there had been foul play, and now that she knew, what should she do? Nothing, according to Zack, the chief, and probably Edie. But she knew she couldn't just leave it. She had some questions and knew she wouldn't hear the answers from Chief Stone.

So, where to start?

With the only other person they knew for sure had been in the castle.

She wanted to talk to Frank White, the butler. Of course, "the butler did it" was trite, and what could his motive possibly be? He was from the Bay, so what connection could he possibly have had to Savannah? Shelby wouldn't know until she asked him. Well, maybe not straight out, but she knew he was at the top of her list of suspects at the moment.

She decided on a visit to the soup kitchen where Frank volunteered, before seeing Liam. There was only one in town, so it wouldn't be a problem to find it. Hopefully that's where he'd be at this hour of the day. Otherwise, she'd have to find another way of tracking him down.

She watched as J.T. slowly uncurled and stretched before jumping to the floor. The chocolate-brown faux-velvet slipper chair was no longer a solid color, matted here and there with cat fur. She'd tackle that and all the other furniture when she got back home. But now, she'd do the floors.

By ten thirty she felt the cleaning part of her day could come to an end and the running-around phase could begin. She started by heading upstairs to get changed. Twenty minutes later she'd turned left on Market Street, a direction she didn't often take. There, close to the corner of Fuller, the sandwich-board sign for the Bay Food Focus caught her eye. She pushed open the door to the soup kitchen, wondering how busy it would be at this time of day.

The room was twice the size of Bayside Books and was filled with tables, each with a white tablecloth and eight place settings. The kitchen was visible at the end of the room, and several tables with heating pan holders were positioned in a line, providing a barrier between the two spaces. At the table closest to the kitchen, three women sat drinking coffee. From the aprons they wore and the hairnets pulled over their heads, Shelby guessed they were volunteers on a break.

"Can you tell me if Frank White is here this morning?" Shelby asked as she approached them, and they turned her way.

"Yeah. He's just taking the trash out," the youngest of the three answered, waving her hand toward the kitchen. "Just hang out and he'll be back in a jiff."

Shelby smiled and nodded. She walked over to a chalkboard on which the day's menu had been written. Beef barley soup, grilled cheese sandwiches, green salad, and chocolate pudding.

She heard the back door open and looked over at the tall, thin man in the beige flannel shirt who'd just entered. He also had on an apron but no hairnet. Probably because he had very little hair, or maybe it was just too light to see. His wire-framed glasses added a look of studiousness, although Shelby could easily picture him in a black tailored suit and white gloves, holding the chair for Savannah Page at breakfast. Sadly, she hadn't been alive to have that breakfast.

Giving her head a shake to toss aside the disquieting thought, Shelby walked over to him and offered her hand. "Hi, I'm Shelby Cox, from Bayside Books. I wonder if you have a few minutes to talk?"

"Nice to meet you," he said. "I'm Frank White, although I gather you know that already. You want to talk to me right now?"

"That's right. I hope you don't mind my stopping by to see you like this. I'd like to ask you a few questions, if you have the time."

"I gather you're not the police."

"No, I'm not. I'm one of the owners of Bayside Books, and Savannah Page had done a signing at the castle location that afternoon. I was just so shocked by what happened. I hope you don't mind if I just try to get a little closure."

He nodded and pointed to the table on the opposite side of the room from the women. He waited until Shelby took a seat, then asked, "What can I do for you? It was certainly a shock all around. I only met Ms. Page briefly, when I arrived at the castle in the evening, and she didn't bother me for anything before turning in. I waited a half hour or so after she said good-night, then turned in myself."

"You were staying in the nanny's room?"

"Is that what it was? I guess, if you say so."

"How would you hear if she needed anything?"

"She had a bell, a real noisy thing that would wake the dead."

"Had she talked about the fact that she would be wandering around, exploring the castle, so that you wouldn't be surprised if you heard something?"

"Nope, not a word about that. She asked me a bit about myself and said she'd try not to be a pest. That's what she said. A pest. Huh." He looked so uncomfortable that Shelby felt sorry for him. He obviously hadn't signed on for a death as part of his duties.

"Had you ever met Savannah before this weekend?"

"Nope, and I didn't really know a thing about her except that my niece is a big fan of her books. I don't read much, but when I do, it's science fiction. Can't get enough of that stuff."

"Really?" *I never would have thought it.* "So you hadn't met her during her stay at the Skyliner Hotel?"

He shook his head. "I retired from that job a good two years ago. I haven't been there much since then. There weren't too many people I wanted to keep in touch with. Most of my friends retired around the same time."

"Hmm. Did you see anyone wandering around outside the castle before you turned in?"

"Nope. I thought I might see that Kessler guy at some point checking things out. I'd met him once a long time ago but didn't see him that night. And, before you ask, I have no idea how anyone got into the castle. From what I could see, the doors and windows were all locked when I turned in. Mind you, I didn't really check them closely. That wasn't one of my duties. And no, I didn't know a thing about those underground tunnels."

So he hadn't heard about them or known if they led outdoors. She tried to think of what else she should ask him but noticed he kept looking at the clock on the wall. He must have chores to do before they opened for the lunch crowd.

"Thanks for talking to me. I won't take up any more of your time," she said standing. She noticed that the women had gone back into the kitchen at some point during her chat with Frank.

"You're welcome, though I know I didn't help much. Like I said, that was a real tragedy, and I feel pretty badly that it happened on my watch." He shrugged. "I don't know that I could have done anything even if I'd been awake. By the way, if you ever have any free time, we can always use a helping hand around here, especially when it comes to dishing out the food. You don't have to be a cook, you know."

"I'll keep that in mind." And she fully intended to do so.

Her next stop was to see Liam, and she power-walked over to the Skyliner Hotel, more for the exercise than to get there quickly. She asked for Liam at the front desk. He was still registered, and she was directed to the house phone in the lobby. After the few seconds it took for the call to connect, he answered fairly quickly and invited her up to his room.

Shelby was totally surprised when she walked into it to find Brad Pitt's double sitting comfortably in the only guest chair. He stood and walked over to her, hand outstretched. "I'm Bryce O'Connell, Savannah's agent. Liam's told me who you are. I came as soon as I heard what happened to Savannah. I'm still in shock. I can't believe Savannah's gone."

They both glanced at Liam, who'd let out a muffled sound.

"I'm sorry, Liam, but we need to talk about it, about her," Bryce said.

Liam nodded. "I know. It's just that I don't think it's totally sunk in yet. Have you heard any details, Shelby? The police chief isn't sharing much information with me." He indicated she should sit on the bed, so she perched on the end of the unmade king.

"Nothing. I was in the store yesterday when they, uh, found her, but the police wouldn't let me open. In fact, the entire castle was closed to tourists for the day. I was questioned and then sent home. I just wanted to tell you, Liam, how sorry I am for your loss. I didn't really know Savannah all that well, but I certainly enjoyed the time we spent together."

"Thanks, Shelby. She spoke highly of you, you know. You did make quite an impression." He walked over to the window and stood staring out at the river.

I did? It was a nice thought, but surprising.

Bryce patted Liam's right shoulder, then walked over to sit beside Shelby on the bed. He lowered his voice. "I'd think, being located right in the castle, that you'll hear things as the investigation continues. Would you consider keeping me in the loop? I feel we both need some closure here." He glanced over at Liam, who hadn't moved. "I understand you were an editor at one time."

"Yes, at Masspike Publishing. How did you know?"

His laugh was quiet and short. "You must remember that very few things are private in the publishing industry. Besides, I looked up your bookstore when Savannah told me she'd arranged some signings. In fact, I checked up on everything to do with Blye Castle."

"Why?" She was curious. She'd never gotten that involved with a client's writing or life. Of course, that might be one of the differences between being an editor and being an agent.

He shrugged. "Savannah could be on the intense side. She'd get an idea, say, staying overnight in a castle or writing about the ghost of a Prohibition-era gangster, and jump right in. I tried to keep her grounded."

"It sounds like you were close."

He glanced at Liam again. "Maybe we could go out for a coffee and continue our chat?"

Shelby also looked at Liam, at his sagging shoulders and air of sadness. She had really wanted to talk to him, but what else could she say at this point? It would border on intrusion. But Bryce was another matter, and it sounded like he might have some answers.

"Sure. There's a restaurant downstairs, or over a few blocks there's a really cool coffee shop, Chocomania, owned by my good friend Erica."

"I'm a chocolate man, myself. I'll just say a few words to Liam and meet you downstairs?"

What could she say to that? "Sure. Uh, goodbye, Liam. Again, I'm so, so sorry for your loss. Please let me know if there's anything I can do."

Liam turned toward her, and she could see that his eyes were red as tears slid down his cheek. "Thank you, Shelby. Thank you for coming over."

She nodded and left the room as Bryce walked over to Liam. After about ten minutes, he joined her in the lobby.

"I feel so bad. I really do wish there was something I could do to help," Shelby said as they crossed the parking lot.

"There might be."

Shelby looked at Bryce. He didn't stop walking but after several more steps continued, "I'm serious about wanting to know how the investigation is going. I think both Liam and I are owed that much, but the police aren't talking. And since you work in the castle, I thought you might pick up on things, like something the officers might let slip as they're investigating or what the talk is around the castle. People love to speculate, and often there's some truth involved."

"I really don't want to get on the wrong side of the police," Shelby said, but refrained from adding *again*.

"I can understand that."

"So, why can't you wait to get the details? The police will inform everyone involved once they've got something to say or have solved the case."

"You saw Liam. He's a wreck, and I'm sure he will be until he has some closure. He's blaming himself for not being there with Savannah."

"But she wouldn't let him join her."

"We all know that, but it still doesn't prevent him from feeling guilty."

"What about you? What's your hurry?"

He stopped and turned to her. "To be perfectly honest, besides wanting this solved, I also would like to get hold of her laptop, and I'm hoping you can help there, too. I need something to give the publisher, some hint of whether there will be a story or not. She might have left detailed notes, or maybe she's even written enough chapters so that I can hire a ghostwriter. So to speak," he added with a sheepish smile.

"She didn't keep you up-to-date about the book?"

"We didn't talk daily, you know. Also, she'd work in spurts." He began walking again, and Shelby scurried to keep up.

"Did you ask the police about the laptop?"

"Yes, but they say they didn't find it."

"Are you sure she had it with her?"

"Of course she did. She used it for everything. Nothing in longhand for her."

They'd arrived at Chocomania, and Bryce reached for the door, holding it open for Shelby as he glanced around the shop. Shelby waved at Erica, who smiled and waved back. Her eyes were on Bryce, though. Shelby gave a knowing smile and followed Bryce to the counter.

"Dynamite," he said, slowly enunciating the word into its individual syllables. "What a cool combination—chocolate and coffee. And beauty, of course," he added, looking straight at Erica.

Shelby smiled and made the introductions, feeling like Cupid. "Erica owns the shop, and she supplies the most amazing truffles for us to sell at the castle bookstore."

"Even better. What would you like, Shelby?"

She placed her order for a latte and a chili-lime truffle.

"The same for me," he said, pulling his wallet out.

"You two sit and I'll bring it all over," Erica said. When Bryce had turned and walked to a table, she grinned at Shelby and licked her lips.

Shelby laughed, then joined Bryce. "Tell me more about Savannah."

"Well, to be honest, she was more than my client at one point. She was a close friend. In fact, we were involved before she met Liam."

"Wow, that must have been hard on you, working with her so closely after that."

Bryce leaned toward her. "At first it was, but my work always takes precedence. She felt the same way, and these days we were totally focused on her career. She was a very savvy writer, you know. She also had a sharp mind when it came to marketing."

He waited until Erica had placed their order on the table, gave her a wide smile, then picked up the truffle. "Excuse me, pleasure before business."

He popped it into his mouth, and Shelby watched as his eyes widened. She noticed that Erica was watching, too, from back behind the counter. In fact, she seemed extremely interested in her new customer. *Interesting.*

"Wow, you were right about the truffle." He took a sip of the latte. "Savannah was my client for eight years, right from the start of her writing career. She queried me and I was immediately intrigued. We worked on her first manuscript a bit, and then I sold it straightaway. She put out a book every two years after that. That was the professional Savannah Page."

Shelby had been savoring her truffle but quickly wiped her mouth with a napkin. "And the personal?"

"As I said, we dated, but for less than a year until I came to my senses. I really prefer not to mix business and pleasure, but for Savannah . . ." He shrugged, his hands lifted in that universal *what's a guy to do* pose. "She met Liam not long after, and they got engaged a few months back. She seemed to be totally happy with him."

He stretched his legs out to the side of the table, looking completely relaxed. "Liam was telling me that you all spent some time together. I was just wondering if Savannah had talked to you at all about this new book she was researching."

"No, not really. She just said she was looking forward to staying overnight in the castle to do research, and she asked me some questions about Joe Cabana. She seemed fascinated by him."

"Between you and me, she seemed a bit scattered about this book at first. She'd never written about a cold case before, but it was more than that. It was almost like she'd lost, or misplaced, her mojo. But then she got this idea about staying overnight in the castle and she was her old enthusiastic self again."

"Do you think that's because of the ghost?" Shelby's grin was mischievous.

"Uh, you've heard. She had this thing about all that stuff—tarot cards, tea leaves, séances. I'm sure she was very open to the idea of meeting a ghost."

"Well, that would have made readers take notice. How did you sell the book to her publisher if you know so little about it? I heard she had a contract for it."

"No, not yet. You can't believe all the rumors flying around. But it would have happened. Guaranteed. They loved her. We all did."

Apparently not everyone.

Chapter Eleven

Tuesday morning it rained. Shelby stared out the window of her houseboat, watching what little activity there was on shore, while she ate breakfast. Her mind focused on the slow day about to unfold. There'd be fewer tourists, that was for sure, and those who showed up would be a soggy lot. She just hoped they'd shake off any clinging raindrops before walking through the bookstore. Since the space was so small, it could be hard to get up close to the shelves without brushing against something, usually books.

She sighed. Oh well, she should be happy for people to show up at all rather than worrying about the splash situation. It would probably be a good day to shift some of the shelves around. Now that they were into the final month before the castle closed for the winter, she was ordering fewer books, and that was apparent in the empty shelves. But some creative positioning would help fill in the gaps. She didn't want to put customers off with too much empty space. She finished her toast and felt better now that she had a plan.

She was just about to grab her raincoat when her smart-phone rang. She was surprised to see that Erica was calling at this hour.

"Good morning, Erica. What can I do for you?" She wondered if she should have planned to stop at Chocomania that morning after all.

"Nothing really. I just thought, in case you didn't stop by, that I would call to thank you for bringing that truly awesome guy into the store yesterday. I'd been wondering who he was ever since seeing him pass by on the street on Saturday as I was closing. In fact, truth be told, I was hoping I'd see him again. And there he was, thanks to you. Did he ask about me?"

Shelby laughed. "Well, he did look interested, but I'm sorry, our talk was all about Savannah."

"Oh, okay. Well, he knows where to find me, and I do hope he'll remember. See you later."

Shelby smiled as she hung up. That shouldn't have been a surprise, after seeing Erica's reaction the day before. But then, as she walked to the shuttle, she wondered how Erica could have seen Bryce on Saturday if he had arrived in town on Sunday.

*   *   *

Once in the store, she carefully took her wet items to the back room and then turned on the coffeemaker. She'd be working alone today, unless Taylor was desperate enough to brave the weather. She hoped not. Alone would be fine, and she worried that Taylor might be taking on too much. That thought surprised her. Or rather, how concerned she was that Taylor have a safe pregnancy. In fact, Shelby realized she'd changed in the few months she'd been in Alexandria Bay from someone whose sole concern was herself to the new Shelby, who seemed worried most of the time about any one of her new friends. That was the secret—she now had several friends and didn't spend all her time wrapped up in her own world.

She thought back to her first day working in the store. She'd been so anxious about talking to the customers that she'd almost fainted. Social situations made her tense, probably because as a child she'd spent many of her nonschool hours with just her dad, a somewhat reclusive college professor. In high school, she'd had a small group of girlfriends but only one date, which she initially thought was a success. But she'd never heard from the guy again. Then came college, and after a few dates with a few guys, she'd fallen hard for one classmate in particular. This time they dated for almost a year, but when he dropped her, she decided that caution was called for in the future. There had been a couple of guys when she'd lived in Lenox, but nothing special. And now, here she was in Alex Bay with new friends, family, and Zack, who might actually be the man of her dreams. It felt good.

She glanced at the clock; there were still twenty minutes before the castle opened for business. Maybe the right time to take a look at the suite where Savannah had stayed. Not that she expected to find any clues. The police would have found anything if that was the case. But she wanted a look at the room, to get a feel for what it would have been like to stay there.

She didn't bother locking up the store behind her as she walked over to the grand staircase, smiling at the volunteers who were heading to their locations. As often happened, she found herself wondering how it had felt for Millicent Blye, walking up this magnificent staircase she and her husband had chosen for the castle when having it built. In fact, how it had felt to leave behind everything they knew, to start a new life in a different country, although at least the language was the same as in England. But the Blyes had been wealthy and, from what she'd heard, part of a large, well-known family. That must have made it even harder for the young wife with an adventurous husband.

Shelby allowed herself to continue the daydream until she reached the second floor. To her dismay, when she reached the newly dubbed guest suite, a strip of yellow crime scene tape still blocked the door. Fortunately, it wasn't sealed but anchored on either side of the doorframe. She glanced at her watch and then looked around. There was no one nearby. She tried the door, and it opened. Ducking under the tape, she pulled the door shut and waited to hear if anyone was coming after her. She took a deep breath and began looking around.

The king-size four-poster bed kept drawing her attention to the opposite side of the room. The pale blue–and–white quilt set off the oak bedframe, making it look comfortable and inviting. It was still turned back, waiting for someone to crawl into the bed. All the walls sported a blue-and-white wallpaper that looked like brocade. She didn't reach out to touch it, though. There was a dressing table, a bedside table, and a tall double-doored armoire, all in a rich dark oak carved in minute detail. On the floor was an almost threadbare multicolored Oriental rug, and a chandelier hung centered in the white ceiling. To Shelby, it looked almost as large as the one in the formal dining room downstairs.

She realized she'd spent more time than she'd planned in the room and glanced around a final time. There was nothing out of the ordinary to be seen, and she had to admit that it hadn't really provided her with anything. It was more the idea of seeing what Savannah had seen during her final hours.

She heard a noise at the door and held her breath. It sounded like the door was being locked. She crept over to it and cautiously tried the handle. Sure enough, it was locked, and she couldn't see a way to unlock it from inside.

She leaned against the door and tried to figure out what to do. The obvious solution was to pound on the door and call until someone came. She'd be reamed out for going inside, but that would probably be the extent of it. Of course, unless Chief Stone had locked it and was still on-site. That might land her in jail, if she was lucky.

After a quick look for another door, which turned out to be a closet, she pulled out her cell phone and called Chrissie Halstead.

"It's Shelby, and I'm locked in the guest suite. Can you find a key and let me out?"

"What are you doing in there?"

"Long story. Please, please?"

She heard Chrissie sigh, although her voice sounded almost like she was laughing. "I'll be right there."

A couple of minutes later, Shelby heard the door lock click open, and Chrissie slipped inside.

"This doesn't look good. What are you doing here? Are you investigating the murder?"

"That's a leap," Shelby said. "I wanted to take a look around; just curious, you know. And then I heard the door being locked."

"That was me. I've been bugging the police since yesterday to take the tape down. It's too lurid for the tourists to see that and draws attention to the suite. Chief Stone finally called and said it was okay to remove the tape but to lock the door for now anyway. Which I would have done anyway. I don't want everyone flocking in there. Now, can we leave? Or did you find something?" Chrissie's shoulder-length blonde hair swung from side to side as she glanced around.

"Nothing except that I've learned my lesson. No more poking my nose where it doesn't belong. Lead the way."

As they left the room, Shelby noticed the tape had indeed been removed. When they stopped at the top of the staircase, Shelby asked if the nanny's room was also under lock and key.

"No, it's not. Why?"

"That was the room used by the butler, isn't it?"

"Yes, we thought it was the easiest one to prepare."

Shelby decided not to waste time with it just then. She could check it later if she wanted. The underground passage was another matter. "Could I please take a look at the secret passageway?"

"It's off-limits."

"I won't disturb anything. I just want to see what they look like and get a sense of what happened to Savannah."

Chrissie thought about it a few seconds and nodded. "Okay, but you need to make it quick. When the tourists start traipsing up here, I don't want them seeing you coming out from the stairway."

Shelby followed Chrissie along the hall to the sewing room. Chrissie turned back to look outside in the hall, making sure no one else was around, then unlocked the door to the passage.

"Do you have a master key or what?"

"Exactly. Now, make it quick." She flicked on the light.

Shelby started with an overview. The walls looked like unpainted drywall, but the steps were stone, some crumbling at the edges. She wanted to look at the bottom and peek along the hallway. She'd really like to follow the passageways and see if there was a way to the outside, but she knew there wasn't time.

She noticed right away how narrow the stairs were and realized it would be easy to trip and fall down them. Is that what had happened to Savannah? When Shelby reached the bottom, the appearance of the passageway changed. It looked rougher, almost like it had been fashioned out of rock. She knew the island was basically solid rock, so that would explain it. She could also feel how cold it had gotten.

She pulled out her cell phone to use the flashlight and studied the floor near the base of the stairs. She noticed some staining, and that brought shivers to her body beyond the colder temperatures. There didn't seem to be anything else to see. She glanced up at the top of the stairs and tried to picture Savannah falling, then wished she hadn't thought about it. Had Savannah screamed? Of course she must have. Wouldn't Frank White have heard it and come to help? Was he hiding something? She might just pay him another visit. She turned to peer along the hallway and noticed that it branched into two farther along.

"Hurry up," Chrissie called out.

"Coming." Shelby walked quickly but with care. When she reached the top of the stairs, she took another quick look behind her, then pulled the door shut.

"Thanks, Chrissie."

"Did you find anything?"

"Not really. Have you ever been down there?"

"No. I knew about the passageways but had no desire to see them. And I still don't. Come on, I hear voices downstairs. It might turn out to be a busy day." She crossed her fingers and held them up for Shelby to see.

They quickly returned down to the main hall without saying anything. Shelby was surprised when Chrissie followed her into the bookstore.

"I was actually on my way to see you when you called," she said.

"Oh, yeah? What's up?"

Chrissie looked from one side of the room to the other, and then behind her. "How is business these days?"

Shelby indicated the empty store. "Slow, but I'm told that it can be like that at this time of year, especially on a soggy day."

"Not so for the rest of the castle, I'm afraid. We've had more than enough crime scene gawkers. I guess that's all they're here for, a look at the second floor, although we've locked the door to the passage. And they're asking a lot of questions, but the volunteers aren't allowed to say much. In fact, I've written a script for them all. The customers don't hang around long once they realize there's not much to see or hear. I'm sorry they don't take the time to shop in here, though."

"If that's the real reason they're here, I'm happy they're giving us a pass. At least you're getting their admission fees."

"There is that. What I want to ask is if you've noticed anything that's gone missing in here."

"Missing? Like what? Anything specific? A few books? There's always a small shrinkage factor, but nothing we're really worried about."

"No, I mean something more valuable." She approached the counter and lowered her voice, even though they were alone. "Do you keep a float here? Or, I don't know, how about a piece of artwork from the walls?"

Shelby followed Chrissie's gaze. There was no space for artwork of any kind in the small store.

"Or maybe you had an expensive clock sitting on the table over by the bay windows?" Chrissie sounded exasperated. "Oh, frig, has anything been stolen?"

"Stolen? Nothing along those lines. It's not easy to get around the counter and open the cash drawer, and we don't keep a float here overnight. I take it home every afternoon and bring it back the next morning. And we don't really have anything of value here, aside from the books. What's this all about?"

Chrissie slumped against the counter. "Well, thank goodness for that. I wish we could say that about the rest of the castle."

"Something's actually been stolen? What? When? Do you have any clues?"

"The only thing we know for sure at this point is that several small items have gone missing, but we have no idea when or how. What's most upsetting is that the architectural drawings for the castle are gone. I don't know if you've seen them, but they're kept in a glass cabinet under lock and key in Mrs. Blye's sitting room on the second floor."

"Seriously? And you think they were stolen? How?"

"It seems like someone jimmied the lock on the cabinet, or whatever they do, in order to get inside the cabinet."

"When were they taken?"

"I have no idea. It's not like we take inventory every day."

Chrissie sounded so distraught, Shelby reached out and squeezed her arm. "That's really terrible. You're right, it was obviously well thought out. It also sounds unlikely that it happened during the day."

"That's just it. How could anyone get in at night? There are motion sensors, and Matt lives close by."

Shelby shrugged. It didn't make sense, but neither did Savannah's death. Unless there was a connection.

"What if the person came in through the underground passageway? It must have a door leading outside. What if the thief came back to steal something larger, something he couldn't take out of the castle during the day? And then there was Savannah, intent on exploring the passageway as part of her research. So, maybe she wasn't the target, but instead she interrupted the intruder."

"Interesting idea, Shelby," said Chief Stone from the doorway. "In fact, I had the same one, so you can be assured, we're following up on that. Which means, this time, you can stay out of this."

Shelby felt her face turning a telltale shade of red. "I wouldn't dream of interfering, Chief Stone."

Stone made a noise that sounded somewhere between a grunt and a laugh. Shelby decided it was time to change the topic. Plus, she was curious what had brought the chief to her store.

"What was it you wanted to see me about?"

Stone looked at Chrissie before answering. "I'd imagine it's the same thing that brought Ms. Halstead into your store. I'd like to know if there's anything missing from your bookstore."

Chrissie nodded, fidgeting with her iPad. "Well, I'll leave you to your questions, Chief Stone. Thanks, Shelby."

"No problem. And thanks again."

"So," Stone continued, "anything missing?"

"Not that I know of. Of course, I've only taken a cursory look around. This is the first I've heard of anything being stolen in the castle. And what would we have of value in the bookstore that would attract a thief?"

"You tell me. Nothing, you say?"

"Right, but if it appears something is, I'll let you know right away. I'll also check with Aunt Edie in case she can think of an item I should check on."

"Good."

"May I ask you a question now?"

Stone looked at her but didn't say anything. Shelby took that to be consent to ask away.

"What about the cleaning staff? Did they see anything useful on Sunday morning?"

Stone's face remained unmoved, although her eyes seemed darker. "Not that it's any of your business, but they didn't show up. The husband was sick, which is good for us because they hadn't yet messed around with things. Is there anything else?"

"Seriously?" Shelby couldn't imagine the chief was willing to answer questions.

"I think I'm better off knowing what you're thinking about rather than finding out after you've stuck your nose in somewhere it doesn't belong. I will tell you one thing, though. Miss Page's laptop is definitely missing. It wasn't in her hotel room either, and the fiancé says he hasn't seen it lately. Now, if you know anything about that, I'd be happy to hear it . . . No? Okay, no more questions on your part, to me or to anyone. Got that? Have a nice day." After taking a final glance around the store, Stone put her hat back on and left.

Shelby sucked in a deep breath. Why did she still feel nervous around the chief? She had nothing to hide.

Yet.

Chapter Twelve

S helby stood with her hands on her hips, slowly scanning the bookstore, hoping to see if anything was indeed missing. Then she ran her hands along the window ledges and frames. Nothing felt out of place, and there'd certainly not been any signs of broken glass at any point over the last few days or weeks. Next, she checked the door lock. Again, nothing wrong that she could detect. In fact, there were no signs at all of someone breaking in or even making an attempt. And although she couldn't think of anything of real value in the store, nor picture anyone stealing something while she or Taylor had been working there, she decided to take advantage of what might be a slow day and do a more thorough search.

She started by standing at the door and taking an objective look at what she could see from that vantage point. If she wanted to steal something, what area would she focus on?

When customers entered the store, they found the fiction section lining the entire left-hand wall, neatly presented in floor-to-ceiling bookshelves. Only books. Mysteries were kept on two freestanding shelving units close to the main counter, and along the right wall, the shorter of the two, were a variety of seasonal nonfiction titles filed by subject. Again, only books.

Of course, there were bookends at intervals, shaped as different wild animals and carved in dark oak. They were beautiful and looked like they might have cost a lot, but she didn't place them in the "worth stealing" category. The occasional book-related tchotchke, placed around the room, fit on that list, also. And Shelby was pretty sure nothing was missing.

The addition that housed the bookstore had been built in 2001, when the Heritage Society had decided Blye Castle should become a tourist attraction. They'd added several large windows, giving the space a light, airy look. Edie had decided on two white wicker chairs set between the largest windows, inviting customers to sit and browse awhile. That part didn't always work out, as their customers usually had a lot of castle to visit in a short time. It made for an appealing working space, though.

To do a more thorough search of the bookshelves, Shelby would need a printed inventory and several hours. None of the books were of interest to antiquarians though, so Shelby wasn't too worried about abnormal shrinkage. She decided that Edie was indeed the one who would best know if anything other than books was missing. She poured herself another cup of coffee and dialed Edie at home. They'd had a long conversation the day before about Edie taking a few more days off, especially since the weather was bad. She really hoped Edie had stuck with the plan.

Edie answered on the first ring, and Shelby quickly explained what had happened that morning. "So, can you think of anything valuable enough to be stolen from the bookstore?"

Edie was silent for a few seconds. "Not offhand, and I'd be totally surprised if I had something there that anyone would want, other than books. I'll keep thinking about it, though, and get back to you if something comes to mind. Now, I was just about to take a quick nap, so maybe my subconscious can figure something out. We'll talk later."

Around noon, Matthew wandered in. "Thought I'd get in out of the rain, but don't worry, I'll be careful around your books."

Shelby smiled. He obviously remembered her rant a couple of months ago after some rowdy toddlers hadn't been so careful with their rain gear. "I have complete faith in you, Matthew."

"Now that's something I don't hear most days." He winked. "Thank you, Shelby."

"Would you like some coffee?"

"I was hoping you'd ask. And I want to ask you if you'd noticed anything missing recently."

"Same question Chief Stone asked earlier, and Chrissie. I haven't noticed anything missing or even out of place. I also phoned Aunt Edie to see if she knew of anything valuable that could be stolen, and she couldn't come up with a thing. So, what's this all about?" she asked as she headed into the back room to pour them both a cup of coffee. She was dying to find out more details.

He'd tucked his raincoat and boots in a corner by the time she got back. He took the coffee and had a sip before answering. "I'm trying to figure that out myself. All I know is what I've been told, which is that some items have gone missing from the castle. They haven't told me what, except for the plan for the castle, but it sounds like most of the items are small and fairly portable, so maybe someone just got creative and lifted them during open hours. Big purses and deep pockets, you know. Knowing the chief, though, this will all be laid on my doorstep. As caretaker of the property, I should have been keeping a closer eye on things, or so she'll say."

"But you're not paid to do security for the castle, are you? What about the security company? That should be their responsibility."

"I'm not paid to do security, but they do like me to keep an eye peeled, which I do. And, as you know, there are only two paid security staff here each day. They tend to do more moving of furniture when that's needed than actual security. And no one is here inside the castle overnight. There are only the motion sensors that are hooked up to an alarm, more to scare someone off, because by the time anyone could get over from the Bay to back me up, the culprits would be long gone. Of course, the night of the murder, the sensors were turned off, so that's of no help. And I certainly haven't heard any alarms at any other time, so it's unlikely someone broke in at night just to steal a few small items." He took a sip and looked up. "None of the locks on the main doors or windows has been jimmied either. I think the murderer knew how to get in but didn't take the time to think it through. The padlock on the door to the tunnels was cut off but not replaced with a new one, just put back on, so it wasn't hard to find the point of entry."

"So, the tunnels do lead outdoors," Shelby said. "I'd been wondering. It sounds like that's how Savannah's killer got in. Do you think the killer and the thief are the same person? Maybe it really was a theft gone wrong. The thief, or thieves, came back to steal some larger items and didn't know that Savannah would be there. She surprised them and they killed her, then got out."

"Slow down. That's *if* she did surprise them at the stairs. You know, it sounds like you're getting too wrapped up in this. Let's get back to my initial question, because I have no idea whatsoever about the rest of it."

He sipped some more coffee as Shelby thought about what he'd said. Then she nodded. "Fine. But nothing is missing from the bookstore; at least, if it is, it's not noticeable. That does make it sound like the theft of the plans was well planned, so to speak. How would he get them out? I'd love to know what else was taken, because I'm sure that's a clue as to how it was done. I guess the cops are checking pawnshops and antique dealers in town."

Matthew nodded. "Pretty sure. And also in nearby towns."

"Well, it would have been obvious if someone had broken in here, and look for yourself—the door lock is just fine."

"I saw that. I'm sure the chief took note of it also."

"And I also checked the windows. So, do you think the plan of the castle was stolen beforehand and that's how they knew to break in through the tunnels?"

"You have too many questions, Shelby. Good ones, but this is not what you should be concerned about."

"Okay, but I do have one more question. Have you heard any more details about Savannah's death?"

He shrugged. "What makes you think I know anything after all I've said about my relationship with the police?"

Shelby remembered, all right. She'd heard all about how Matthew had at one time been suspected of murdering his wife, but it had never been proven. When he'd moved to the Bay, Chief Stone had been on his case, suspicious of his every move. And she still seemed to be.

"Well, maybe a security guard let something else slip." She raised her eyebrows.

He shook his head.

"Okay, make that two questions. Do you know Frank White, the butler on that night?"

"Nope. They told me his name, in case we ran into each other, I guess. But that's it. We weren't formally introduced. I hate to ask, but why do you want to know?"

"Well, he was here when it happened, right? Didn't he hear Savannah screaming when she fell? She must have screamed, unless she was already dead before being shoved down the stairs."

Matthew put his hands over his face for a few seconds. "You're giving this far too much thought. I hope this doesn't mean you're thinking about getting involved again. Remember what happened last time? You almost ended up a statistic. And think of poor Edie. She'll get positively apoplectic if she thinks you're getting in harm's way again."

That sent a shiver down Shelby's spine. "I'm not seriously thinking about investigating. I'm the first to admit I don't have a reason to get involved except for the fact that I knew Savannah. And it happened here in the castle. But, having said that, I am very curious. Did you know anything about Savannah? I mean, you having also been a true-crime writer?"

Matthew shook his head. "That was a long time ago, well before she started writing. I haven't had anything to do with publishing since then. That's not someplace I want to go, Shelby."

She felt bad that she'd brought it up. She knew the story about his past and also how he didn't like to talk about it. She felt embarrassed for her lack of empathy.

He cleared his throat. "Well, just remember what I said. Now, I should be going. I'm keeping an eye out for leaks. Thanks for the coffee." He slid into his jacket and tugged on his boots, then gave her a small wave before leaving.

* * *

As it got closer to closing time, Shelby was thoroughly depressed. There had been so few customers and no Taylor to talk things over with. She had been relieved, though, when Taylor had called to say she'd be staying home. She didn't want her to slip and fall in the awful weather.

Shelby had put the long afternoon to good use, dusting and rearranging some shelves. Those seemed to be endless jobs around a bookstore. Just another of many details she'd never even thought about before stepping into her role as part owner and manager. She had also made some lists of how to box things up when it was time to clear out the store.

She leaned against the counter and glanced around the room, something she'd been doing all day. But this time it was to let the feeling of the whole bookstore sink right in. She did love being in this space, she loved being surrounded by books, and she acknowledged that it hadn't taken her too long to feel a part of the castle. Funny how life worked out sometimes. She'd never really looked beyond living in Lenox and continuing on in her small life. This felt much bigger. This was where she belonged.

Some late-in-the-day customers wandered in, and she set aside her dust cloth and her musing.

An hour later as she was about to leave, the phone rang. She thought about letting it go to voice mail, but the caller ID showed it was Edie.

"Do you mind coming here before going home?" she asked.

Shelby agreed but didn't have time to ask any questions. The horn signaling the imminent arrival of the boat had just sounded. She locked up and hurried to the dock, careful not to slip on the wet surfaces. She huddled in the cabin for this trip, as the rain had returned, along with a hefty wind.

She gave a moment's thought to driving up to Edie's, given the weather, but admonished herself for being a wimp and instead tied her hood tighter and did her best to hurry. She didn't take time, as she usually did, to stop and admire the outside of the two-story white clapboard house before rushing up to the front door. It had been home to the Cox family since the mid-1920s. Even Edie's impressive garden seemed shrouded in sadness today, though.

By the time Shelby knocked, then opened the door at Edie's house, she was soaked and back in a foul mood.

"It's me, Aunt Edie," she called out as she shrugged out of her wet things in the entry.

"I'm in the kitchen."

"What a miserable day. I don't think even the ducks are happy," she complained as she entered the warm, aromatic room at the back of the house.

Edie chuckled. "We're getting into fall weather. Better get used to it, although we do get a lot of beautiful sunny days, too, along with some wonderful fall colors."

"Huh. It's good to see you getting around, but not too much, I hope."

"I'm doing just fine. Don't you worry about me. Now, I wanted to run something by you."

Shelby plopped into one of the wicker chairs by the back window. She took a deep breath and looked around the homey kitchen. Although it had been updated over the past ten years, she guessed, it still had retained the cozy feel. She could feel her foul mood passing. "Shoot."

"I got to thinking some more about things going missing," Edie began, "and I still can't think of anything valuable at the castle store, although I will come by tomorrow if I feel up to it and double-check. But then I started wondering about the main store, so I asked my neighbor to run me over so that I could take a look around. Trudy hadn't noticed anything, and I couldn't see anything out of the ordinary, but I did check in the back room. Not that we keep anything valuable in there. But I noticed that one of the plans was missing from where I'd left them. Either that or it was misplaced, which would mean someone had looked through or under them. Trudy said she hadn't touched them."

"You mean, one of the batch of plans you recently bought at that garage sale?"

"Yes. I had them spread out in the back because they'd been rolled up for so long. I was going to frame a couple of them and hang them. One, I'd meant to take to the castle."

"Are you sure one was missing? What type of plan was it?"

"Well, I hadn't looked at it recently, but it was a preliminary architectural sketch of the castle. I looked through the remaining ones and also checked the room pretty thoroughly. It's gone."

"How did you even get that plan? Shouldn't it have been with the Heritage Society?"

"You'd think, but there it was, along with a lot of other old plans of the Alex Bay area. I hadn't decided whether to donate it or hang it on our wall. The society does have a similar one already on display, after all."

"Not any longer."

"What do you mean?"

"It was stolen at some point."

"Really?" Edie sat down abruptly, her skirt fanning out. "What's going on? And why is ours missing also?"

"It's all very mysterious. Who knew about the plans in the back room?"

"All of us, of course. But Cody seemed the most interested."

Chapter Thirteen

The next morning, Shelby went over her conversation with Edie once again, as she'd done the night before when she'd gotten home. Fortunately, she'd been able to convince Edie not to come to the island to check things out. Not just yet, anyway. Slippery walkways and all.

The fact that Cody had asked all sorts of questions about the castle plans meant nothing more than that he had an inquisitive mind. Shelby knew this from all his research just a few months earlier on the Prohibition days and smuggling in the area.

Shelby had pressed Edie to let Chief Stone know about the missing plan. This might have been how the thieves had found out about the secret passages, which they had then used to get into and back out of the castle. But then, why steal the second set of plans? Or had the one from the castle gone missing first? Then why take the one from the store? Were they even the same plan? None of it made any sense.

But to think that Cody had anything to do with any part of it was ridiculous. In fact, she'd even asked Edie not to mention his name to Chief Stone but to say instead that they would check with the staff to find out when the plans had last been seen and if anyone had expressed interest in it. After all, the back room did not have a door but rather a screen in front of it. Anyone could have slid in behind the screen, if he or she had been so inclined. But that person would first of all have had to know about the existence of the plans.

She finished her granola and quickly ground some beans for an espresso. She'd drive herself crazy if she thought about this any more right now. She'd wait until Edie had spoken to Trudy, Cody, and even Taylor. Of course, talking to Cody would have to wait until the weekend when he came home from college. Shelby had insisted she be in on that conversation.

J.T. jumped on the counter and rubbed against her arm, becoming pushier until she finally gave him her full attention and patted his head. It seemed to be constantly itchy. She'd wondered at first if this meant a trip to the vet was in order, but Erica had convinced her it was not unusual behavior, which just drove home the fact that owning a cat wasn't an easy process. It seemed she had so much to learn . . . about many things.

Shelby listened to the purring as she drank her espresso and decided it was all worth it.

She made it to the main dock early for a change, giving her a chance to get caught up on castle gossip with some of the volunteers while waiting for the shuttle, not that there was anything of major importance happening these days. No one knew anything more about the most important topic, the murder. Shelby enjoyed touching base with the volunteers, though, something she didn't get a chance to do during the day, although she could track down a lunch buddy if she wanted. She admitted that, way down deep, she still felt that old tug to keep to herself during most breaks. Unless she spent them with Matthew. She was fairly pleased and surprised that she had felt so comfortable with him so quickly. Of course, that could be because of his relationship with Edie. She wondered if it was going anywhere permanent, and then, as she usually did, stopped herself from being overly nosy.

At least the weather was more agreeable today. The sun occasionally peeked from behind fluffy white clouds, and the forecast said it would eventually win the game and stay around for the afternoon. The shuttle ride turned out to be pleasant, with the gentle breeze blowing through her hair, and she was almost reluctant to disembark. A longer boat ride would have been fun. Today she wished she were a tourist.

She paused at the bottom of the stone walkway that led from the dock up to the castle. The scene before her never failed to take her breath away. This castle was the smallest of the three that were the main tourist attractions in the Thousand Islands, and to Shelby, it had the most charm. Maybe that was because she'd actually been a part of its existence for the past four months. She spent more time in the castle bookstore than at home, it seemed. That made it a sort of second home, she felt.

The expanse of green lawn flowed downward from the castle to the water's edge. It could make you feel like a kid again, seeming to invite a roll down the hill. But watch out for the trees. They dotted the landscape at uneven intervals, and many were now starting to lose leaves as they changed into various harvest colors of orange, gold, and brown. The evergreens remained true to the surroundings, some guarding the sides of the castle, others gathered beside the Sugar Shack, the snack and ice cream booth that was now closed until next spring.

The many flower beds were also in fine form, the plants and colors of summer having been swapped out for the more traditional fall beds of asters and helenium. That's what Matthew had called them. Shelby readily admitted she didn't have a clue when it came to gardening. Matthew had tended the flower beds with great care after the professional landscaper had come around to make the seasonal changes. She could tell he thoroughly enjoyed that part of his job as caretaker on Blye Island.

She sighed, feeling happy to be heading to work, and took the walkway up to the castle. Once inside the front door, she stood in the massive hall for a few minutes, soaking in the sound of the indoor fountain to her right before she passed in front of it and into the bookstore. The castle made all seem right with the world. She thought she'd never tire of the feeling that enveloped her each day.

Shelby was in a positive frame of mind as she approached the door to the bookstore. But that plummeted when she saw Chief Stone leaning against the doorframe.

"Good morning, Chief. You're here early." Inwardly, she cringed.

Stone nodded. "I came over on the police launch so that I could have some time walking around without all of you in the way."

She smiled when she said it, but Shelby knew it was the blunt truth. "And I take it you have some more questions for me."

"That I do." The chief pushed herself off from the doorframe and followed Shelby into the store. "I had an interesting call from your aunt last night. I'm seeing her next. Now, I wouldn't say no to a cup of coffee. Black."

Shelby couldn't think of a thing to say as she turned on the lights and got the coffee going. It seemed the chief couldn't either. Finally, a mug in each hand, Shelby emerged from the back room and found Stone running a finger along the titles in the local-authors section.

"Here you go," Shelby said. "Are you also interested in buying a book, by any chance? We have a great anniversary sale on right now." Unlikely but worth a try.

"Not today." Stone blew on the coffee and took a cautious sip. "Good brew. Now, do you have any thoughts about what happened to those plans? The one from the main store?"

At least she hadn't come right out and asked about Cody. Edie must have stuck to the plan.

"Not really. I hadn't even seen them. They weren't laid out in an obvious location, and Aunt Edie had told me about them but she didn't go into any detail. Of course, you've seen what the back room is like. Anyone could get in there if Edie or Trudy was distracted."

"That would have been my next question. You're anticipating me. Seems to me you've been giving this a lot of consideration. Is there a reason for that?" Stone peered over the rim of her mug.

Uh-oh. "It all seems so bizarre, but I'd hate to think the store was involved in any way in a theft from the castle. Or, worse yet, Savannah's death."

Stone's eyes narrowed, and the steely look settled on her face. It was a look Shelby had seen a lot in the spring during the last murder investigation.

"That's an interesting conjecture. How did you get there?"

"Well, from what I've heard, the thief or thieves may have gotten into the castle through the secret passages." She paused, but the chief didn't react. "The plan that went missing from the bookstore was an early architectural design for the castle, according to Aunt Edie, and although I haven't seen them, they must have shown the passages, wouldn't you think? So, if someone knew about our plans and wanted to get into the castle unseen, he'd be smart to steal them first. Right?"

"That makes sense." The chief looked like she was taking it all in.

"But"—she might as well jump right in—"why steal two sets of plans that are basically the same? Or I assume they are. And, if our plan was stolen first, why then take the ones from the castle? Unless"—the thought just hit her—"it's the other way around and the castle ones were stolen first, not on the night of the murder, though. And they didn't have the secret passages noted, so maybe ours did and that's why they were stolen."

"That's an awful lot of conjecture," Stone answered after a few moments. "If that were so, the plans from the castle had to have been taken during the daytime, or how else would the thief get into the castle at night before he knew about the passageway? And that's a reasonable assumption, because there was no other sign of a break-in in any other part of the castle. The main question is, I guess, when did those plans go missing?"

Shelby just stared at the chief. Her mind felt like it was working overtime, and more questions were popping up than being answered. She'd leave all of that to Chief Stone, she decided. She was also surprised the chief had shared so much information with her.

"What about the murder?" Shelby asked.

"Do you have a theory about that, too?" Shelby could hear the sarcasm in the chief's voice but pushed ahead anyway.

"Just what I've already mentioned. Was it a coincidence that Savannah's body was found in the secret passageway? Maybe the murderer did have another way in, although I know nothing's been found yet to support that, and found Savannah wandering around doing research, and pushed her down the stairs. So, back to the plans. Did the castle set show the passages? And how do you figure out which set was stolen first? If ours at the store have, in fact, been stolen. Edie did say they could just be misplaced."

Stone snorted. "Edie may be a bit scatterbrained when it comes to some things, but I do know she has a need to keep things organized. That hasn't changed over the years, I hear. If the killer came in through the passageways, he had to have the plans to know about them and where they led. So, the main question is, who stole the plans? I think it's possible we could have two thieves and one of them is the murderer. Now, I want you to trust me to follow through on this, and don't you go messing in this investigation. Do you hear me?"

Shelby nodded. She guessed this wasn't the time to ask the chief if she'd talked to Jenna Dunlop yet. Or whether Liam was on the suspect list. She also wondered what Frank White had told the police. That might turn out to be something she'd have to find out for herself. She tried to appear sincere.

Stone nodded, apparently satisfied with Shelby's supposed acquiescence. "Now, I know I don't have any control over your thoughts, so if you happen to come up with something I need to know, I trust you'll tell me right away. Right?"

"Oh, yes."

"But you will not follow up on anything on your own. Right?"

Shelby nodded again. Stone held her gaze with that look she had and then visibly relaxed. She finished her coffee and thanked Shelby.

At the door, Stone turned back. "Remember, this is not your business." She stomped out the door, pulling it closed behind her.

Shelby leaned against the counter, realizing how tense she'd been. What had she just promised? She knew it wasn't possible to carry through on it. She heard the boat whistle and shook her head, trying to get the chief out of it before the first customers arrived.

Just before noon, Shelby looked up from the catalog she'd been thumbing through to see a striking raven-haired woman about her own age entering the store. She wore a pair of navy-and-light blue checked leggings, the same ones Shelby had bought a couple of weeks earlier. She was so lucky she hadn't worn them to work that day.

After browsing the shelves, the woman approached the counter. "Are you the owner?"

"That I am. What can I do for you?"

"I hope you have a copy of Savannah Page's latest book. A signed copy," she hastened to add. "You see, I couldn't make it to her signing, and I just love her work. I'm really kicking myself for not getting here. I don't see it on the shelves, although maybe I was looking in the wrong place. At least, I hope I was."

"Just let me check the inventory," Shelby answered, turning to the computer. "I'm sorry, we don't have the book here, but our main store in Alexandria Bay has four copies."

"I'll stop in there and pick one up, if you don't mind asking them to put it aside. I'll do that later this afternoon."

"Happy to do that. And your name?"

"Rachel Michaels. What was she like? Savannah Page, I mean."

Shelby put the note she'd written to the side and considered Rachel's question. And also wondered why she wanted to know.

As if reading Shelby's mind, Rachel said with a lopsided smile, "I know it sounds nosy, but like I said, I was a fan. And I'm totally devastated about her death. From a purely personal perspective, I'm also really sorry we didn't get a chance to meet, although she'd agreed to talk to me."

"She had?"

"Oh, yes, I was so excited." Rachel kept nodding her head so emphatically, she had to push her peach-framed glasses back to where they perched partway down her nose. Shelby's gaze wandered to Rachel's hair, admiring it's deep and shiny color and the smoothness of the style. She'd always wished her naturally curly hair would morph overnight into a straight style like that.

"I'd emailed her," Rachel was continuing, "and explained that I'm also a fiction writer with some publishing credits, but I want to branch into writing true crime. I'd asked if I might buy her a cup of coffee and ask her some questions. I was blown away when she agreed. We were supposed to meet after her signing on Friday, but as I said, I couldn't get here on the weekend."

She looked disappointed or sad or both. Shelby felt bad for her, although she thought it odd that Savannah would have agreed to meet at that time. After all, she had been scheduled to dine with Edie and Shelby. It had been arranged several weeks in advance.

"That was a shame," Shelby agreed. "I'm sure you would have liked her as a person as well as a writer. In answer to your original question, she came across as friendly and engaging. I know that sounds trite, but she obviously enjoyed meeting readers, and she handled both signings with warmth and a great deal of patience." She thought she'd leave out any mention of the incident.

"That's what I thought. I knew she'd be nice and generous with her ideas, since she'd agreed to meet me and look over my work. At least, I'd hoped she would. It doesn't really matter now, though." She sniffed, then replaced the sadness with a smile.

"Do the police have any leads? I'd hate to think this is another murder that ends up in a true-crime novel as an unsolved story."

"I haven't heard. The police chief is on top of things, though. She's good at her job."

Rachel nodded. "That's good to know. And I'm really happy you have a copy of the book. Thanks for talking to me about Savannah."

"You're welcome."

Shelby phoned the main store as soon as Rachel left, relaying the message to put the book aside before she forgot to do so. She also told Trudy that she needed at least one of the remaining copies for the castle.

She felt a bit down after that conversation. Rachel had seemed very sincere and disappointed. And Savannah had been really pleasant to talk to. Generous was probably a good description, also. And now she was gone.

It wasn't right.

Taylor phoned a little bit later to apologize and say she wouldn't be in. "I really am sorry," she added.

"That's all right. You know you don't have to come in, right?" Shelby reiterated. "In fact, I usually hope you won't."

"Yes, I know I don't have to, but I feel like I'm using you. I come in when I can't stand it at home, and then I opt out when she's being reasonable."

Shelby laughed. "Well, I don't feel like I'm being used at all. And it's all good. I'm glad you two are getting along these days."

"For now. But you're right, it is good. I'd hate to think we were destined to be at odds for the rest of our lives, especially with children involved. And I know it upsets Chuck if I talk about how I feel, so I admit that I'm using you as a sounding board. Thanks for being so understanding. Is the door still open when I need it?"

"You bet, but part of me is hoping not to see you unless it's at your house."

"Yippee. That sounds like you're thinking of stopping in sometime. If you're free for tea next Monday, hope you'll come by. Although I know how precious your day off is. You probably already have a dozen things booked. Just be sure to give me fair warning so I can make myself presentable."

Shelby chuckled. "I can't imagine you being anything but. Take care."

The call left her in a good mood, shaking away the earlier gloom brought on by thoughts of Savannah.

Before locking up at the end of the day, Shelby tracked down Chrissie, hoping she hadn't already left. She had questions to ask about the missing plans, and since Cody wasn't around to supply more details about the plan from the store, Chrissie was next on her list. Chrissie had said that her day would be filled with shadowing the volunteers and talking to them, all with the intent of drawing up new guidelines for the following year.

Hearing some excited chatter in the back kitchen, Shelby headed there, and she was pleased to find Chrissie and two middle-aged women and one teen huddled around the table. Even though the kitchen was not in use as such, it had been set up as a working kitchen, and the area around the table was off-limits. Unless you were a coordinator, obviously.

She knocked on the doorframe, and Chrissie looked over. "Can I talk to you when you have a minute?" Shelby asked.

Chrissie nodded. "Now will work. Okay, ladies, that's it for today. Thanks for your input."

The three rushed out and could be heard still chattering all the way down the hall.

"What's up?"

Now that she had Chrissie's attention, Shelby wasn't quite sure what she wanted to ask. "I'm just really curious about the theft of those plans. There's no way of knowing who took them or when?"

Chrissie paused a moment, as if digesting Shelby's questions. Then she smiled. "You're thinking of investigating this, aren't you? Just like before."

"Not really. I mean, I don't have a reason to do anything, but I'm wondering just how easy it would be to do such a thing. Have thefts of large items happened before all this?"

Chrissie looped her arm through Shelby's and steered her out of the room and toward the grand hall. "I'm all for you looking into it, you know. This is not good publicity for the castle, and that's my main priority as PR person. And, if it got out how easy it appears to be to get in here and steal something . . ." She left the thought hanging but punctuated it with a shudder.

"So, are you saying it *has* happened before?"

"Nothing large or awkward in size but like I said, there have been a few small items that have disappeared over the years, but nothing major, as in something large enough that it had to have been taken overnight. And it must be widely known that we have an alarm—well, at least a motion sensor—so that's got to be a deterrent. But since those were turned off the night Savannah stayed over, well, it was almost an invitation to someone wanting to break in."

"But who would know that it was turned off?"

"The board. Matthew Kessler. Savannah and her fiancé, I'd guess. Security. The butler. Quite a few people, actually."

"What's Matthew's role in security?" Shelby knew what he thought it should be. She was curious if that's how the board saw it, too.

Chrissie snorted. "None. What can an old man do? People are aware he lives on the island, so I guess that's a bit of a deterrent, but his main job is taking care of the grounds, not guarding the contents. I don't fault Matthew at all."

That's good, Shelby thought, remembering how everyone had jumped on the bandwagon to accuse Matthew last time there had been a murder on the island. She bristled on his behalf at his being labeled an old man, though.

"So, what specifically has gone missing and when?"

Chrissie stopped walking and turned to face Shelby. "We don't do a daily or weekly or even monthly inventory, as I've already told you. That would take too long, and besides, it would be ridiculous." She paused for a moment and then shook her head. "No, it's not necessary. It's been mainly items that can be slipped into a pocket or a backpack, like the brush from Millicent Blye's dressing table and Thomas Blye's collapsible cane. It's just those frigging plans that are causing the major headache."

"But don't you think it's odd that the thief would steal the plans *after* breaking into the castle? Aren't those something he would need beforehand? Just saying . . ."

Chrissie's jaw dropped. "I hadn't thought about it much. But I guess he must have known about the tunnels already but wanted the plans to find specific rooms quickly."

"And there was nothing significant missing from any other rooms?"

"Not that I know of. The surrounding area was thoroughly searched, and we're continuing to do so throughout the castle on a segmented basis."

"Which means?"

Chrissie rolled her eyes. "There are two volunteers who have broken down the rooms into sections, and they are doing an inventory one section at a time. So, you see, we have it in hand."

Shelby gave her a reassuring smile. "It sounds like you do. That's good. Let me know if I can help in any way. Gotta run now." She wiggled her fingers and set off in a fast walk.

Chrissie called out as Shelby walked away, "You know, I doubt we'll recover any of the items, and I don't think we'll ever find the thief. At least, Chief Stone doesn't hold out a lot of hope."

Shelby turned and replied, "You never know. Fingers crossed." *If only there were cameras.*

Chrissie nodded and walked in the other direction. Shelby kept returning to the same dilemma that two plans had gone missing, one from the castle and one from the bookstore. She wondered yet again why the thief, or killer, would need the one from the castle after taking the one from the store.

Obviously, he wouldn't. So, there must be two different suspects. Two different motives was also a given. Which left one major question—who had wanted Savannah Page dead?

Chapter Fourteen

Shelby's landline light flashed to tell her a message was waiting as she walked into the houseboat that night. It was a request from Savannah's agent, Bryce O'Connell, to meet for a drink later that night. She glanced at the clock and thought, *I can do that*, wondering why he wanted to see her. She had to content herself with leaving him a message that she'd be at his hotel bar at eight PM. Then she dug through the fridge until she found the beef patty she had stashed in the freezer along with a frozen bun.

It still looked like summer outside, even though the temperatures had certainly dropped. Still a good time to barbecue a burger. She intended to make as much use as possible of the small portable charcoal grill she'd purchased at the beginning of summer, before it became too cold or too white outside. But of course, by then she'd be off the boat and living with her aunt.

If only it were available year round, in which case she'd seriously consider trying to buy it. The sale of her dad's house in Boston had left her with a comfortable sum she hadn't dug into yet.

She wondered if it was possible to remain living on the houseboat when it was in dry dock. Her landlord hadn't even suggested it, but she might ask the question next time she spoke to him. He might have assumed she wasn't interested. She wondered about insulation and if it would be warm enough, although she'd think that once it was in dry dock, it would be warmer than in the water. But what did she know? She had already arranged with him that the furnishings could stay on board during the storage.

After supper, she quickly washed the dishes, then looked at the clock. She still had plenty of time before she needed to leave. Maybe Cody would be available for a quick phone call. She really did need to talk to him about the plan, now that the chief knew about it, and she didn't want to wait for the weekend. She pulled out her cell phone and gave him a call. No answer after four rings, and she didn't feel like leaving a message. Tomorrow would have to do.

She decided to upgrade to a warmer jacket for the evening, then took off at a brisk pace to the Skyliner.

When she arrived, she spotted Bryce at a table for two beside a large window overlooking the bay. He was obviously watching for her and waved her over. He greeted her with a large smile and asked what she wanted to drink. After she placed her order for a glass of red wine, he leaned forward, arms crossed on the table.

"Thanks for meeting with me, Shelby. I just wanted to know if you'd heard anything more about the investigation." Lines of concern creased his forehead.

That surprised her, although why, she didn't know. When she'd gotten his message, she'd thought maybe he wanted to ask her some questions about Erica. What was she doing thinking of playing matchmaker, anyway? Better question, how much could she tell him about either Erica or what she'd learned? Of course, he didn't know she had been asking questions. His main interest was the police investigation. The theft wasn't public knowledge yet. So, really, she didn't have much to say.

"I haven't heard much. I know the police are going all out, but they don't share information with me, and anyone who I've talked to at the castle is as much in the dark as I am. How's Liam holding up?"

"He's getting a bit antsy and would like to get back to Buffalo. I guess I can understand that." He hesitated before continuing. "He does have a job, although he works from home and has been telecommuting from the hotel, but as he says, there's nothing he can really do here."

Something in his voice alerted her. "What? Do you fault him for wanting to leave?"

"Well, I know if it were my fiancé who had just been murdered, I'd want to have as much to do with the investigation as possible." He picked up his empty glass and signaled for another. Shelby declined.

"What about you?" she asked. "Are you also anxious to leave?"

Bryce shrugged. "Not really. I know I can't be much help, but I do want to keep on top of what's happening with the investigation. I guess it's still sinking in. But I think I should try to stay on top of it all, in case something negative turns up, and get right on damage control."

That totally surprised Shelby. "Like what?"

He leaned closer. "Like, what was she doing wandering around at night? Why was her body at the bottom of the stairs? Oh yeah, the police told me that much. Was she just being curious, or did she have something else in mind?"

"I'm not sure what you mean. You don't think Savannah was planning on stealing anything?" Did that make sense? Was she involved in the thefts? No, it didn't.

Bryce shrugged. "I can't imagine that, but then again, I couldn't have imagined she'd steal someone else's research subject either. I believe in her, I truly do, but again, just in case, I have a business to run, and that means doing damage control wherever and whenever needed."

He leaned back in his chair. Shelby realized he was watching her for a reaction. She was flabbergasted, to say the least, but tried not to look it. "I hope you're wrong."

"Believe me, so do I, but I've had stranger things happen with clients before. But I'm also thinking of the next book, and if there's any way to salvage it. As I already mentioned, I'm not sure how far she'd gotten in writing it. I need her laptop, and the police haven't had any success in finding it. Do you think you could have a look around the castle, in the room she stayed in, maybe? It might have fallen down behind some furniture or something."

"The castle is cleaned on a regular basis, and I'm sure they would have found it if it was there. Plus, the police thoroughly searched the room."

Shelby felt a shiver snake across her shoulders. It all sounded a bit heartless. She had to wonder, why he was *really* still in town?

He took a long swig from his beer glass when it was brought over, and looked straight at her. "I know that sounds cold, but there's nothing I can do for Savannah except maybe publish something posthumously. And if you knew her, you'd know Savannah would have wanted that."

Shelby had no doubt that it would have been Savannah's choice. She'd seen that drive in her actions and heard it in her voice. But it still sounded cold.

Bryce sighed. "I'm probably in your bad books now, aren't I? And I know this really isn't the right time to be asking, but what can you tell me about Erica? Does she have a boyfriend?"

At that moment, after the way he'd talked about Savannah, Shelby didn't want to tell him anything about her friend, but she thought Erica deserved the chance to make up her own mind about him.

"She's not seeing anyone at the moment. Chocomania is her business, you know, and she's great at making chocolates. But it does take up most of her time." *Let him find out the rest for himself.*

He grinned, and Shelby relented. "She's really nice, a good person who'd do anything for her friends."

"That's sort of what I thought, even though we met only briefly. Do you think she'd say yes if I asked her out to dinner?"

"Sorry, I'm really bad at reading people."

Understatement of the year.

* * *

Edie phoned a few minutes after Shelby arrived home.

"Are you all right?" Shelby asked, surprised at the late-evening call.

"Fine, fine. Just getting antsy, you know. My brain and all parts of my body, except for me knee, are raring to go. So, my mind has been working overtime."

Uh-oh!

"What's on that overly busy mind of yours?" Shelby asked hesitantly.

"Well, you should expect a phone call from Cody at some point, hopefully not too late tonight. I tried reaching him, but there was no answer, so I left him a message to call you. I just want to know more about our missing plan, in case he has any information. I can't wait until Saturday. It's really bothering me not knowing if this was part of what led to Savannah's death."

Shelby sighed. "I know. I'm wondering too, and I tried calling him also, but there was no answer. Okay, let's hope he does as you ask. I'll let you know when I hear from him."

"Would you? Thanks, honey. It will put my mind at rest. I hope."

"You're sure you're feeling okay, aside from the restless brain?"

"Oh, sure, sure."

"By the way, do you know where Frank White lives?" Another unknown on Shelby's list.

"Frank? Why? Are you planning to visit him and ask some questions? I don't know him all that well, since he's about ten years older than me, but I think he's a pretty straight-up guy."

"You're probably right. I already talked with him, but I thought in case I miss him at the soup kitchen when I go back, I'd try his home. I'm curious why he didn't hear Savannah scream, because she must have. I mean, that makes sense. Right?"

"I would think so. Where are you going with this?"

"I'm not sure. I just want to check back with him again, but I'm assuming he works over the lunch hour, and I'm usually at work then."

Edie chuckled. "That place is on my list of volunteer jobs when I finally retire. You're right, though, it does conflict with running a store unless you give a midday shift to someone else."

"You mean, like the other part-time employee we don't have as yet?" She couldn't resist saying it but hoped she didn't come across as too sarcastic.

"Yup. My fault, I know. I will get organized again someday soon. I promise."

"Good to know. Now, I hope you get a good rest tonight."

"Oh, I will. In fact, Matthew has just brought me a hot chocolate. Gotta go. Sleep tight."

Shelby was smiling as she hung up, although she realized she hadn't gotten an answer to her question. At least somebody would be getting a good night's sleep.

Chapter Fifteen

The phone call came at eleven, just as Shelby had turned off the reading lamp on her bedside table.

"I wasn't sure if this was too late to call," Cody explained to a sleepy Shelby.

She glanced at the bedside clock. "No, it's okay. I gather you got Aunt Edie's message."

"Yeah, and I'm really curious, you know. Does this have to do with my weekend shift? Is anything wrong? Did I do something I shouldn't have?" He sounded nervous.

Oh, boy. How to put it so as not to upset him? "We just had a question about the castle plan in the back room at the bookstore. Did you happen to borrow one of them or put it aside somewhere?"

"What? No, I didn't. I haven't touched any of them. Is one missing or something?"

"It looks like it. We can't find the ones of the architectural plans for the castle."

It took Cody several seconds before he answered. "Is that tied in to the murder at the castle? Why else would you be asking?"

"It could be. Or maybe not. We just want to track down the plan. You see, there were some items that went missing from the castle. They're not really sure when they were taken, but it could have been at the same time as the murder."

"I didn't do anything to them, I promise."

"Okay. I have another question. Do you think anyone else besides us would know about them?"

"Uh, well, yes, now that you mention it. I guess so. I guess I sort of told some friends of mine. Well, not close friends, but guys I knew from high school. They were talking about the castle and how cool it would be to sneak in one night and hang a sign from the second floor, you know, a message from the grad class."

"And how did they think they'd pull that off?" She hoped he hadn't shown them the plans.

She heard him take a deep breath. "I told them it couldn't be done, that there was security. And one of them wondered if there were secret passages or something, being a castle and all. I said I'd seen the plans, that they were in the back room at the bookstore, and there were no passages. I didn't know if that was true, but I wanted to derail their planning. I was pretty sure there was more involved than just hanging a banner, and I didn't want any trouble."

"Good idea, but it may not have worked. Do you know if they attempted to get into the castle?"

"I haven't seen them since then, so I have no idea."

"Are they the type of guys who might give it a try?"

"I don't really know. Like I said, I knew them a bit from school. They were a year behind me, and we didn't hang or anything like that."

"Who are the guys?"

"You think they broke into the bookstore and took the plan?"

"I think it's possible that one or more of them stole it, yes. But maybe not. I don't think you owe them anything though, Cody. Just in case they did it, the police need to know."

It took even more time before he answered. "You're right, of course. Oh boy, my bad. Am I in any trouble? No, don't answer that. I don't think I should tell you their names, I'm sorry. What if they're innocent? But how about I call Chief Stone tomorrow morning?"

Shelby wanted to know the names of the boys but thought this might be the better plan. Cody needed to feel he was doing the right thing, but she'd be sure to call the chief herself later in the day, hopefully for an update. *As if . . .*

She checked the clock and decided to wait until morning to fill Edie in on what had just happened. She tried to fall asleep quickly, but her mind wouldn't stop turning, trying to figure out how the hellions had possibly broken into the bookstore without leaving a trace. She knew Edie would want to know. too.

*   *   *

The next morning, Shelby gave Edie a quick call before heading to work to fill her in on her talk with Cody. As the morning progressed, she saw a bit of what Chrissie had been talking about earlier in the week. The store got very busy for a while, and most of the questions the visitors asked were about the murder, not about books. However, if she'd had more copies of Savannah's book, she probably would have sold out several times. She didn't mind in the least that that didn't happen. She didn't want to profit from the death, and she was sure that's what had driven up the interest.

Edie called just before lunch. "I know how they broke into the store."

"What? You didn't go there, did you?"

"No, but Tekla Stone did. Looks like they jimmied the back door but then managed to glue the wooden frame back in place so we didn't even notice. In fact, I don't think that door's been used in a while. They were smart and came prepared."

"Did she manage to get any fingerprints off it?"

"That she did, although we're not sure if they belong to the hooligans or not. You'd think since they thought to bring glue, they'd also be wearing gloves."

"You'd think. Well, I'm glad that's sorted out. Cody's not in any trouble, is he?"

"Not in my books, and I don't think Tekla's thinking he's part of it. Apparently he called her this morning and that's why she went to the store. So, we know how they got it, but I would hate to think that some teens were responsible for Savannah's murder, though, if it turns out that's who stole the plan. It's bad enough they broke into the bookstore."

"Do you buy their story about wanting to hang a banner from the grad class in the hall?"

"Anyone who would break into a bookstore—I mean, who would do that?—would probably do much worse, like maybe graffiti the hall. That would have been a terrible mess. But that didn't happen, nor did the banner. So maybe they didn't get around to breaking into the castle after all."

"I hope not. You're right, they're teens, and although the plot doesn't surprise me, a murder would. Oops, gotta go. I've got an official visitor," she added as a familiar-looking face walked through the open door and headed straight toward her.

"Chief Stone, hi."

"Shelby. We need to talk." Stone walked over to where Shelby sat behind the counter. She looked rather stiff, and Shelby wondered if she was in pain. Maybe bad knees, like her aunt? They were the same age, after all. It probably wouldn't do to ask.

"Sure. How are you?" She couldn't help herself.

Stone grimaced. "My arthritis is acting up. It happens. But that's not what I'm here to talk about. Tell me about Cody and those pals of his who were so eager to find out about the plan."

Uh-oh. "Would you like some coffee while we talk?"

Stone's eyes narrowed. "That sounds like you're stalling, but I would definitely like some."

Shelby felt Stone's eyes on her as she went to the back room and returned quickly with two mugs of coffee. She waited until the chief had blown on it and taken a sip before she told her what she knew.

"Well, all I know is what Cody told me when he called last night. It seems some guys from his high school told him they wanted to sneak into the castle and hang a banner for their grad class or something equally ridiculous. They weren't really friends of his, though."

"I know, I know . . . one of those grad pranks. So, he offered them the plans of the place?"

"What? No. He said he didn't. Cody happened to mention the plans to them but told them there were no secret passages. That was their original question. But he tried to throw them off. He didn't, and wouldn't, give them the plans."

"Well, it sounds like they very well may have wanted to see for themselves."

Shelby didn't have an answer to that. "But Cody tried to throw them off by telling them there weren't any passages. He wasn't part of it. I'd stake the store on it."

"I like how you have that boy's back. He called me this morning, by the way. But I'll bet you already knew that. I just wanted to get a better take on it all. But I'll be talking to him some more this weekend, and I hope you'll encourage him to give up the names of these boys. He said he wasn't comfortable telling me this morning."

"I can understand that."

Stone snorted. "So can I. I was young once, you know, but this is serious business. If they did break into the castle, they could also be murder suspects."

"But they're just kids. It would have to have been an accident, in that case, or so I'd bet. Are there any other suspects right now?"

Stone took a few minutes before answering, choosing instead to walk over to the local-authors section of the bookshelves and run her finger across the titles. "I can't share that with you, as you well know. But let's just say there are a lot of questions I'd like to get answers to before I close this case."

"Do you know when Savannah's agent, Bryce O'Connell, arrived in town?"

Stone swung around. "That's out of left field. Why do you ask?"

"Just wondering. I had a drink with him last night."

"I thought you and that Coast Guard smart-mouth were . . . you know."

Shelby felt her face catch fire. She decided to ignore the comment. "Uh, Bryce was wondering about Savannah. And Erica." She probably shouldn't have mentioned her friend, but she also didn't want to talk about her own relationship.

Stone chuckled. "Interesting. Well, he says he arrived Sunday around noon, after the fiancé called him."

Best not to say anything about Erica's seeing him on Saturday night until she had confirmation.

Shelby stood as two customers entered the store. She gave the chief an inquiring look.

"I'll talk to you again, I'm sure," Chief Stone said. She put her mug down on the counter and nodded to the newcomers as she left.

Shelby let out the breath she'd been holding since she had asked about Bryce. What was he up to, anyway? Maybe she should double-check with Erica. She could have been wrong, after all.

Of course, seeing the chief of police in the bookstore seemed to be all the permission the new customers needed to ask questions about the murder. What was it with this day? Shelby tried to downplay everything as best she could, and she made sure not to give out any relevant information, short of saying *no comment*. She did manage to make some sales at the same time, though.

Her final customer of the day left an impression. The man looked to be about Edie's age, meriting the distinguished graying at his temples. His short sideburns were totally white. His jaw was square and stern, but his smile softened the look. Although he was casually dressed in beige chinos and a dark-brown windbreaker, he looked as if he usually hung out in a suit, tie, the works.

"Are you the owner?" he asked, sticking out his hand. "I'm Nathan Miller, from Buffalo."

"Shelby Cox, and yes, I'm one of the owners. My aunt and I have the two stores, this one and the main one in Alexandria Bay."

"I've seen it; in fact, I stopped in there earlier today. This is the more enchanting store, though."

Enchanting. That was a good word, Shelby decided, but it surprised her to hear this man call it that. "Thank you. I totally agree."

"Are you the only staff person over here?"

What an odd question. But Shelby felt comfortable answering him; after all, the castle did have a lot of people in it. And he seemed trustworthy.

"I'm the main person, but we usually have a part-timer as well. She's off on maternity leave right now. Why do you ask?"

He nodded. "And I already know that in the main store there are two people working plus one weekend part-timer."

"Yes." She wondered where this was going.

He nodded again, more to himself this time. "Just curious."

He wandered around, looking more closely at some shelves than others. Shelby continued to watch him. Finally, he came to a stop in front of her again. "I'm just looking for someone, a friend. I'd heard she'd moved to this area. Do you know a woman by the name of Margo Delore?"

Shelby thought about it a few moments. "No, I don't think I do. Should I?"

"Not necessarily. I just wondered if she was a customer or had maybe even applied for a job. She's very knowledgeable about books."

"Uh-uh. It still doesn't ring a bell. I'm sorry."

"That's okay. I'd sort of lost track of her over the years, and I was just hoping to locate her at some point. I thought the Bay area would be to her liking. I really do like this store, by the way. You're to be congratulated." He glanced at the watch on his right wrist. "Guess I should be going and catch the next boat. Nice meeting you, Shelby Cox."

"And you." She watched as he left the store, wondering if he'd ever again meet Margo Delore. Was there a tale of romance there? Or maybe unrequited love—that seemed more logical. She sighed. It was fun to be thinking about romance rather than murder.

Chapter Sixteen

At the end of her shift, Shelby caught the shuttle, keeping to herself and enjoying some thinking time, then headed for Chocomania once the boat had docked. She was pleased to see Erica was alone, although she felt momentary guilt for thinking that. A full shop would have meant good sales for the day.

Erica waved as Shelby walked through the door. And although Shelby had promised herself all talk and no truffles, she couldn't resist ordering an espresso and a sea-salt dark-chocolate truffle. She grabbed a table close to the counter so they could talk while Erica did the end-of-day clean-up.

"I have an odd question, so please, just indulge me," Shelby started. "You told me you'd seen Bryce in town early Saturday night. Are you sure it was him?"

Erica leaned on the counter, arms folded. "Why do you ask? Are you playing detective again?"

The door opened, interrupting them. Shelby looked over and knew her feelings must be pretty obvious, what with the big smile that had sprung to her face. "Hi, Zack. What are you doing here?"

He squeezed Shelby's shoulder as he walked past her up to the counter. "I think I'm doing the same thing as you." He smiled at Erica and pointed at Shelby's treats. "The same, please."

"Right away. Good to see you, Zack. You haven't been around much lately."

"It's called work, unfortunately. I hope my not being here hasn't cut into your profits too much."

Erica chuckled. "I'm coping." She handed him his purchases, and he settled across from Shelby.

"Am I interrupting anything?"

Erica answered before Shelby could. "Not really; we're just catching up. And, Shelby, I'm very sure."

"Sure about what?" Zack asked.

"That I should buy some of her new flavors for the bookstore." Oops, that lie had come out entirely too easily. She hoped she didn't look as guilty as she felt.

Zack didn't seem to notice. "How could anything from this store not do well?"

"Well, thank you, Zack. It's good someone has total faith in me," Erica answered, then got back to packing away the remaining truffles before closing for the evening, but not before she gave Shelby a meaningful stare.

"So, tell me what's keeping you so busy, or can you tell me?" Shelby asked Zack.

"I can tell you a lot of things and would be happy to do so over dinner." He raised his eyebrows to make the statement a question.

"You mean tonight?"

"Right now, yes. Let's consider this dessert."

She smiled, suddenly very happy. "I'd love to."

He reached over and squeezed her hand. "I was hoping you'd say that." After several seconds he looked over at the counter and asked, "Would you like to join us, Erica?"

"What? Have you never heard the adage *two's company*, et cetera, et cetera? Not on your life. Thanks anyway."

"I like what she's implying," Zack said.

"Yes, subtlety is not Erica's strong suit." Shelby glanced over in time to notice the look Erica shot her. A friendly set of daggers. Shelby finished the rest of her drink, feeling very content sitting there with her two best friends—well, one definitely more than that.

As soon as Zack finished the last of the espresso, they bid goodbye to Erica and walked hand in hand toward the Ripe Tomato, a new bistro that had opened earlier in the month, just down the street. She wished she'd worn something more striking—no, something sexier, but that wasn't a look she cultivated for work. If ever. She'd just have to pretend her blue striped silky shirt and navy leggings were sexy.

It wasn't very crowded, so they chose a table next to the window. As they settled in, Shelby thought back to her first dinner out with Zack. Not a date, but it had been a start. In some ways it felt like a long time ago, even though it had been only about four months earlier; in other ways, it felt like it had just happened. She had to admit she'd done an about-face in her feelings about not getting involved with him, with anyone.

She smiled at the realization that she'd been wrong. This felt so right.

Zack caught her smile and sat with his arms crossed on the table, saying nothing but watching her.

"What?"

"I'm just enjoying being here with you," he answered. "I'm really not happy when it gets so busy at work and I don't get to see you as often."

There was that smile again, and the tingle it sent down her spine.

"I totally agree, but I know that your work with the Coast Guard means unusual hours." She wanted to say more but suddenly felt shy. She blamed it on old habits learned from living most of her life with only her dad as a guide. And he had liked his privacy. She mentally squared her shoulders. She was her own person now, and this was a part of that life that she really enjoyed.

She looked around the room, pointing to the variety of paintings of tomatoes that hung on the walls. "They really get into it, don't they?"

Zack followed her gaze. "You know, I like it. It could have been overdone, but they've got just the right mix of sizes and colors. Who knew there were purple tomatoes?"

"They're not something I've tried, but I like the vivid colors. It makes me feel relaxed. Look, even the chairs have been painted to coordinate."

Zack peered at the table next to them. "Huh. I hadn't noticed that. What else haven't I paid attention to?"

His gaze had shifted to her, and it was so intense, Shelby didn't know whether to smile or squirm. They ordered, and then as they waited for their meals, she sipping wine and Zack with a beer, he asked the question she'd been hoping they could stay away from.

"How's the murder investigation going?" he asked.

She tried to look surprised, but knew from the look on his face that she hadn't done so.

She tried anyway. "What makes you ask that?"

He leaned forward. "Because I know you, and you're right in the thick of this, given that it happened at the castle. You might as well admit it." His blue eyes were even more so. She had fallen for those eyes right off. They looked crinkly at the edges, like they were always smiling, which she took to be a sign of a gentle soul. Tonight, though, his eyes seemed to be mocking her. He knew her so well.

However. "You missed the fact that Savannah had done two book signings for us, so I knew her. And we'd also had dinner together on Friday night."

"Hmm. I did know that. And even though I'd like to point out that doesn't give you permission to do any poking around, and I'm sure you've already heard that, I also know it won't make any difference. So, what have you found out?"

"Do you know anything?" She turned his question back at him. "Has the chief shared any information?"

"This isn't my investigation. I'm not involved in any way, and therefore, I'd be the last person she'd tell. Next to you, that is." He grinned.

She pretended to pout. "So, why are you asking if you're not involved?"

He reached out to touch her arm. "As I've often said, it's because I worry about you and I know you're probably up to your neck in it."

She felt a shiver, but she wasn't sure if it was from pleasure or dread. She cleared her throat. "I haven't found out much, I'll readily admit. But there are a lot of interesting suspects involved."

"Suspects?" Zack asked, eyebrows raised. "Such as?"

"Yes, or at least persons of interest, whatever that means. There's Liam, the fiancé. Was he really in love with her and okay with her staying overnight at the castle, or jealous about her past relationship with her agent? Bryce, said agent, lied about when he arrived in town and is anxious to get his hands on Savannah's laptop, which may or may not mean a thing. Then there are two writers involved. One of them, Jenna, is local, and very publicly accused Savannah of stealing her plot. She did it right in front of customers at the first signing. And now a second writer, Rachel, has shown up saying she's upset she missed getting to the signing and didn't get a chance to meet Savannah."

"And how is that suspicious?"

Shelby shrugged. "Maybe it isn't, but Rachel said Savannah agreed to have coffee with her after the signing, but she and Liam were already supposed to have dinner with Edie and me. So why would Savannah have made other plans?"

"That's hardly damning."

"I know. It's just one of the things that doesn't really make sense." Shelby took a long sip of her water before continuing. "And it's possible the butler did it. I know, that's so corny."

"I was going to say you're starting to sound like Erica."

Shelby shot him a quizzical look.

"You know, *two's company*, et cetera?" He chuckled when she groaned. "I'd heard there was a butler hired for the night. So, what would his motive be?"

"I don't know. I haven't finished talking to him."

"You haven't?" he asked in a mock-shocked tone. Then his voice and expression turned serious.

"Why are you doing this? I thought we had a conversation about you not getting involved."

"You didn't sound too concerned a few seconds ago."

"I'm exasperated, Shelby. I don't know what to do or say. I thought maybe by humoring you I could dissuade you, but I can't keep it up. I worry about you. I really do like you, a lot, and I don't want anything happening to you."

Before Shelby had a chance to gather her thoughts, their food arrived. They both made busy with the silverware and taking their first bites; then Zack leaned forward. "Did you hear what I said?"

"I did, and I know what you want to hear, but I can't say it." She shifted uncomfortably on her chair. "I can't just ignore the fact that Savannah was murdered, and that affects everyone who had anything to do with her. I know I hadn't known her long, but it is on my mind. I'm sorry."

He gave his head a small shake. "Just promise me you'll be careful and call me or Chief Stone if you feel in danger."

She let out the breath she'd been holding. "I will."

She wished she could take a photo of the smile Zack gave her. It easily put any thoughts of any investigation on the back burner.

Until later that night, when she ran through all she knew about the murder. Which left her puzzling once again over why Bryce had lied.

Chapter Seventeen

The message light on the landline in the bookstore flashed at Shelby while she set up a small display on the counter, preparing for another day of what she hoped would be big sales. When she finally noticed it, she realized she hadn't thought to check it when she'd first gotten in. Too many other things on her mind. Well, one, really. The murder.

On her way to the shuttle, she'd stopped by the main store and picked up a bag containing two copies of P. K. Pitt's book *Cruising the Castles*. It had turned out to be the best seller of the local bookshelf, and even though the season was nearly over, she wanted to have what was in stock on hand at the castle. Thus, the counter display. The other book was a special order for Mae-Beth, the workshop coordinator.

Shelby had discovered very early on at the castle that even though the late Loreena Swan had held the title of volunteer coordinator, Mae-Beth was the person who had the better rapport with the volunteers and was, therefore, the one they all turned to when any issue arose. It seemed they still went to her, even though Chrissie tried to do a good job in her new role.

Shelby looked from the display to the phone and decided to check the message first, and then if there was time before opening, she'd go in search of Mae-Beth.

The southern accent alerted Shelby immediately, even before Prissy Newmarket identified herself. Prissy was an old friend of her mother's, one who had been in the store a few months earlier. She'd been the first contact Shelby had had with anyone, other than Edie, who had known her mom. But even though Prissy lived in nearby Clayton, they hadn't seen each other again.

Prissy wanted to do something about that, she explained, and invited Shelby for brunch in two weeks, on a Monday, when she and her husband would be back from a short holiday.

Shelby was pleased that Prissy had followed up and also that she'd apparently remembered her day off. She made a note to call back and accept the invitation. Prissy had seemed friendly, and Shelby was also anxious to learn more about the mother she could barely remember.

She shook her head—this was not the time to dwell on all that—and grabbed the book for Mae-Beth, whom she found in the music room.

"The book you ordered is in," Shelby explained, handing it over.

"That's wonderful. Thank you so much for ordering it, Shelby. I'll come by and pay for it right now if you like. My purse is tucked away in the office."

Mae-Beth looked a bit more harried than usual, but Shelby thought it best not to comment. Her black-and-brown-striped nylon blouse was untucked on one side, and her silver-blue pageboy had sprouts of hair sticking out in places. Shelby did wonder about the workload Mae-Beth had taken on since Loreena Swan's murder a few months before. Even though an honorarium was involved, it seemed like Mae-Beth should be considering retirement very soon. She had to be at least ten years older than Edie, but then again, it wasn't Shelby's place to judge. If Mae-Beth wanted to keep active, that was great. And Shelby was the first to acknowledge the lure of the castle.

"Don't rush. Anytime you're able to come by is all right. I was wondering if I could ask you a question, though."

Mae-Beth stopped thumbing through the book and gave Shelby her full attention. "Of course, my dear. What is it?"

"Are you aware of anything going missing in the castle over the last several months?"

"Missing—you mean, as in stolen? Is this what Chrissie has been tiptoeing around?"

Shelby nodded. That's exactly what she meant.

"Well, not that it's being referred to as stolen, but what else could it be? The old spyglass in the east bedroom has mysteriously disappeared. Now, if I believed in Joe Cabana's ghost, I might have attributed it to him, a prank or something. But since I'm not a believer, I'd have to say someone did in fact walk off with it. I did mention it to Chrissie, by the way."

"I don't remember it. Was it very valuable? Would it be hard to conceal during the day?"

"That depends on what the person was wearing. I've seen some videos of shoplifters in stores wearing roomy coats, and it's amazing what gets stuffed in inside pockets. As to the value of it, I have no idea." She paused before adding, "That's not my area of expertise, but it looked very old."

"So, what do you think happened to it? Or have you heard any speculation about it?" Mae-Beth was turning out to be a wealth of information.

"I don't know, and I haven't heard anything, nor has Chrissie gotten back to me about it, but you'd think it would have come up at the board meeting or something. Does Edie know about what's been happening, and more importantly, does the board know about it?"

Edie had been a member of the Heritage Society board for the past five years but was unable to attend all the meetings while resting her knee. And although Shelby had gone as her stand-in to one of the meetings, she hadn't heard any mention of anything going missing. Unfortunately, neither of them had attended the most recent meeting.

"I'll ask her. She has her ways of knowing even when she's out of commission. Thanks."

"How is she doing, anyway? I was really sorry to hear about what happened. That must have been very painful, falling on her new knee. I know how much she hates having to stay at home and recuperate. I do plan to stop by with a casserole later this week, if she's up to company?"

"She'd love that, I'm sure. You know Edie."

Mae-Beth nodded and smiled. Her expression changed,

though, as she asked her next question. "That was certainly dreadful about that young author, wasn't it? Do you know if the police are any closer to figuring out what happened?"

"I haven't heard, unfortunately." Should she mention there might be a tie-in to the thefts? Better not, in case the police were trying to keep any connection quiet.

"I thought it was a bad idea letting her stay here, in fact," Mae-Beth continued. "I disagree with the idea of offering the suite on a seasonal basis."

"Why's that?"

"Because this is the kind of thing that happens. Oh, I don't mean murder, nor am I suggesting that the poor girl was responsible or anything like that. But once you let the public in after hours, bad things are bound to happen. It's such a large and special place. You'd think they'd be doing background checks on anyone they allowed to stay here. Of course, I'm sure everything was aboveboard with your author, but what about if they open to the public? I'm even against renting the castle out for special occasions, and I have heard rumors about that, too. Do I sound very judgmental?"

"It's hard to say what the repercussions could be, but I'm sure the board will have to look very closely at all possibilities. From what I've seen, they take their roles very seriously." In fact, she thought, recalling the one meeting she had attended, it seemed almost like a calling for some of them.

Mae-Beth's smile looked a bit shaky. "Good. I don't want to sound too negative if it really is a good promotional move for the castle."

They had begun walking together into the main hall, and Mae-Beth sighed, running her gaze along the wooden paneling. "It is such a precious place."

Shelby patted her arm. "It is, but I don't think you need to be worrying about it." She heard the tourist boat sound its horn as it approached the dock. "There's the warning. Here they come. I hope it's a good day for us all."

"Especially for you, dear. Thanks again for the book."

Shelby nodded, then crossed the hall to the bookstore. She paused a moment, her eyes closed, at the edge of the indoor fountain, listening to the waterfall for several seconds. Feeling refreshed, she took a final look around the hall. It looked like it might be a busy day, for the castle at least.

The phone rang as Shelby propped the store door open with the large stone painted like a cat. It surveyed anyone entering the space and had turned out to be a big hit with schoolkids in particular. Shelby allowed herself a pat on the back for spotting it at a craft sale earlier in the spring. She had given it the perfect home.

Edie was on the phone wanting to know if Shelby had heard anything further from Cody. "I just wondered if he'd given it some more thought and might have gotten back to you with the names of those boys. He seems to have a good rapport with you, after all."

"I was actually out last night, but he didn't leave a message if he did call."

"Out? As in a date?"

Shelby felt her face heat up, even though there was no one to see her blush. "I had an unexpected dinner invitation from Zack, and it was a late night." An understatement, but she hoped Edie wouldn't pursue it.

Edie chuckled instead. "Glad to hear it. Okay, I guess we'll have to wait until he's home to find out what's on his mind. Even if he doesn't tell us, I hope he'll let Tekla know. While I do believe he's not involved in what happened at the castle, I know he feels some of that macho 'no snitching' stuff, but in this case, given that there was a murder, I'd bet he'll do the right thing. He's a good kid."

Shelby heard some paper rustling and wondered if Edie was reading the newspaper. Her aunt was notorious for multitasking.

"Other than all that," Edie continued, "anything planned for today? Maybe another romantic dinner tonight?"

Shelby stifled a grin. "Not that I'm aware of. How are you feeling?"

"I'm raring to get back to work, that's how I'm feeling."

Shelby felt a tinge of panic. "I just hope you don't rush it. You want to be in top form for winter, and we need you to be."

Shelby heard a muffled sound, and she hoped it meant acquiescence. "Do you want some company tonight? Are you getting bored?"

"Not tonight, thanks, dear. Trudy is coming for supper. I'll let you get back to work now."

Edie hung up without the usual sign-off. Shelby had quickly gotten used to her aunt's quirky mannerisms. She had worried about it at first, wondering if it had anything to do with early dementia or something similar, but she was now convinced it was just Edie. She was thankful she'd not pursued that line of thinking. She smiled as she pictured Edie settling back with the newspaper and a cup of coffee at the kitchen table.

The phone rang again before Shelby could get away from the counter. Surely her whole morning wouldn't be spent on the phone.

"Hello, Shelby. It's Felicity Foxworth. I hope you're not swamped with customers. I mean, I hope you will be, but not at this exact moment. I wanted to have a little chat. Is now okay?"

Shelby guessed that Felicity wasn't swamped either at her art shop, the Gallery on the Bay, located next to the bookstore in town. "Now is fine, Felicity."

Besides, her curiosity was piqued. Felicity seldom called; in fact, she hadn't called in months, not since the grisly events of the previous spring.

"Well, you know I've been thinking about this new murder, and I assume you're involved, that poor girl having been signing at your bookstores and all, so I thought you'd want to know."

"Know what?"

"Well, I saw them arguing late Saturday afternoon."

"Who?"

"The author and that young man who hung around with her. You know, he was helping out opening the books at the signing."

"Her fiancé?"

"Oh, I didn't realize they were in a relationship. Nobody said. The poor, poor man."

"When did you see them?"

"Well, the first time was when I got my book signed, but of course that wasn't when they were arguing. The next day, later in the afternoon, they were walking towards the dock, and I assumed she was taking the boat over to the castle because I'd heard she was sleeping there overnight. Wasn't that a creepy thing to do? And, as we now see, dangerous, too."

"Could you hear what they were saying?" Shelby asked.

"No, I heard raised voices, but I didn't want to appear too interested. I was walking over to Riley's, and they were a bit ahead of me on the sidewalk. She did grab his sleeve, though, and he shook off her hand and stomped away from the dock." Felicity took a deep breath. She sounded breathless, like she'd had to run for the phone, although she was the one who had placed the call.

"Are you sure it was them?"

"Absolutely. I quickly went to the other side of the street, though, so she wouldn't think I'd overheard. She didn't even glance around. She just stood there a few seconds watching him, while I looked in a store window, not wanting to intrude. And then she headed for the boat. And now she's dead." She paused. "Do you think he did it?"

"I have no idea, Felicity. I'm really trying to stay out of it." Shelby wished that were true.

"Oh, I do understand, dear. Chief Stone made it really difficult for you last time, didn't she? Well, you did a marvelous job solving that one, so if you're pulled into this one, just remember what I told you about the argument, all right? We can't have another murderer walking around our town."

"Yes, I'll remember. Thanks, Felicity."

Relationships. That always seemed to be at the bottom of things. Was that what this was all about? Was that why Savannah had been murdered?

Chapter Eighteen

Shelby had little doubt Felicity had been right about what she'd seen. But the big question was, what had that argument been about? Savannah and Liam had looked like a happy couple at dinner that night.

Should she tell Chief Stone about the argument? Maybe not. She shook her head. *No. Maybe.* But if it turned out to be just a small lovers' tiff, it would be a shame to expose the grieving fiancé to Chief Stone's probing. That was not her decision to make, but she thought she'd wait until the evening before making up her mind about whether or not to give Stone a call. And, if she happened to run into Liam before then . . . well, it couldn't hurt to ask him some questions.

Taylor arrived just before the first customers of the day. "Sorry I didn't let you know first, but it was either escape today or end up with a criminal record."

Shelby shook her head and tried to hide the smile forming. "That bad, huh?"

"After being cooped up during the rainstorms, I needed some distance." She sat down after depositing her jacket in the back room and let out a small sigh as she settled. "Being pregnant was easier in the summer when sundress and sandals were all I needed. Now, with rain gear added, it's getting tedious. I just hope we have a mild start to the winter, or I'll go bonkers."

"How are you feeling, aside from exasperated?"

"Fat."

"I think you're brave to take on the boat ride over here and the walk up the path to the castle." Even though there had been early-morning showers, they were lucky there was hardly any wind.

Shelby paused before having another sip of the coffee she'd just poured. Taylor did look frustrated and tired. She wondered what she could do to help.

"Well, I want to be doing something useful, to keep my mind active and off the downside of all this. Can I stay, please?" Taylor's large, dark eyes appeared even more so now that they were filled with emotion, and Shelby thought Taylor's husband Chuck must be a goner at times like this. *How do you say no?*

"Of course, but you have to tell me the minute you're getting too tired or, you know . . ."

Taylor smiled, patting down a single stray blonde hair. Shelby marveled at how her pixie cut hadn't appeared to be ruffled by the boat ride. Maybe that was the style she should get.

"Will do," Taylor replied. "So what can I do?"

"Take charge of the purchases when customers decide to appear. And, oh yeah, please try to think of something for Edie to do. You're both in similar spots, you know. She needs to have her mind occupied also, so that she doesn't head back into the store too soon."

"Just like before. You'd think she'd be used to that convalescing routine by now and that she'd realize if she goes back too soon, it could set her back. But I get how frustrating it can be. Did you have anything in mind?"

Shelby crossed her arms and leaned on the counter. "We've got truffles from Chocomania in this location, and they're a draw on their own. I wonder if there's something we can do at the main store over winter. There can never be too many reasons to tempt customers to come in."

"Hmm. You can't do truffles because Chocomania is just down the street. And with Driftwood and Seawinds close by, you can't really do small gifts." She shrugged. "I like the idea of bringing in something new, but what could you mix and match with books? Maybe that's the question you should ask Edie to spend her time thinking about."

"You could be right, but I'll bet she's done this before, so I'd like to have at least one suggestion to get the conversation started."

The bell over the door tinkled as the first customers, an elderly couple, wandered in. Obviously tourists, even though there wasn't a charter bus group expected that day.

"Huh. Leave it to me and I'll try to think of something. Oh goody, let the fun begin," Taylor said in a quieter voice.

"Welcome to Bayside Books," Shelby said to their new customers. "Is there something I can help you find, or do you prefer to browse?"

The woman tucked a strand of curly hair behind her left ear and answered, "Thank you, but we're not quite sure what we're looking for. Can you point out the local section? I usually like to buy a book, preferably something coffee-table size with lots of pictures, from the really unusual places we visit. And I'd say this castle qualifies. You do have a local section, don't you?"

Shelby smiled. "Of course. It's right over here."

She left the couple and winked at Taylor, who settled back in her chair and tried not to be too obvious about watching them.

"Penny for your thoughts," Shelby said as she walked back behind the counter to grab the coffee mug she'd just put down.

"I was thinking what a sweet-looking couple they are and wondering if strangers will say that about Chuck and me when we're that age."

Shelby chuckled. "I can't picture you two at that age. Don't rush it. Although you may have gray hair sooner than later, depending on your offspring," she added in a hushed voice.

"Are you speaking about the well-behaved, angelic Chuck Junior?" Taylor grinned, then pulled a bag out from under the desk, anticipating a sale.

Shelby gave her a thumbs-up and walked to the back to refresh her coffee. Chuck Junior. Zack Junior. Now where had *that* thought come from? She gave her head a shake.

Voices reached her ears, a different male and female discussing the title of a book. She glanced at Taylor as she reentered the room, noting the phone receiver held to her ear.

"May I be of help?" she asked the younger couple.

The woman, who looked to be in her late teens or early twenties, grinned. "You bet. I hope you still have some signed copies of Savannah Page's latest book. I understand she did a book signing here before, uh, before, you know . . ."

Shelby felt that shiver again but smiled at them. "I'm pretty sure we have at least one copy left. Let me check for you."

She found the one remaining copy of *Lies and Deaths: The A. R. Smith Story* she'd brought over from the main store and handed it to the woman.

"That was nice," Shelby said after she'd left. "I guess I'll need to order even more copies of Savannah's book. Would you mind checking the system to see if Trudy already did so?"

Taylor tapped the keys and read the screen. "Yes, she ordered four copies a couple of days ago."

Shelby nodded. "Thanks for checking. I wonder if the sales will continue even without a signature. And just how long the notoriety will last."

"At least until the killer is found. And maybe it will start up all over again once the trial starts."

"You're awfully confident they'll catch him. Or her."

"Of course I am. Chuck would disown me if he heard I said anything different." She folded her arms across her belly as she leaned back in the chair. "It just takes time."

"But that's just it. On all the cop shows, it has to be done quickly or the trail runs cold. Or the suspects leave town. I wonder when her fiancé and agent are leaving."

"You think they're suspects?"

"Well, yeah. They were both close to her," Shelby pointed out. "And also, I'd hate to think the murderer was someone from around here."

"But neither of them is in jail, so they must have good alibis."

"Hmm. Or maybe they don't have strong motives. That we know of."

"What are you thinking?" Taylor sat upright, immediately attentive. "I thought you were giving this a pass."

"Well, I can't help but wonder what the lovebirds were arguing about on the wharf just before Savannah came over to the castle."

"You didn't mention that before."

"Oh, well, I only just heard about it, from Felicity of all people. She called just before you arrived this morning."

"Why don't you ask the fiancé what it was about? As you said, he's still in town, isn't he? He might not tell you, but wouldn't that prove something in itself?"

"I'm sure he'll have a well-planned answer just in case the police find out and confront him. But I won't know until I ask, will I?" She looked around the store. It was slow just then.

As if Taylor had read her mind, she said, "Why don't you leave early today and go have a talk with him? It's kind of quiet around here."

"Uh-uh. I'm not leaving you, in case . . . well, I'm just not."

"Okay, thanks. I do feel more comfortable with someone else here."

As if to prove how much two staffers were needed, it turned out to be a busy day. Taylor tired quickly, and Shelby sent her home on the early-afternoon boat. After closing the store a couple of minutes early, Shelby made it to the last shuttle with time to enjoy a slow walk, taking in the scenery. Once back in the Bay, she headed straight to the hotel.

A few minutes later she was knocking on Liam's door. He opened it a crack and, when he saw who it was, opened it wider.

"Shelby, what can I do for you?" He sounded and looked surprised to see her. In fact, he looked like he hadn't been expecting any company. His hair was tousled and his clothes needed the power of an iron or maybe just a laundering.

"I just hoped you'd have a few minutes to talk. Do you?"

He looked behind him and Shelby peeked around him, noticing the open suitcase on the bed. "Are you heading somewhere?"

He looked embarrassed. "Well, yeah. I'm driving home tomorrow. I've missed a lot of work. But okay, I'm good with talking. Let's just go down to the lobby for that. It's sort of messy here, as you can see."

He ran his hand over his head, smoothing his hair flat, grabbed the key card from somewhere behind the door, and then pulled it shut behind them. They made their way downstairs, not saying anything until they were seated next to each other at a small grouping of chairs across from the reception desk.

"What's on your mind?" he finally asked.

"I was wondering how you're doing." Shelby wanted to come across as sincere, especially if she wanted any information from him.

"Oh, I guess as good as can be expected." He sighed. "I still can't believe she's gone, and hanging around here hasn't helped any. The memories of our last few days are too fresh."

"I understand. I hate to bring it all up again, but I do have a question for you. I was wondering what you and Savannah were arguing about on the wharf before she headed over to the castle on Saturday."

He shifted in his seat. "Why do you think we were arguing?"

"Someone saw you."

"Who?" His face had gone ashen and his hands gripped the arms of the chair.

"It doesn't matter. Will you tell me what it was about?"

He turned away for several seconds, and Shelby wondered if he'd even bother answering her. It was a rather bold thing to ask, but she was as interested in how he would react to the question as she was in the answer.

"Well, if you must know, although it's really no business of yours or anyone's, I was upset that she wouldn't let me stay the night with her. In no way had I thought she'd be in any danger, but I had thought it would be romantic."

"And she was adamant that she do it alone." Shelby didn't bother to phrase this as a question, since she already knew it to be the truth.

He nodded. "Yeah. She said that I would be a distraction. She didn't want romance that night, she wanted to work. As usually happened, she buried herself in her research. I'm afraid I just got a little tired of it and lashed out. I mean, it was such a great opportunity, staying in such a historic place. I truly and deeply regret what I said, especially since those were the last words we spoke."

"No late-night makeup texting?"

He shook his head and took a deep breath. "This is upsetting to talk about. I really don't have anything to add. You'll have to excuse me."

Shelby sat, watching him leave. He didn't look back as he waited for the elevator, and once she saw it stop on his floor, she left the building.

Back home she debated about what to do with what she'd learned. Did Chief Stone know about the argument? Did she know Liam was leaving? She probably needed to know that much anyway, Shelby thought as she picked up the phone.

"I'm just heading out the door, Shelby," Stone said upon answering. "My day is at long last over . . . unless it's not?"

"I just . . . well, there's something I wanted to tell you."

"Okay. Out with it. Or is this something that should be said in person?"

"No, I don't think so."

She heard Stone sigh. "I'll take it that what you're about to say is related to the murder, even after I've asked you, politely, I might point out, to stay out of it. So, what is it?"

Shelby needed to keep in mind that the chief was usually unfriendly and not take it personally. Why did the woman scare her so much? "I know it's none of my business, but I just wondered if you knew that Liam Kennelly is planning on leaving town."

"How do you know this?" Her voice had sharpened, and Shelby was suddenly very glad they weren't in the same room.

"I was just talking to him, and he told me he's leaving first thing in the morning."

"Oh, is he now? No, I didn't know that." There was a pause, and Shelby wondered if she should be saying something. But the chief took care of that. "Just why were you talking to him?"

"I saw him and asked him a question."

"Like you bumped into him, or you went to see him?"

"Does it matter? You said you didn't know he's leaving. That's important, isn't it?"

"So, what was the question you had for him? I know what my question will be."

She paused, seeing no way out of it. The chief did need to know. "Uh, I had heard he was seen arguing with Savannah on the wharf just before she left for the castle. I wondered what it was about."

"And that's your business because?"

"That's more or less what he asked."

Stone snorted. "And who is your source for this?"

"Felicity Foxworth may have mentioned it in passing."

"Why does that woman not come to me with such information? Is she dense, or is she scared of me?"

"Uh, I don't know the answer to that." *Not going to touch that.*

Stone was silent for such a long time that Shelby wondered if she'd missed the sound of her hanging up. But surely there'd be a dial tone.

"Okay, tell me this," Stone finally said, "did he explain what the argument was about?"

"Yes. He told me that he'd wanted to stay overnight in the castle with her. He thought it would be romantic, but she said she wanted to concentrate on her research. I thought it sounded totally believable and not at all suspicious."

"I'll decide that for myself. And there's nothing I can do about you knowing, but will you now please gracefully bow out of my investigation? Again, I'm asking politely. It really is none of your business."

"Well, Savannah did two signings for us. And, more importantly, I liked her."

"Yes, that is true, but unless you or your aunt is the killer, I repeat, it's no business of yours." Shelby could picture Stone's cold blue eyes and the tightly drawn lips. "Or maybe you're trying to clear Matthew Kessler's name. Again. He did have a motive, after all."

"No, he didn't." She was pretty certain of that. "Uh, what was it?"

"Ms. Page was the competition. A best-selling true-crime writer and all. Maybe he had an insane fit of jealousy."

"Matthew?"

"All right, maybe it's not the best motive, but it is motive. He could at any time decide to start writing again. She was younger, probably a lot smarter, and a hell of a lot prettier. That must make some difference on book tours and these signing events."

"You think that's what a reader is looking for when choosing a book? What the author looks like?" Shelby couldn't keep the incredulity out of her voice. She might be relatively new to the bookselling business, but she did know rubbish when she heard it.

The chief was not to be deterred. "Look, I know he's the darling of the Coast Guard right now, but that doesn't hold water with me. I've got him in my sights. And the more you get involved, the more reason I have to check up on you and those around you."

Now that sounded like a threat. Or a challenge.

Chapter Nineteen

Saturday morning came all too early, but Shelby couldn't complain too much about the reason. Zack called just as she was wavering on the edge of opening her eyes. She'd been luxuriating in the comfort of her bed with J.T. curled up beside her, knowing the alarm would go off shortly but hoping it wouldn't. When she saw Zack was calling, her mind snapped to attention.

"I'm sorry for calling so early. I was hoping you'd be awake and getting ready for work."

"Close enough," Shelby admitted. She liked the idea of his voice being the first one she heard in the morning.

"Good. I have to go out of town for the day so won't be in touch, but I'm hoping you're free for dinner tonight."

She smiled at the tone of expectancy in his voice. "I am, and I'd be delighted."

"Great. How about I pick you up around six. Is that enough time after work?"

"That's plenty. You'll pick me up? Where are we going?"

167

"It's a surprise. Casual dress, though. Have a good day and stay out of trouble. See you later."

"Uh-huh."

She realized as she stepped aboard the shuttle an hour later that she'd been smiling since hanging up. What a great way to start the day. Which was a good thing, because several times during the next six hours, she teetered on the edge of frustration. Who knew that she should have put in a final order for copies of Loreena Swan's book? Fortunately, she'd managed to interest that customer in another local book. She placed the order now to make sure she'd have enough copies when the store reopened in the spring, anyway. She couldn't believe it was that late in the season. Well, part of her brain did know that, but she hadn't mentally prepared herself for all that the end of the season would mean.

The last few weeks had flown by, but she didn't really feel like she'd accomplished much. Maybe she'd have the chance over winter, when there was only one location to focus on, to come up with some creative new ideas to bring in more business to both locations. She'd already tasked Taylor with thinking along the same lines. Maybe between the two of them and Edie, something would occur to them.

Last spring, they'd toyed around with the idea of stocking a variety of magazines, but somehow the conversation had never reached the decision stage. Her initial enthusiasm for the project had waned in that time. Maybe the reason it hadn't caught fire. She glanced around the bookstore, hoping to envision a solution. None came. With a small gift shop already run by the volunteers, the last thing needed in the island bookstore was gifts. What else could a bookstore offer? The book club run by Trudy, Bayside Book Babes Plus One, was happy with how it was going, so there was nothing to do there. Space for writing groups? Not possible at the castle, but what about at the main store? Something to think about.

*　　*　　*

She felt her dock moving later that day, after she'd gotten back home from work and was getting ready for her date. Someone was walking toward the houseboat. She scurried downstairs, hoping it was Zack, but when she looked out the window, Liam's face appeared. Should she be worried? She had alerted the police that he was leaving, after all. This could be a payback visit.

She took a deep breath and pulled the door open a fraction. "Hi, Liam. What can I do for you?"

His smile looked tentative. "Look, I know you told the police chief that I was leaving, and although I'm a bit ticked off, I understand why you did it. And I'm not plotting my revenge or anything. But I think I owe you an explanation. Can I come in?"

How foolish did he think she was?

"Why don't we go up on the top deck and talk? I'll get us some coffee."

"Okay." He glanced to each side.

"The stairs are at the back, although that ladder to your right works also." She pulled the door closed and listened to his footsteps until she heard him settling into a chair. So it wasn't the warmest of nights, but she didn't intend to be alone with him, out of view inside, until she knew what was up. And besides, if Zack arrived early, he'd be sure to see them. She grabbed a heavy jacket as she waited for the Keurig to work its magic. Then she joined him, kicking the door shut behind her.

"So, what's on your mind?" she asked after they'd both had a sip.

He shifted in his chair so that he more or less faced her. "There was actually more to the argument than I'd originally told you. I acted like a kid, getting jealous about Bryce, when she stood firm about my not joining her. I accused her of not wanting me on the island because he was meeting her there."

"That must have gone over well," Shelby couldn't help saying.

"Tell me about it. She was mad, but I know now she was probably mostly hurt that I basically said I didn't trust her."

"Why didn't you? You seemed all right about the castle arrangement earlier."

"That was before I spotted Bryce in town. Savannah had said he was coming up on Sunday for a brief meeting in the afternoon. But there he was, in the hotel lobby, as we were leaving for the shuttle."

"Did you talk to him?"

"No, I was surprised. And I didn't point him out to Savannah, either. I really wish I'd done it all then. Or not said anything at all. I can't get over the fact that my last words to her were so cruel."

He looked so despondent that Shelby almost reached over to hug him. Almost. She needed to keep her objectivity. What he said made sense, but it was possible that, once again, he was lying.

"I'm sorry for you, Liam. And I do understand why you didn't want to say anything about this. So, why are you telling me all this now?"

"Because I thought you might hear about it from the chief, and I didn't want you thinking I had lied. I've heard that you have a reputation for finding killers, and I want you to know I didn't do it." He finished his coffee in a couple of gulps and stood. "I still can't believe all this happened. I don't know what I'll do without her."

Shelby also stood and patted his arm. "I can't begin to imagine how you feel. It will take a while, but at some point, you'll figure it out. Thanks for telling me, Liam."

He nodded and left the way he'd come, while Shelby stood on deck watching him and wondering what this meant for Bryce.

Her thoughts were interrupted several minutes later by the sight of Tekla Stone sauntering along the dock. She didn't look to be in a hurry, but Shelby sensed the chief was uptight about something. She really hoped it wasn't something she'd done.

"Good late afternoon, Chief Stone," Shelby called over the edge of the deck. "I'll be right down."

"Shelby."

Stone had removed her hat by the time Shelby joined her at the door. She walked in when Shelby held the door wide open.

"I see you've had another visitor. What did he want? He wasn't giving you a hard time, I hope?"

"No, no, actually he was apologizing for his earlier abruptness. And he explained some more about the argument he had with Savannah. I presume he told you the same thing."

"That depends on what he told you."

This wasn't going to be easy. Since the chief was obviously waiting for Shelby to go first, she obliged. "He said he was jealous of Bryce . . . and thought he might be staying over at the castle with Savannah. Especially since he'd suggested he stay the night with her and she'd refused."

Stone nodded. "That's the same story he told me."

"You sound like maybe you don't believe him."

"It sounds plausible and I have nothing to contradict it, so I'm going with that, until proven otherwise. What I want to know is why you didn't tell me that Bryce O'Connell was spotted in town on Saturday." She stood with her legs planted slightly apart and was fingering the brim of her hat.

"It wasn't my story to tell. I hadn't seen him. Why do you think I already knew?"

Stone snorted. "What is it you *don't* know?"

"Well, a lot, when you get right down to it." She decided she'd better not sound flippant. "Is there anything else I can do for you?"

"Yes, but I may have mentioned it already: stay out of this." She plopped her hat back on her head and pulled it down snuggly.

Shelby felt the boat rock before she heard the knock. Stone, who stood closest to the door, pulled it open. She looked from

Zack standing in the doorway back to Shelby. "You are a busy gal. Enjoy your evening."

Stone winked and then nodded at Zack as she passed in front of him.

"Wow, wish I'd come earlier," he said as he filled the space Stone had just vacated. He looked at Shelby. "Is everything okay?"

"Uh, sure. She just wanted to ask a few more questions."

"Well, I have a question for you. Are you ready to go?" He nodded at her jacket she hadn't yet removed, a quizzical smile on his face.

"Oh, uh, not quite . . . just give me a minute, okay?"

"Are you sure everything is okay? You seem sort of distracted, although I know the chief can have that effect on people."

"It's not only her. Liam Kennelly—you know, Savannah Page's fiancé—came by just before. I guess I'm getting a lot of information at one time and just need to process it."

"This doesn't sound good." He put a hand on each of her shoulders. "Why would he be talking to you about this?"

Shelby saw the concern on his face. "I'll tell you all about it after. I just need a couple of minutes to freshen up."

Before she knew what had happened, Zack pulled her toward him into a long, deep kiss. She felt breathless when they pulled apart and not quite sure what to say.

"Keep that on your mind while you're getting ready. Tonight is for us, okay? It's not a night for solving murders."

She nodded and placed her hand on his cheek for a moment before going up the stairs. She felt dazed and just hoped she wouldn't trip. That man did know how to get her attention.

She wondered if the outfit she'd chosen was just the right touch of casual and sexy. The red cashmere off-the-shoulder sweater was an extravagance she'd bought before coming to Alexandria Bay, and one she'd not worn before. The length begged for it to be paired with black leggings, and the black suede booties added the final touch. She took a look in the mirror and wondered if she needed to change into something less . . . She wasn't quite sure what; maybe less contrived. She had never been a fashion plate and was even less comfortable wearing something out of the ordinary, but somehow this felt right.

Zack's face confirmed it when she reached the bottom stair.

"Wow. You look amazing. And you never cease to amaze me," he added as he kissed her cheek.

She wondered briefly if he'd felt a heat transfer from the blush that took over her entire body. Her smile never left her face as they made their way to his Jeep. A few minutes later, he pulled into his driveway. The blush seemed to be her default for the evening.

Although she'd been to his house a few times for barbecues over the summer, he'd planned to take this meal up a notch, she realized when she saw the table set, complete with a tablecloth, flowers, and candles. Was there an occasion?

"It's just finishing off in the oven," Zack said as he hung up her coat and led her to the sofa. "May I get you a glass of red wine?"

"I'd love one." She tried to relax while waiting but felt keyed up. She took a deep breath, knowing she should just be enjoying, not analyzing. When he brought her drink, she was mentally ready.

"Is this a special occasion?" she asked, wondering if she'd missed his birthday. She realized that was information they'd never discussed.

He grinned. "It's special because I wanted to spend more time with you and not be bothered by servers or other diners. And I keep telling you how talented I am in the kitchen, so I think I have to prove it."

She could tell he was being playful about his kitchen skills but truly believed he wanted more time for them both. Well, that worked for her.

"I like that, both the spending time together and being fed. And I have been treated to your feasts before."

"Ah, barbecuing is fun, but not quite the challenge of cooking indoors and from scratch. No prepackaged ingredients here."

"Just how did you have time for all that? I thought you were out of town all day."

"I didn't say it wasn't prepared beforehand, which some of it was."

"I'm still impressed."

"Good. That's my goal."

Shelby smiled. "You know, a girl could get used to this."

"Not just any girl. I hope you know, you're the one who's got my attention, don't you?"

Shelby nodded, not quite certain she could speak without getting overly emotional. Zack watched her intently for several seconds.

"Good. Now, let's eat."

She helped him bring the dishes to the table and then sat when he pulled out her chair.

"That's the good thing about fall," he said, lighting the two candles on the table. "The earlier darkness encourages romance."

So does the right man, she thought as he topped up her wine glass.

Chapter Twenty

Sunday meant another dinner out, this time at Edie's. Family time. It had been a surprisingly busy afternoon at the bookstore, much to Shelby's delight, so she was ready to be pampered. She just hoped her aunt hadn't gone to too much trouble nor spent a lot of time on her feet. Matthew arrived just after Shelby, something that was happening increasingly, and voiced the same concerns.

"Believe me," Edie said, sitting at the kitchen table, "there's nothing easier than putting a roast in the oven. Especially since I've left the veggies for you two. I'm ready for a drink, thank you."

Matthew looked at the bottles set out on the counter and poured the women each a sherry and a Jack Daniels with water for himself.

"Why don't you two go and relax in the living room while I take care of these?" Shelby suggested.

When she was on her own, she took a sip of the drink, let out a sigh, and set about peeling the carrots, then cutting them up and setting them to boil. She added sugar peas for the final few minutes and sat at the kitchen table to wait for it to be ready. Besides, she probably wasn't being missed.

She'd taken the chair closest to the window and tried to relax, looking out at the garden. Edie had the green thumb in the family, that was for sure. She couldn't remember her dad having had even a houseplant at their place, while she enjoyed buying some cut flowers every now and then. She knew the shelf life for those and didn't feel bad when it had been reached. At least she knew it wasn't her fault.

She'd often wondered if Matthew was partly responsible for the colorful scenery out there. Whatever, or whomever, was to thank, it provided a restful spot. She wondered briefly what it would look like in winter.

She checked the clock and tested the carrots. Nicely done, not too crisp nor soggy. She transferred the food to the serving dishes Edie had set out and brought them out to the dining room table, announcing that it was time to eat.

It didn't take long for everyone to serve themselves. After taking several bites, Matthew leaned toward Edie and said, "You're an amazing cook. You really know what to do with a roast."

Edie looked pleased, and Shelby felt like a third wheel. She was content to enjoy her meal without feeling she had to offer a lot to the conversation. She'd been right; it seemed the other two had a lot to get caught up on.

Shelby had just finished clearing away the final dishes and carried her cup of tea into the front room, having decided she'd drink quickly and discreetly leave, when a sharp knock at the front door had her jumping to her feet.

"Are you expecting someone? Trudy?"

Edie shook her head.

"I'll get it." Shelby decided to be cautious and open the door a fraction; after all, it was dark outside. "Chief Stone, what are you doing here?"

Stone shoved her way inside and looked into the front room. "Ah, I thought I might find Mr. Kessler here." She walked farther in, uninvited. "I'd like to have a few words with you."

Edie struggled to stand. "This is very intrusive, Tekla, even for you."

Stone ignored her. "Now, I thought I was being discreet, talking to you here, Kessler. I could, however, take you down to the station and do it more formally. Your choice."

Matthew looked at Edie and shrugged. "Here's fine, if Edie doesn't mind."

Edie looked like she did mind but shook her head. "You're welcome to use the dining room," she said as she lowered herself back into the chair.

Stone grunted. She held her hand out to the side, indicating Matthew should lead the way. Before she stepped into the room behind him, she turned to Shelby. "You might as well come, too. That way you won't have anything to go sticking your nose into later."

"You don't mind this nosey parker being here, do you?" she asked Matthew after they'd both sat.

Matthew looked at Shelby, his eyes hooded. She wondered what he was thinking. "That's okay."

Shelby sat down as quietly as she could, not wanting to draw attention to herself.

"So," Stone began, "we have Ms. Page's laptop, and I've spent time going through it. What gets my curiosity up is the fact that you had corresponded with her several times. Something you hadn't mentioned before. Would you care to enlighten me?"

Shelby sat up a bit straighter. She hadn't known Savannah and Matthew had been in contact. Why hadn't Matthew said something? *Like what?*

Matthew shrugged. "You've read the emails, I'm sure. I don't have much to add."

"Well, we'll get to why you didn't mention this before, a bit later. It looks like Ms. Page wanted to do a book about your wife's murder. But you refused to cooperate. Is that right?"

Shelby had noticed a slight jerk in Matthew's body at the mention of his wife. She guessed that answered her question. He didn't like to talk about nor be reminded of her, even now.

"Yes, that's right."

"Why did you refuse to take part?"

He shifted in his seat, looking more uncomfortable than Shelby had ever seen him. Finally, after a few minutes of staring at his hands, folded on the table, he looked back up at Chief Stone.

"Because it was a painful time . . . and still is, when I think about it. The case was thoroughly looked at by the investigators and by me, with no satisfactory outcome. I didn't want it dredged up again, just so some hot new writer could publish another book. Not unless she had new information, but I highly doubt that. There was no way she'd find the killer. I'd been there and failed." He paused and sighed. "I mainly didn't want to have to relive it all again."

"And that's it? Here's a . . . how did you describe her? A hot new writer, and she's writing in your field, where you've been a best seller for many years? Now you're a forgotten name and she's heading for the top. There was no feeling of jealousy? Maybe after a few years of hiding out on an island, you've been longing for the limelight again? How did this make you feel, Mr. Kessler?"

Matthew's expression hadn't changed, and it didn't look like he was about to provide an answer anytime soon. His body had tensed, though, and his fingertips turned red as his clenched hands tightened still further.

Shelby was glad Edie was in the other room. She'd have felt dreadful for Matthew, just as Shelby now did. She wanted to run over and put her arms around him but knew the chief would definitely frown on that. She looked at Tekla Stone, wondering how she had known Matthew would be at Edie's. Had she been following him? That wasn't something she should ask. She searched the chief's face for a hint of compassion but couldn't find it. What she did see was annoyance and impatience bordering on anger. Now it was her turn to sigh.

"Are you finding this tedious, Shelby?" Stone asked, glaring.

"No, not tedious." She decided to leave it at that.

"Well then," Stone said, her voice rigid as she stood, "we'll leave it at that, for now. But you think long and hard on this, Matthew Kessler, and if there's anything you should be telling me, you'd better do it, and soon. Before I find out on my own."

Shelby decided this was not the right time to ask the chief where Savannah's laptop had been found.

Chapter Twenty-One

S helby found it hard the next morning to concentrate on her weekly household cleaning. That wasn't a big surprise. She had to admit, this was her least-favorite task of the week, but she forced herself to do the most obvious chores. All the while her mind kept wandering back to how Sunday evening had ended. Chief Stone had really dropped a bomb. After she'd left, Matthew had been quick to follow. Shelby could see how upset he was, even though he tried to hide it from Edie. It was left to Shelby to soothe her aunt's worry while keeping her own mind from wondering about those emails. She had believed in Matthew when Loreena Swan had died; she needed to do the same now. Besides, this didn't count as a valid motive, she was sure of that.

Of course, Edie had known just how to add to all those concerns running through Shelby's mind when she'd phoned earlier that morning, telling Shelby she would be working at the main bookstore that day. Shelby had to do some talking to get her aunt to agree to put in a half day only. She wanted Edie back at work as soon as possible but remembered the hazards after the knee replacement surgery. Edie had often felt exhausted after short work periods, which could, and had, led to falls.

She'd just given the countertop a final swipe when her cell phone rang. The number didn't look familiar, but she answered anyway.

"Is this Shelby Cox?" The caller was female and sounded like she might be around Edie's age.

"Yes, it is."

"That's good. It always helps to have the right person on the phone." She chuckled. "I'm Izzy Crocker. I was a friend of your mama's."

Shelby already knew the name and had been meaning to track her down, but that hadn't prepared her for this surprise call.

"It's nice of you to call, Mrs. Crocker."

"First of all, please call me Izzy. And secondly, I've been wanting to get in touch with you since I'd heard you'd moved back to the Bay. I thought you might want to hear more about your mama. We were good friends, your mama and me, as you've probably been told, but only for a few years. And that was so long ago. My memory isn't what it should be. But I'm happy to try to fill in the gaps for you. Would you like to come over?"

"I'd love to. When is best for you? I do work most days, though."

"Well, it sounds like you're not working today. How about afternoon tea, at three? Do you know where I live?"

"Yes, I do, and I'll be there. Thank you. I look forward to meeting you."

"And me you."

Shelby stood with her hand over her heart, willing her pulse to stop racing, trying to comprehend what had just taken place. Suddenly, her mother was foremost in her thoughts again. This was what she'd been hoping for when she'd moved back to Alexandria Bay, information about her mom, who she'd believed had passed away almost thirty years ago. Although she now knew Merrily hadn't died but had instead run off with a banker from Georgia, never to have contact with her daughter again, Shelby had been trying to put those upsetting thoughts out of her mind. But she still wanted to know more about the woman who had given birth to her. She needed to know more.

Shelby made herself some coffee and sat at the counter to make a list of questions she wanted to ask Izzy. Then she ripped up the list, deciding that was too rigid. She just wanted to hear the memories.

So, instead, she started a new list . . . of suspects. She doubted that Frank White should be on the list but decided to put him in the *Unlikely* column. He was the only name there. She glanced at the clock. He should be at the soup kitchen by now, if he was going in that day. This would be the perfect time to pay him another visit. As much as logic told her he wasn't the murderer, there was a part of her that couldn't quite give him up. He wouldn't have killed Savannah, but might he have been complicit in some way? Maybe without even knowing it? She thought briefly about Cody and his mentioning the plans to the boys.

She knew it was foolish to get so involved in another murder, but really, she'd been drawn into the investigation. Again. It wasn't her fault. Besides, it would keep her mind off thoughts of what she might, or might not, learn that afternoon.

She quickly changed and did a fast walk to the soup kitchen, pausing outside to slow her breathing. She really must be out of shape. Inside, the kitchen looked busy, with even more volunteers than the last time she'd been there. She spotted Frank at the same moment he looked over at the door. She gave a small wave, and he nodded. A couple of minutes later he joined her at the table she'd chosen close to the door.

"I assume you've thought of something else to ask me," he stated. "Not that you're here to volunteer?" He added a small smile, which put her at ease but made her feel a bit of guilt for bothering him in the middle of such worthy work.

"I think it's a great cause, and someday I'd like to try to get involved. But right now, I just have a few quick questions. I hope you don't mind."

He looked resigned, even though he didn't answer, so she continued.

"I guess you'd been to the castle before."

"Are you kidding? Of course. I grew up in the Bay, after all. In fact, I knew your dad."

"You did?" That threw her off. She'd been so busy trying to get information about her mom that she hadn't wondered much about her father's earlier years. She felt ashamed.

"Well, not so well. He was a few years younger than me, and he didn't really hang out with any gangs. I see that look on your face, but in those days *gang* didn't always mean the same thing it does today. We were just a bunch of kids hanging out together because of where we lived or what sports we played or, in your dad's case, what clubs we were in at school. As I seem to remember, he was the brain, used to play chess and such things. It's your aunt who everyone knew. She was quite the figure, all hippie-like all the time. A real ball of fire and always into everything. I haven't seen her in a while, though. I hope she's doing okay."

"Well, she had a recent knee replacement, but other than that, she still runs the bookstore."

He chuckled. "I can relate to the replacement part. Had a couple myself."

Shelby felt she'd completely lost control of the conversation. How had this evolved into a discussion of old times and new ailments? *Time to get back on track.*

"I should have asked the other day—did you hear Savannah when she got up and was wandering around?"

"Not a thing."

"Not even when she fell? She must have screamed."

"Like I said, nothing."

She stared at him. That didn't sound right. Finally, he shifted in his seat and added, "I wear hearing aids, and I take them out at night. I would have heard the bell, though. I'd tested it."

It made sense, but she was curious to know what the chief had made of it. Or maybe Edie would be a good one to ask. She was always saying how her hearing wasn't what it used to be. Perhaps she could relate.

"Thanks for telling me. I'm also curious, after you'd been hired to do that shift at the castle, did anyone approach you about what you'd be doing there or ask you any questions about the castle itself?"

He hesitated a minute, and Shelby hoped that meant something. She was disappointed when he shook his head. "Nope."

"Did you know about the secret passages?"

"Yup. At least, it was a rumor, but we all believed it. I hadn't seen them myself, though."

"Did you tell Savannah Page about it?"

He shook his head. "Like I'm sure I told you last time, I didn't really talk to her. She found out about them on her own, I guess."

Shelby couldn't think of anything else to ask. It had been a long shot at best. What she'd actually been hoping for was his admitting he'd gotten so carried away talking about the castle that he'd mentioned the secret passages, which seemed less secret by the moment. She thanked him for his time and headed home for a quick lunch.

At three precisely, Shelby knocked on the front door of Izzy Crocker's home. She'd decided to drive, since it had appeared to be rather a long walk. Besides, her car needed to be driven occasionally, although she knew that what it really needed was a long run. Like to Clayton or Cape Vincent. One day soon, she promised it, as she surveyed Izzy's house. From the outside it looked charming, like a picture from a Thomas Kinkade painting. The deep blue of the clapboard siding contrasted vividly with the white trim around the roof, the door, and the windows. Even the shutters were white.

The yard looked just as inviting, with beds of fall flowers across the front of the house and individual groupings of shrubs and plants scattered seemingly randomly across the lawn, but Shelby realized it had a purposeful look.

The door was pulled open before she even knocked, and an older woman of medium build, her white hair pulled back into a bun, welcomed her inside. Shelby guessed she was in her sixties or seventies, probably a few years older than her mother would be.

"I'm Izzy Crocker," she said, giving Shelby a hug. "You look so much like your mama, I would recognize you in an instant."

"Thank you," Shelby said, suddenly at a loss for words. She'd heard that before, but it still seemed unreal. Any photos she'd seen of her mom since coming back made her feel like she was looking at a stranger. She felt totally detached from the images, and she wasn't sure if that was a good thing or not.

Over tea and an assortment of sweets, Izzy filled Shelby in on what it was like growing up in Alexandria Bay. Her family had been there for generations and had been involved in everything from farming to shipbuilding, but Izzy had married a banker. Her life had been good, even though they'd stayed in the same town for their entire lives.

"A banker?" Shelby echoed. "I understand that a banker caught my mother's eye, too." There, she'd said it, she'd introduced the topic. She just hoped she was ready to hear what Izzy could tell her. She took a sip of tea and tensed.

Izzy looked at her and reached over to touch her hand. "That's right, dear." She sat back and stared out the window before continuing.

"Maybe I should start at the beginning. You may get a better sense of who your mom was. We met only a few days after she'd moved here with your dad. They'd been married less than a week and had come straight from a honeymoon weekend in New York City. They actually rented that cottage you see to the left of this house. My papa had originally built it for my older sister and her husband, to help them get a start. Then we, Hector and I, put it up for rent. We'd been married and living in this house about six years at the time."

Shelby glanced out the window but realized she'd have to wait until she left to be able to see the cottage. She focused again on Izzy.

"Your mom was a beauty and, I thought, a social butterfly totally out of her element. There was nothing in Alex Bay to compare to the life she'd known. We became good friends and did a lot of things together, but she was restless, right from the start. At one point, she and Edie opened that store, but I don't think Merrily lasted more than a week in there. She'd always be wanting to go out to tea, although she seldom entertained. I was sure she thought the cottage was too small and a bit beneath her. I don't mean to make her sound flighty or vain, but she had been brought up differently from your dad, and they'd been too infatuated with one another to realize it. At least, that's what I sensed."

Izzy stopped her tale long enough to pour herself some more tea after filling Shelby's cup. After taking a bite of a sugar cookie, she continued.

"She also loved to go out to dances, and in those days, there were a lot of those held at the community center and also the church basement. Your daddy, though, he wasn't one to take to the dance floor. But there were a lot of husbands willing to oblige. We wives just sat back and smiled, although I know a few of them were silently fuming. When Merrily got pregnant, she was filled with joy. She was so looking forward to being a mother."

Shelby felt a catch in her throat and tears filling her eyes. Why had she left her behind, then?

"But, you know, after a long dreary winter with little social activity, Merrily became less, well, animated, I guess. She stayed at home and took care of you and really tried to be a good mom, but I could see the gradual change in her. She had several friends, but she started withdrawing from them. I think we stayed close because, well, we lived next door. These days I think they'd diagnose her with a massive case of postpartum depression, which lasted a few years. Until she met Gerald Steiger. He was a banker from Georgia visiting town to do business with my husband. Merrily and Gerald met here one afternoon, and I could see her transforming. He came back to town three more times, and each time I saw his car parked at the cottage. She didn't talk to me about him, nor did she tell me she was leaving with him. I found a note in my mailbox one afternoon, and that was it. I never heard from her again."

Shelby felt the same sorrow that had engulfed her when Edie had first explained what had happened. She couldn't think of a thing to say.

"I know it's not easy to hear, Shelby. She didn't run away because of your dad or because of you, but because she needed something more, something to keep her alive and vibrant. Like I said, they were just too different to start with."

Izzy moved over to sit next to Shelby on the couch and put an arm around her shoulders. "I'm sorry, dear. It's not a story with a happy ending for anyone but her."

Shelby thought about it a few minutes and then pulled herself together. "Thank you, Izzy. I needed to hear their story, and now maybe I can start to move beyond it. It came as quite a shock when I found out she hadn't died when I was younger. That's what I'd been led to believe."

Izzy gave a final squeeze before removing her arm. "Anytime you have any questions, just come on over. In fact, I hope you'll feel free to come by and we can enjoy afternoon tea again. I'd like to get to know you better, my dear."

Shelby nodded, not sure if that would happen. Or maybe it would, once she'd resolved all the ghosts in her life.

Chapter Twenty-Two

Chocomania was the first stop for Shelby the next morning. She needed to stock up on fresh truffles both for the store and for herself, particularly after the rough night she'd had. She'd hoped no one would call her because she didn't want to talk nor explain why she didn't. Fortunately, she'd had only J.T. demanding her attention. That afternoon visit had been a lot to process, and she was sure there was still a lot more to learn about her mom. Most importantly, why she hadn't been in touch with her only daughter all these years. Or maybe Shelby wasn't her only child. Maybe she had a family with her new husband and she wanted to keep that life totally separated from Shelby. So many questions. But she knew Izzy Crocker wasn't the one to supply those answers. But now, she could get on with things. Like work.

Like truffles. She waited, debating which flavor would be her special treat for the day, while Erica finished serving an older couple some hot chocolate.

"I'll have to try your hot chocolate one day," Shelby said after Erica greeted her.

"Pure chocolate. It will rock your world. Want one now?"

"Um, no. I'll save it for a treat on a thoroughly miserable, rainy, foggy day. What I do want is my usual truffle count and a latte. And I'll also take the order for the store. How was your weekend? Anything special happen?" *Like, any word from a certain literary agent?*

Erica shrugged. "Not really. Oh, right, Bryce asked me to dinner on Sunday."

"Wow, and was it fun?"

"I turned him down."

"You what? I thought you were ready to go out with him."

Erica leaned across the counter and lowered her voice. "Not after the bits of conversation I heard Chief Stone having with him in here on Saturday."

"Really, what did she say?" Shelby had lowered her voice as well and felt like a true conspirator.

"I didn't hear much, but she did tell him she'd found Savannah Page's laptop and had gone through it. She said she wanted to know what Bryce had to say for himself. Then she glanced at me and suggested they go to the station to discuss it. So, you see, if he's in any way connected with the murder, I don't want to go out with him. Besides, he sort of snuck into town, remember?"

She sounded so dejected that Shelby reached out and squeezed her hand. "It could be nothing, or it could be something. I don't know what to say. I'm sorry, though, because you both looked interested in each other."

Erica sighed. "Story of my life. There's always something. Now, let me get your order. Do you think you need as many truffles in the store at this time of year?"

"Oh, they won't go to waste. Believe me," Shelby guaranteed, already salivating.

*   *   *

It turned out to be a two-truffle day, which meant not very many customers. After Shelby had straightened the shelves, changed around some displays, and spent far too much time thinking about the murder, thinking about the bookstore, thinking about Zack, and avoiding thinking about her mom, she decided to call Taylor.

"Hey, Taylor. How are you?" She hoped for good news.

"Great to hear from you, Shelby. I meant to call. I even thought about coming in today, but I just got too comfortable to even move. And my MIL is even being somewhat agreeable."

"You sound tired, and maybe she's realized what it takes to stay on your good side. I'd think she'd want to do that."

Taylor chuckled. "One would think. How are things at the store?"

"Quiet doesn't even cover it. But the shelves are sparkling."

"Good job. And how is the murder investigation going?"

"You know me too well. I'm finding out a lot, but I don't know how it all ties in, if at all. I don't think I'll quit my day job, as they say."

"Well, Chuck isn't sharing anything these days. I've tried to get him to talk about it, but all he wants to discuss is the baby. Go figure."

"Yeah, go figure. I appreciate your efforts, but I don't want you dwelling on it. You need to be enjoying these last days of freedom."

"Ouch. Just wait till you're a mom, Shelby Cox. I look forward to saying those same words to you."

When I'm a mom, Shelby thought later as she locked up the store. That might never happen. It wasn't something she was working toward, anyway. Not at this point. She was only twenty-nine, after all. Still a lot of time left. She hoped. She wondered if Zack wanted children. That was a conversation they hadn't had. Yet. That thought brought a smile to her face as she rushed to catch the shuttle.

* * *

Shelby noticed Bryce coming out of a shop as she sauntered on her way home. It could have been Chocomania. She hadn't been paying close attention. That might be interesting. She picked up her pace and met up with him before he could cross the street and head to the hotel.

"Hi, Bryce. Do you have a minute?"

"Oh, hi, Shelby. Sorry, I was lost in thought." He focused on her and smiled. "Anytime. Would you like to go for a coffee, or are you off to a hot date?"

"Hardly. I'm just getting back from the castle, and yes, a coffee would be great."

She noticed he steered her to the Coffee Café across the street rather than to Chocomania. Maybe he was still smarting from Erica's rejection. She looked around the shop as they entered. They were the only customers. She ordered an espresso, wanting a smaller drink in case the conversation became uncomfortable so she could leave quickly. She tried to formulate a plan. She hadn't really been thinking ahead when she'd stopped him. But she would make good use of the time.

"Can I ask you something?" He surprised her by starting the conversation, although his attention was focused on his coffee mug.

"Sure."

"Did Erica say anything about me?" He seemed to be searching her face, looking for any trace of a reaction.

"Like what?" *What to answer. Stall for time. Keep a straight face.*

"I'm not sure. I thought she was interested, but when I asked her out, she shut me down." He paused to take a long drink. "Did it have anything to do with Chief Stone questioning me?"

An opening. "You'll need to ask Erica about that. But I *am* wondering what the chief thought of your explanation, you know, of what she found on Savannah's laptop."

Shelby couldn't quite read the look that passed over Bryce's face. Anger, fear, malice? Whatever it was, he looked uncomfortable, and she sure felt the same. Well, she'd asked the question. She had to see this through.

"So, Erica did hear about that. Why don't you just ask the chief? But I will tell you, as I told her, it's not what it seems. We had worked out our problems."

Curious. She took a stab. "So you're saying it wasn't a strong motive for murder?"

He bristled. "Murder? Like hell. I didn't kill Savannah. I wouldn't kill anyone. And as you said yourself, the chief obviously doesn't think so, either, or I'd be in jail." He took a deep breath and seemed to calm down.

Shelby considered pointing out that that wasn't what she'd said but thought it best to leave well enough alone now that he seemed more settled. Should she ask about the laptop again? What was on it? A new book suggestion he didn't like? Hardly a motive. Blackmail? About what? Was Liam's fear founded after all? Did Bryce want to get back together with Savannah?

Would the chief tell her?

"I'm sorry I got so exasperated," Bryce said, finally adding a faint smile. "I'm still on edge after everything."

Shelby decided she might as well jump in, even if she alienated him. "I can understand that, but you did say you wanted me to let you know what I heard about the investigation. Right now, what I can't understand is why you won't tell me what you and Savannah had worked out. Were you two seeing each other again? Was that it?"

He stared at her for a few seconds, possibly trying to decide what to do about her. Finally, he answered, and she let out the breath she'd been holding.

"All right, I'll tell you, but this goes no further. Do I have your promise?"

"Yes." She hoped it wasn't something Erica should know.

"And the only reason I'm telling you this is because I have the feeling you won't stop otherwise, which could end up badly for me." He folded his hands, tent style, on the table. "Savannah found out that I'd borrowed some money from her royalties before passing them on to her. I knew she never checked the statements, and I needed some quick cash to pay off a debt I'd incurred to cover a bad investment." He glanced at Shelby for a reaction. Her mind was racing, wondering what kind of investment that could be, but she didn't interrupt.

"Fortunately, I had the money to repay her right away; in fact, that's what I'd originally been planning to do. I promised her it wouldn't happen again. And she promised she'd start paying attention to her statements."

His smile was due to the memory of Savannah rather than anything to do with her, Shelby realized. That made it seem believable. Besides, even if it had ended acrimoniously, what was the worst that could have happened? Savannah dumped him as her agent? Would that have led to murder? Unlikely. Or what if she had threatened to call the cops? Again, a reason for murder? Possibly, but he must have realized the police would be checking out every aspect of their relationship and everything would come out. So, murder? She guessed not.

"Okay, thanks for telling me."

"And you won't tell Erica?"

"No, I won't." She might have to reconsider if they reached a serious stage in their relationship, though.

He reached across the table and put his hand on her arm. "Thank you, Shelby. And I won't hurt Erica, I promise. On the other hand, she baffles me. But you're right, I need to talk to her." He glanced at his watch. "It's getting late. I don't want to keep you from dinner."

"Thanks for the coffee," Shelby answered, knowing when it was time to leave. She grabbed her bag and stood. "Good luck."

She felt his eyes on her back as she left. When she glanced back in, he had pulled his phone out and was punching in numbers.

Should she let Erica know he was calling? He might be already talking to her. She debated with herself about it all the way home.

Which is why she didn't notice that she was being followed.

Chapter Twenty-Three

S he heard the footsteps as she neared the houseboat. She could also feel the wharf rocking as the person picked up speed. Fear choked her, but she forced herself to turn around rather than make a dash for the door. She wasn't sure she could have made it in time anyway. When had she gotten so on edge?

In the gathering dusk, she could see it was a woman, but she couldn't see the face. She slowly let out her breath.

"I'm sorry to startle you," the woman said, getting closer. She was a girl, really, and Shelby recognized her after a couple of seconds. Rachel Michaels.

"I'm surprised, that's all. Was it me you were looking for? How did you know where I live?" She tried slowing her breathing without it being too noticeable.

"I saw you in the coffee shop just a few minutes ago and followed you. I know, not cool, but I wanted to talk to you, and I didn't want to have to pay the boat fare again." Her smile made her look like an embarrassed teenager.

"What can I do for you, Rachel?" Shelby still wasn't sure if she wanted to invite her on board.

"I want to ask you something; a favor, really." She hugged herself, and Shelby realized that, with the sun going down, the dampness from the river was settling in.

"Why don't you come inside?" she said. She'd met Rachel, after all, and they had a mutual interest in Savannah's book. Shelby opened the door and stooped to scoop up J.T. before he made it outside. She liked to keep him in overnight now that it was getting cooler. Who knew what four-legged creatures were out there getting ready for winter.

"Have a seat," she said, indicating the chairs to her left.

"What a cool cat. What's his name?" Rachel reached out to pat him, but J.T. didn't stick around for long.

"Would you like some coffee or something?"

"No, thanks, I just want to talk, if that's okay."

Shelby slung her coat over the back of a chair as Rachel sat in the paisley slipper chair closest to the door.

"You see, I'm a writer," Rachel began. "I'm sure I told you that last time. At least, I'm trying to be. I've written a couple of books now, which have done okay, but I can't seem to get a big-name publisher."

"What do you write?" Shelby didn't want to prolong the conversation, but she did want to come across as friendly.

"I've just branched into true crime; that's why I wanted a copy of Savannah Page's latest. Like I said, I'd actually hoped to get here and meet her in person and then go out for coffee, but I got delayed. I wanted her to read over my outline, and I'd hoped she'd have some suggestions about how I could advance my career or maybe even put me in touch with her agent. That would be a big help. But I missed my chance."

"That was too bad." Shelby wasn't sure what to say, nor was she sure where it was leading.

"Uh-huh, it sure was. So, I was hoping that maybe, instead, you could help me."

"Me? How?"

"Would you introduce me to Matthew Kessler? I've seen you talking to him at the castle. I'm a big fan of his, and I'd like to see if he might help me, to pick his brain. I'm sure he could give me some great pointers on research. Maybe he'd even read my new manuscript."

That wasn't what Shelby had expected. But she was pretty certain what Matthew would say. Also, she wondered when Rachel might have seen them together. That sounded odd.

"I'd have to ask him first, of course, but I'll warn you, I don't think your chances are very good."

"Why not? I'm a serious writer. I'm just asking for a break now that Savannah isn't here. I'm sure she would have helped me. All the big-name authors know people who have helped them over the years. There's a lot of networking going on. I just want to get in on some of that. I've put in the time honing my writing skills, but now I want what I deserve."

Shelby had stiffened at the increasing irritation in Rachel's voice. She could give her a tip right now that this wasn't the way to make friends and get people to help you. However, it wasn't her place to tell her any of that. She would mention it to Matthew, but that would be the extent of it.

Shelby stood, hoping her intent was clear. "I will ask him, Rachel. Do you live around here? How can I get in touch with you?"

Rachel stood, back to her original self, all smiles. "I live just outside Cape Vincent, but I'm staying at a B and B in town. I'll give you my number and you can text me. I can meet him anytime, really. This is so, so cool of you." She pulled a piece of paper from her pocket and spotted a pen lying on the side table. She wrote down her number and handed it to Shelby. "Thank you so much."

She left quickly, and Shelby once again stooped to grab a scampering J.T. She wasn't quite sure what to make of her visitor, but she was glad Rachel had refused the coffee. There had therefore been nothing to keep her lingering.

Shelby locked the door and took a deep breath. She would have to ask Matthew, of course, but she was certain he would want nothing to do with this young author.

*   *   *

After a quick supper of pasta, pesto, and chicken strips, Shelby felt restless, in need of a walk. She could head up to Edie's, although they'd had a long talk on the phone earlier in the day. Or maybe she'd walk over to the James Street Wharf and enjoy the lights playing on the water. Something that was mindless and would help settle her down.

She dressed warmly and found a small flashlight, then ducked out before J.T. could rouse himself from his sleep on the chair. The sky was overcast, and she felt pleased she'd brought the flashlight. The parking lot had a lot of cracks in it, and even the sidewalk into town could do with a redo. By the time she reached the wharf, she realized the restless feeling had given away to one of feeling spooked. Her hand found the smartphone in her pocket, and she thought about calling Zack. Maybe he'd like an after-dinner walk, too. That might sound romantic, rather than someone giving in to foolish fears. Unfortunately, the call went to voice mail. She left a short message so he'd know the call didn't need to be returned.

She thought about going into Riley's to warm up with a coffee but suddenly had the desire to get home as quickly as possible.

By the time she stuck the key into the doorknob, she'd worked herself into a tizzy. *Too much thinking about murder*, she decided. A good book, a cup of tea, and a cat on her lap were what was needed.

Chapter
Twenty-Four

By the time Shelby was ready for work the next morning, the light drizzle had turned to a heavy, pelting rain. She took a look out the window and wished it were Monday. Then she could have just gone back to bed where it was cozy and enjoy the sound of the rain pounding on the roof. But no such luck. Of course, she reminded herself, if it were Monday, she'd have had to get up eventually and clean.

She opened the door for J.T., but after he stuck his head out to sniff the air and got sprinkled with some drops, he scurried back to what had become his favorite chair. The love seat with its wide back, placed under the window, allowed him to keep an eye on the outside world while enjoying the warmth and security inside.

It hadn't taken him long to give up his wandering ways and settle in at the houseboat, Shelby thought, as she gave him a thorough scratching on the top of his head. She realized how much that pleased her. She hadn't previously given a thought to owning a cat or a dog, but that had certainly changed.

Although, of course, she didn't own J.T. It was more the other way around these days. She thought of all those adages she'd read about cats having servants and such. *How true.*

"All right, here I go, and I'm sure I'll be the only one in the store all day." She looked at J.T. for support, but he was busy grooming himself and didn't even give her a look.

Hmph.

It turned out that she was right about the lack of foot traffic. By noon she'd made only two sales and was feeling discouraged. She looked up expectantly as the bell over the door rang, but instead of a customer, Chrissie Halstead walked in.

Chrissie glanced around the store while Shelby admired her moss-green pantsuit. "I see it's as busy in here as the rest of the castle," she said, smiling. "Don't worry, it's quite normal at this time of year, especially when the weather is this bad."

Shelby sighed. "I understand. It just makes for a long day. Do you know if our contract states we have to be open all day, until our stated closing time?"

"I don't. I've never seen it. What are you thinking?"

"Well, if we can discern a pattern, maybe we can shorten the hours here. I could work more at the main store." Shelby was pleased with the thought but wasn't sure if it was possible, or even if Edie would agree. "So, what are you doing here today? I noticed the number of volunteers has been cut back."

"Yes, we're on a fall schedule for sure. I don't know if that's a good thing, though." She twirled a stray piece of blonde hair that had worked its way out from behind her ear.

"Why is that?"

"I still haven't mentioned this to the board as yet, but I think we're missing some more objects."

"More? I thought steps would have been taken to prevent any more theft." Shelby cast a quick glance around the store, wondering if she, too, should have remained more vigilant. She'd be sure to have a thorough look after Chrissie left.

"Well, if I'd told the board, there probably would have been. It's my bad. But it's kind of brazen, don't you think, after the murder and all. You'd think the thief would be worried that we would all be on high alert, which we obviously aren't."

"So, what do you plan to do now?" Shelby still couldn't get over the fact that Chrissie hadn't taken steps to upgrade security. But would that have done the trick? She didn't know the answer to that.

"Well, I'm telling only you because I need a sounding board."

Shelby liked the sound of that. It was important to her to feel a part of the castle. "First of all, what do you think is missing, and more importantly, why?"

Chrissie walked over to the counter and leaned against it. "I have to admit that, once again, it's nothing too obvious; otherwise we would have found out sooner. I'm trying to track down a master list of which objects are in each room, but I can't find it. Which is very odd, because Loreena was so organized."

"That was part of her job, then?"

"It was, at least at first, anyway. She was on the committee right from the start, but when they hired an executive director, Loreena's role changed."

"So maybe the ED, Pat Drucker, has the list."

"That would make sense, but I wanted to confirm a few things before I go involving her and the board, because she'd have to tell them, of course."

"Is there anything concrete I can do?"

"Brainstorm with me. I know we've gone through this before, but how could someone steal these things? Some are pocket size, although others aren't, though they could be slipped into a backpack, I guess. And they're not incredibly valuable. We have many antiques that are, but not these items. So, why would anyone even bother taking them?"

"Maybe it's someone who doesn't know antiques or doesn't care. Maybe someone was doing a little redecorating at home. Or maybe we're dealing with several different thieves. The ones who took the plans and wanted to steal something they couldn't take out during the day, and also these guys who take the smaller items. Do they have any resale value? You could check with the pawnshops, although I'm sure the police have done that already."

Chrissie cocked her head. "I knew it was a good idea to talk to you. Yes, there's at least one pawnshop, so I'll check there, just in case the police haven't gotten to it. I know they're more concerned with the murder right now. I guess my next problem is, as you pointed out, how to prevent further thefts, because it doesn't look like they'll stop on their own. It's going to be an ongoing problem until the thief is caught, if ever," she added with a sigh.

"I would think that's something the board should have to deal with. You do really have to tell them. I'd think it would help to have some cameras placed around the castle. Not only would they act as a deterrent, you might even find the culprit."

Chrissie sighed. "You're right. And I will tell them. It's just that I want to impress them with how I'm handling everything. I've heard that Pat may be considering moving on, and if so, I have my eye on the ED position. Please don't tell anyone, though."

"Of course not. But why would she be leaving?"

"Her daughter and grandchildren live in Maine, and she wants to be near them. That's what my source says, anyway."

"I can understand that. Well, good luck with the search. I guess with all of it, really."

"Thanks again." Chrissie returned Shelby's smile and left.

Lots of interesting news. And lots to think about. Shelby wondered if the thefts had had anything to do with the murder after all. Maybe not. Maybe the students hadn't been totally honest about what they had wanted to do in the castle. Small-time thefts for some quick cash? If so, from all she'd been hearing, it seemed like they might never discover who the thief or thieves were, unless the board made some changes in security and did it very quickly.

So, if that was the case, maybe there was yet another person, or other persons, who should be on the suspect list.

But how would she ever figure it out?

*   *   *

Shelby really wanted to talk to Chief Stone. Try as she might, she couldn't shake that thought while she was finishing her evening meal of pizza, fresh from the freezer. She'd just finished the washing up when Edie phoned.

"I thought you might like to join me for dessert and tea. It's been a couple of days since I've seen you, you know."

"I'd love to. Be there shortly. Can I bring anything?" She knew better than to ask, since Edie always declined, but she wanted to be polite.

Twenty minutes later, Shelby knocked on Edie's front door before opening it and stepping inside. As usual, her aunt hadn't locked it. She was glad that the rain had finally stopped and she'd arrived without being soaked. She glanced in the living room, wondering if Matthew might be there, as she made her way into the kitchen. Edie appeared to be alone.

"Hi there. What's on the menu?" Shelby asked, trying to peer over her aunt's shoulder.

Edie waved without turning around from whatever she was doing at the counter. "I made an apricot Bundt cake this afternoon and wanted to share it. There." She turned to face Shelby, holding the tray with two slices already plated. "Would you mind grabbing the tea tray?"

Shelby nodded and followed Edie to the living room with it. "This is a nice treat, although I really don't need the extra calories. And when did you have the time to do this? I thought you were at the store this morning."

"That's the key; I only worked half a day. Just as you suggested. I had plenty of time for baking after a short nap. Now, eat, relax, and fill me in on what's been happening in the castle."

Shelby did as her aunt asked, enjoying a couple of mouthfuls of cake before speaking. "Since you're on the board, I shouldn't be telling you this, but I didn't promise not to share it with you. Chrissie stopped in to see me and said she's concerned that a couple of more items have gone missing. She thinks they might also have been stolen and was wondering what to do about it."

"She has to tell the board, that's what to do. She must know that."

"She has her reasons for trying to deal with it herself."

"And that part you're not going to share?"

"Exactly. Anyway, that left me wondering if those kids, our supposed thieves, did indeed break into the store to take the plan. What if we assume they did it and they used the plan to break into the castle? It's not the right time for a grad prank. So, what if they were planning to steal something?"

"Well, first question is, would these items be expensive?"

"Not according to Chrissie."

"So it seems unlikely the lads would break in just to go to the trouble and risk of stealing, unless it was part of the prank."

"True. And if they did, that proves they actually ventured beyond the passageway and into the castle."

"You're not thinking of them as suspects in Savannah's murder?" Edie sounded shocked.

Shelby shrugged. "Well, if so, it would probably have been an accident. Maybe she appeared and they pushed her out of their way and down the stairs." Shelby couldn't hold back any longer. She took a larger bite of the cake. *Delicious.*

"Hmm, that might have happened, I suppose. I hate to think they'd cover that up, though, rather than call the police. Anyway, we have no real proof that they even took the plan, much less put them to use."

"You're right, of course," Shelby continued, "Maybe the thief is brazenly mixing in with the tourists so as to not attract attention, and swiping the objects. And that may have nothing to do with the murder."

"Too bad we don't have CCTV cameras throughout the castle."

Edie looked at her. "We never thought there was a need before. I wonder if it's something we should be considering, though. I'll mention it at the next board meeting, after Chrissie brings everyone up to speed, that is." She took a bite of her piece of cake slowly finishing it before continuing. "Now, why are you still thinking about this? It's really not up to you this time."

"You're not concerned that Matthew was being questioned?" Shelby asked.

"Of course I am, but I also know what happened last time I asked you to clear his name. Look where that landed you. I don't want you in danger ever again."

"Okay, but I would like to talk to the chief about it all."

"She may have mellowed in her dealings with this family, but she is still the chief of police. I wouldn't expect too much of her." Edie sat back in her chair and savored another forkful of cake.

"So, you don't think I should talk to her about it?"

"I would say no, but I know you'll make up your own mind about it," Edie said, pointing her empty fork at Shelby.

Shelby smiled. *You know me so well.*

Chapter
Twenty-Five

Shelby was just about to plug in the coffee machine at the store on Thursday morning when the phone rang. Hearing Taylor's voice on the line made Shelby hold her breath until she heard the reason for the call.

"It's one of those days. I really need to get out of the house today. Do you mind if I come in for a few hours?"

Shelby took a breath. She wasn't sure what she'd expected, but she did realize she'd been on tenterhooks for the last few days when she hadn't heard from Taylor. The thought flittered through her head, and she wondered when she had turned into such a negative person, thoughts going directly to worst-case scenario. Like Taylor having another miscarriage.

"Sure, if you're certain you should be taking the shuttle. I'd love to have the company, but you might be wiser working at the main store if you're that desperate to get out. I'm sure Trudy would be glad to have you. You know, the dock and walkway might be slippery after yesterday's rain."

There was a long pause. "I guess you're right. The whole boat thing might be too much right now. I've been feeling a bit queasy, but I'm putting most of the blame for that on my mother-in-law. You don't think Trudy would mind?"

"I'm sure she'd be thrilled. Why don't you call her? How are you feeling, besides queasy and restless?"

"Well, now that the initial concerns about the pregnancy are long past, I'm feeling as I should be. Or, as I'm told I should be. I know I'm being a bit unreasonable, but I really do wish these last few months were over and I was complaining about the lack of sleep instead."

Shelby chuckled. "I'll remind you of that, shall I?"

"Uh, maybe not. Okay, thanks a lot, Shelby. It would be nice to see you, though. Maybe you could stop in on your next day off? For some coffee?"

"I know, I've been meaning to. I'd thought about that on Monday, but something came up. I will call you first, though, and make sure it's a good time for all in your house."

Taylor laughed. "Might be a good idea. Have a good day."

"You, too." Shelby was smiling as she hung up the phone.

"That looks like it was good news," Matthew said as he pushed the door open.

"It was Taylor, who's getting antsy. I suggested she work in town today rather than taking the shuttle."

Matthew nodded but said nothing. "I just wanted to stop by and tell you that if you're starting to pack anything up for winter storage and need a hand with boxes, just let me know."

"Okay, I will, thanks. But to tell you the truth, I hadn't even thought about that yet. Edie hasn't mentioned anything either. Is that odd?"

"No, probably not. She's always hated to close up over winter, so I have to remind her, too. You've still got plenty of time, but there may be some things you can take back to the Bay ahead of time and cut down the final job."

"Sure. I'll think about it. Thanks, Matthew." He turned to leave, but Shelby spoke up. "Do you have a minute?"

"Sure. What's on your mind?"

"I've been thinking about something Chrissie Halstead said yesterday, about more items that have gone missing around here, although it's hard to pinpoint when it happened. Do you have any ideas?"

"And why do you want to know? I'd say it's a matter for the board to deal with. I'm just surprised they haven't done so already. No one has even asked me for my suggestions. It's not something you should be getting involved with, you know. Just like you shouldn't keep asking questions about the murder."

"Well, I'm trying not to, but information keeps landing in my lap. That reminds me, I also have a request I said I'd pass along to you."

"I'm all ears."

"I had a visit the other night from a fairly new author, although she is apparently published, who was supposed to meet with Savannah and get some tips from her or have her read her manuscript or something. She couldn't get here on the weekend so missed seeing Savannah, and now she's wondering if I could introduce her to you. For the same reasons."

The look on Matthew's face was hard to pinpoint. "That's not my thing anymore, Shelby. I've left that world and everything to do with it behind. Please tell her I'm not interested."

"I hope you don't mind, but I felt I had to ask. I hope that's okay. I'll let her know it's not going to happen."

"Thanks, Shelby." He nodded and eventually managed a smile.

After he'd left, Shelby busied herself dusting and shifting stacks of books. Again. Anything to keep busy. When she'd finished, she stood back to appreciate her handiwork. Not much difference. Huh.

She decided to get it over with and called Chief Stone, who answered on the first ring. She was in the office and ready to listen.

"I'm sorry to bother you, but I have a question, if you don't mind."

"Sure, go ahead and ask. That doesn't mean I'll answer. But I am curious."

"It's a *what if* question. What if the boys who broke in were planning to do more than trying to hang a banner? What if they were really there to steal items to sell?"

"And what makes you think that?"

"Well, nothing specific, but if it were true, and they were there the night of the murder, they could have bumped into Savannah, literally. That would make her death an accident. What do you think?"

"I'd like to know what you're basing this on. I know you have specific information to make you think this. It's not a random thought. I have dealt with you before."

Shelby cleared her throat. Did she have to mention Chrissie?

"You've been talking to Chrissie Halstead again and she's figured out that more items are missing, right?" the chief continued before Shelby could make a decision.

"Maybe."

"So, my question is, why hasn't she come to me about this? Has she even told the board?"

"You'll have to ask her, but I know she's trying to figure out what's going on. It does seem possible that this could go either way. Either the thief is someone who had nothing to do with the murder, or the two crimes are linked. So, what about the boys? Could they have been looking for loot, maybe what they thought were antiques they could sell? Like I said, could it have been an accident after all?"

"And if I had my doubts, what makes you think I'd share them with you?"

"Well, I just shared a lot of information with you." Shelby could hear the exasperation in her own voice and thought she'd better dial it back.

"You think I didn't know anything about this? Or have similar thoughts? Me, the police chief?"

Shelby wasn't sure, but she did know she was through sparring. She might not have any answers, but she had shared some information, and hopefully it was new as well as useful.

"May I ask one more thing? You said you found the laptop. Where was it?"

There was silence for longer than Shelby liked, but finally Stone said, "It seems she forgot it. Her fiancé had it, but he'd been upset about not staying with her that night, so he didn't take it over to her. He also said he'd then forgotten about it. Since I can't prove otherwise . . ."

Another few seconds and then Stone continued, "I appreciate that you're sharing information with me, even though you shouldn't have that information at all. Be careful."

Shelby hung up with a smile, even though she couldn't help but think what a frustrating person Chief Stone was. She guessed that might be a good thing for a police officer.

A half hour later, the phone rang, and Shelby started to feel like she'd been on the phone all day. She hoped it was some good news. It was Rachel Michaels.

"I'm sorry to bother you, but I couldn't wait any longer. I just have to know; did you ask Matthew Kessler yet?"

"Uh, yes, I did, Rachel. And I'm sorry to say, he's declined. He's been away from the publishing world for so long he doesn't think he has anything to offer." Maybe that wasn't exactly what he'd said, but it sounded right.

"I see."

Shelby thought it sounded like she really didn't see but decided to say nothing.

"I wonder if he'd be more inclined to meet with me if he knew I'd decided to write about the murder of his wife."

Seriously? "What made you think of that? It's an old case now."

"Well, it is, but it's still unsolved. A cold case, and maybe I could put a new spin on it. Who knows, maybe with the right research, I could explore new angles, and maybe even find the killer."

"You don't think that's been tried over the years? Besides, I'm pretty certain Matthew Kessler would not want to go through all those details again. It's a part of his life he doesn't want to revisit." *Odd that Savannah had the same idea.*

Rachel was silent for several minutes, but Shelby was certain she was still on the line.

"In that case," Rachel said, "I guess you did try, so thanks." She hung up without saying goodbye. For some reason, that didn't surprise Shelby.

*   *   *

A short while later, Shelby caught the final boat back to the Bay. She decided she needed a short walk to help relieve the tension she felt.

As she passed Driftwood and Seawinds, she glanced through the window and saw the Noland sisters, Peggy and Deanna, behind the counter, deep in conversation. It looked warm and inviting inside and she knew there would be a good reason to shop in there, but she kept walking. She had been trying to stick a bit more to her budget these days.

A couple of stores had already closed for the day, but Chocomania's lights were still on and it looked busy. Shelby thought briefly about stopping in for a truffle, for energy, but kept walking. When she'd gone several blocks up the hill, she turned around and looked at the view. There weren't many cars driving the streets and even fewer walkers out. She guessed people were home getting supper ready, which she should be doing. She lingered longer, though, focusing on the lights starting to twinkle in the water beyond.

She wondered what it would look like in winter and tried to imagine the same scene blanketed in snow. That was something she was looking forward to, even though she'd be relocated to Edie's house by then. Her thoughts wandered to Christmas, realizing it would be an entirely different experience for her. For so many years, she'd celebrated with only her dad. Occasionally they'd be invited to the home of a colleague and she'd get a glimpse of what it could be like for other families. But this year, she'd be celebrating with Edie, and she was certain Edie knew how to celebrate.

She could picture the stores with brightly colored lights in their windows and the same draped across the houses. She wondered what the town council would do. Did they hang wreaths, lights, candy canes? So many possibilities, and she knew she was looking forward to it all.

Maybe she'd spend some of it with Zack. She hoped so, unless he was heading home to see his folks in Seattle. He hadn't mentioned them since he'd explained about the tense relationship with his dad, so it seemed unlikely he'd be going. But not impossible. She crossed her fingers, hoping he'd be around, and then hurriedly uncrossed them, feeling a bit foolish.

She wished she'd brought her car, as she was getting hungry and a bit chilled. That would have been silly, though. She knew that too many short trips were hard on the car's battery so, unless it was an emergency or an extra long walk, she left it parked in a lot close to the houseboat.

As she neared the Lower James Street Dock, her mind wandered back to possible motives for Savannah's murder. There were still too many suspects. And she had a lot of questions about Jenna's version of what had happened with her story idea. It didn't seem possible that somebody as successful as Savannah Page would have needed to steal someone else's plot, or taken the chance on it. Jenna must have it wrong, but it wouldn't hurt to find out why she was so certain. Maybe Shelby would eat at the pub tonight—if Jenna was working, that was—and get in a few questions.

Maybe she could find out if a still-angry Jenna Dunlop thought Savannah hadn't been punished enough.

Chapter
Twenty-Six

S he opened the door of the Brew House and was hit by a blast of warmth and noise. There was a good crowd tonight, but what had she expected? She'd heard it was a popular spot. At least they sounded like they were having a good time. Her thoughts briefly flickered to Zack and his explanation about having to work that night. *I'd better get used to it, I guess. It goes with the job.* That was, if she wanted something more from this relationship. But now wasn't the time for soul-searching.

She scanned the area around the bar for Jenna and found her behind it. Great. When two guys who she thought should have been carded picked up the drinks they'd just been served and moved to the side, Shelby slipped around them and sat. She asked the older man next to her to pass down a menu from the stack at the end of the bar. By the time Jenna stood in front of her, she'd made her decision. She ordered a cheeseburger and fries along with a draft beer. Why not?

Jenna nodded and poured her a brew, placing it in front of her, then went to serve someone else. So much for time to talk. Shelby was determined, though, and decided the trick was to drink and eat slowly. Things had to quiet down, even a bit, at some point. And she'd be ready.

The burger turned out to be tasty but salty. And messy. It had been a long time since she'd had one, but she was enjoying it. She watched Jenna as she ate. Without the hat, Jenna's hair was a mass of curls, and the intense black didn't seem natural at all. Shelby could sympathize with the curls. She'd chosen to wear her hair long, knowing she could at least tame the curls by trapping them in a ponytail.

By the time Shelby realized she'd been drinking faster than intended, Jenna was back in front with raised eyebrows.

"I guess I'll have another," Shelby said. "Do they come in half sizes?"

Jenna laughed. "Seriously? Okay, I don't often get asked that question, but yes, I can do that." She was back in a flash with the order. "Enjoy."

Shelby smiled and took a chance. "When you have a few minutes, can we talk?"

Jenna frowned. "Sure, I guess. Do I know you?"

"I'm Shelby Cox, from Bayside Books."

Jenna's eyes narrowed. "Oh, yeah. I've seen you in there sometimes. Not often, though."

"That's because I'm usually at the store in Blye Castle. I know you're busy tonight, but it won't take long, really."

Jenna hesitated. "Sure, I guess that's okay. I get a break in half an hour."

By the time seven PM rolled around, Shelby had finished her meal but hadn't had much of her second beer. She watched while Jenna talked to one of the servers, who then replaced her behind the bar. Jenna nodded at Shelby to follow, and they went into one of the back rooms. It appeared to be an office, although it looked more like a storage closet with a small desk and seating shoved into it. Shelby sat on the love seat while Jenna relaxed in the chair behind the desk.

"Okay, I have fifteen minutes, but I'd like to have a few of those to myself. This is an exhausting job, not my first choice, you know."

"I do know. You want to be a writer."

"Yeah, and how did you know that?" She looked intrigued.

"I was working at the main bookstore during Savannah Page's signing, so I heard what you said."

Jenna straightened her shoulders and looked wary. "That's right, I said things. They needed to be said. And what's more, I'm glad I did it. So, what do you want to know?"

"You were pretty steamed when you confronted Savannah at the bookstore."

"You're damned right I was. Still am. She stole my work." She sat with her lips in a tight line that matched her eyes.

"Your idea, you said, if I remember correctly."

"Yeah, well, that's how it started out, but now it was on the way to becoming her work. The idea was mine and she stole it. That's plain and simple to me. The story about Joe Cabana? My idea. Even the plan about staying overnight in the castle to do research. Mine."

"Had you already approached the Heritage board about it?"

Jenna shook her head. "Like I said, it was in the idea stage, but it was mine."

"And how do you think Savannah heard about your idea in the first place?"

Jenna sighed and crossed her arms on the desk in front of her, relaxing slightly. "We were at the same writers' festival. Savannah, of course, was the big name, while I, along with another local writer, were on the same panel talking about where we get our ideas. Of course"—she gave a short laugh—"I mentioned that I live in Alexandria Bay and we have this great local legend about the castle and Joe Cabana. I didn't go into too much detail, but afterward, over coffee, Savannah began asking me questions about it. I guess I should have known something was up. I mean, why would she talk to me, anyway? She had lots of adoring fans wanting to meet her."

"So, you gave her some information . . ."

"I gave her the entire plot. My fault, I admit. But I was hoping to get some pointers from her, you know, what direction to go in."

"What did you plan to do about her stealing the plot, as you claim?"

"What do you mean? I emailed her first and asked if we could meet for a coffee while she was in town. She said she had time after the signing on Friday. But the more I thought about it, I decided that confronting her in private wasn't enough. I wanted to confront her and, hopefully, embarrass her in front of her fans. I did what I'd planned to do. She didn't have an answer, did she? They'll remember that and not buy her books anymore. That was my goal." Jenna gloated and settled back in her chair.

"Well, I don't think you'll prevent future sales; in fact, the numbers may be up because she won't be writing anymore. Her book that's in the works won't be coming out, though, unless it's already finished. That's guaranteed. How did you know Savannah was working on that idea anyway?"

"She tweeted about it, not that she said much. But there was enough that I knew where she had gotten the idea."

"You followed her on Twitter?"

"Of course. And on Facebook and Instagram. Like I said, I was a big fan of hers, but I was totally blown away when I read that tweet. I couldn't believe it. She'd even put a teaser about it on her website."

"You could have called her out on Twitter."

"Not good enough. I wanted to see her face when I exposed her. And you know what, I was going to tweet about it, too."

"And did you?"

"I chickened out. What if she'd called me on it and threatened to sue? I had a computer crash and lost a lot of data, including my notes about the book. So, I had no real proof."

"But you still pulled that stunt in the store. She could still have sued you."

"I hadn't stopped to really think it through. I just got so angry when she started her reading."

Shelby paused, trying to gather her thoughts. She felt they were going around in circles. Jenna seemed to have an answer for everything. And what was that about Savannah agreeing to meet after the signing? She'd also told Rachel Michaels they would have coffee, but she'd had dinner plans with Shelby and Edie. What was going on?

"What do you plan to do now?"

"What do you mean?" Jenna looked surprised by the question.

"Well, the book idea is probably wide open again. Are you going to start writing it now?"

"Uh, to tell you the truth, I hadn't given it much more thought. She only just died. I know, that sounds cold, but it's true. Besides, I've been sorta busy here." Jenna looked at the ceiling, then focused on the wall behind Shelby and sighed. "Coming to your bookstore may not have been my best idea. It was overly dramatic, wasn't it?"

"A bit."

"I didn't mean to draw attention to myself, really. I only wanted to embarrass her in front of her adoring fans. I knew she'd never in a million years admit it. It was an act of desperation." She paused and focused again on Shelby. "Like I said before, do you think I choose to work here? That I enjoy working here? All right, maybe I do a little, but I'm not making anything from my writing, so here I am."

Shelby didn't know what to say, so she sat quietly. She was sure Jenna wasn't finished yet.

"And," she continued, proving Shelby right, "the worst thing is, I really, really loved her writing. She was my hero; that's why I was so stoked when she actually talked to me at the festival. Me, unpublished Jenna Dunlop. But look where it got me. I should have taken my friend Kyra's advice."

Shelby was almost afraid to ask, but she didn't have to.

Jenna stood and started pacing in the small space. "Kyra told me to trust my instincts when it comes to writing. She reads my stuff and says I'm good, that I just have to keep working at it to hone my skills. She also says I should start sending it out, to agents and other writers, and get some real feedback. You know, there's not really anybody in town here to ask, except maybe Judy Carter at the library or"—she paused and took a good look at Shelby—"you, maybe, if you'd agree. You own a bookstore, so you know about good writing."

Shelby was dumbfounded. This wasn't where she'd thought this conversation would lead. But she realized she didn't have to answer right away.

"Or maybe you know somebody," Jenna plowed on ahead, plopping back into the chair, "like a writer maybe, who you could check in with and ask if I could get in touch with her. Or him. That's all; I'd get in touch, then, and do the asking about reading my manuscript. I know this puts you in an awkward position. I really don't want to impose, but I don't know where else to turn."

Jenna sat back and gripped the arms of the chair. "I'm babbling, aren't I? I do that when I'm nervous. You see how important it is to me? I wanted to cause Savannah Page some embarrassment and anguish. And I hope I did."

Not much of a plan. And it didn't sound like she'd included a detour to kill Savannah, but Shelby had to ask. "Did you see Savannah again after that confrontation?"

"No, I didn't. I was working a day shift here. You can ask." Her jaw jutted forward, and she crossed her arms across her chest.

"I was thinking maybe later that night?"

"What? Are you accusing me of murdering her?" Jenna sputtered. "I did not. I'm not a murderer. I'd never, ever do something that evil. Besides, when you get right down to it, it was just a plot for a book. I told you, I embarrassed her, and that's what I'd planned to do. Don't you go trying to pin a murder on me."

"I was just asking." Shelby knew it was time for her to go.

"Yeah, well, it sounded like an accusation to me, but you don't have any proof because I didn't do it." She sounded like her feelings were hurt. "Now, can I get on with my break? Alone?"

Shelby smiled, hoping to generate some goodwill. "Of course, I won't take up any more of your time. Thanks for talking to me, Jenna." She paused at the door. "I hope you have good luck with your writing."

Jenna looked surprised, then asked, "She didn't really plan to meet with me, did she?"

"Why do you say that?"

"Well, she must have known what was on my mind. That's if she even remembered me. So, I'm glad I did what I did." Jenna sighed. "She probably didn't even remember me, right? That's even more depressing."

Shelby made sympathetic noises and then pulled the door shut behind her.

She took a few moments deciding what to do next. She actually believed Jenna, so what next? Home seemed like the best idea. She threaded her way through the chairs and people to the door and was reaching for it when it was pulled open and Zack stood there along with two guys she didn't know.

"Shelby. I'm surprised to see you here." He looked behind her toward the bar. "Or maybe I'm not."

The two guys chuckled and pushed past him, turning back to face them after they'd moved inside. Zack did the introductions. "Shelby Cox, owner of Bayside Books. This is Jeff and Kevin. I work with these guys. We finished up much earlier than expected," he quickly explained. "I'll catch up in a minute, guys," he said to them as he pulled Shelby out of the doorway and shut in the noise. "Would you like to join us?"

"No, thanks. I'm actually tired. It's been a long day."

"I have a feeling you've been asking some questions," Zack said. "Doesn't Jenna Dunlop work here?"

"Actually, I had a fairly good supper, and a few questions may have been involved. I'm surprised you remember her name, not being involved in the investigation. Or are you now?"

He shook his head, smiling. "Nope. I just like to keep track of what possibilities there are for you to get in trouble. I do have a vested interest in your well-being, you know."

His face was so close, she was sure he'd kiss her, but instead he asked, "Are we still on for the Wine Festival on Saturday night?"

"Of course. A date is a date." They'd made the plans a couple of months earlier when the tickets went on sale. "Or are you having second thoughts?" she asked, with mock seriousness.

"The thought never crossed my mind. How about if I come by around six, or is that too early?"

"No, that sounds good. I look forward to it."

"Me, too." He gave her a quick kiss, lingering on the sidewalk as she walked away.

Her entire body was still tingling as she stepped onto her dock.

Chapter Twenty-Seven

S helby spotted Matthew when she got off the shuttle the next morning. She'd spent a few minutes standing on the dock, soaking up the rays of sun peeking through the clouds, possibly for the final time that morning, and breathing deeply. She felt good as she started up the walkway. And there was Matthew, walking slowly, head down, scanning the path between his house and the castle. He had his New York Rangers ball cap pulled down over his forehead and a small flashlight in his right hand. It definitely looked like he was searching for something. Something he'd lost?

She hurried over to him, wanting to know what was up, but also because she wanted to get indoors before the rain started. The sky looked ominous despite the occasional sunny moments, and the wind seemed to be picking up. She longed for the sunny fall days and colorful trees she'd been promised when she'd moved here, but it looked like she'd have to wait a little while longer for those. At least until tomorrow.

"Did you lose something, Matthew?"

"Huh? What? Oh, Shelby." He looked surprised to see her.

"I was." He paused and looked around them. "Well, the thing is, I'm pretty sure someone broke into my place last night, and I'm looking for, I don't know, anything suspicious."

"In the underbrush beside the path? What could there be? Do you think you'll find footprints? There must be so many. How will you know what's what?"

"I'm thinking that if anything was taken, maybe part of it was dropped, and that might give me a clue to either who it was or what he wanted." He straightened up and looked toward the water. "That doesn't make a lot of sense, does it? Someone went through my papers, I know that. I'm just not sure yet if any were taken. If so, maybe whoever it was was in a hurry and dropped one. Doubtful, though. And how did they get here? It must have been after hours."

"I take it you weren't here overnight." She felt embarrassed stating the obvious.

He didn't look at her but shook his head. "No, no I wasn't. And nobody else should have been either. I doubt anyone would be brazen enough to tie up at the main dock with all those lights." He turned in the direction of the Grotto. "I wonder if that's been put to use again? I'd better check it out. Or maybe they just used my small dock, although I've already checked the pathway there and found nothing."

"Do you think it could be the murderer? Maybe he came over the same way, whichever way that was, as the night he murdered Savannah."

"I had thought about that, but what could he be looking for in my place?"

"Maybe he'd hoped to find you."

Matthew stopped walking. "What are you saying?"

Her answer had just popped out, but she gave it some thought before answering. "What if he thought you had some evidence or saw him or . . ." She stopped, not quite sure what else to say. It sort of made sense as a motive, but didn't really.

"That's highly unlikely. Don't you think the killer would have tried something before now if that were the case?"

"Sure, I guess you're right. That would make more sense. But what else could it be?" Shelby stared at the ground, willing a clue to present itself. She hated the thought that the privacy of the ever-reserved Matthew had been invaded. She zipped her jacket up to the neckline as a stronger gust of wind rocked her. "Don't you think you should call the police? Maybe there are fingerprints."

Matthew shook his head. "I'm not going to get them involved in what's only a supposition at this point. My desk and file cabinet look . . . different, and I could tell the papers on my desk had been rifled through, but nothing's dreadfully out of place." He passed his right hand over his forehead. "Maybe I'm getting old and forgetful. Maybe I didn't straighten things the way I usually do."

He looked up at the sky. "Hadn't you better get inside and get your store opened? Not that I don't appreciate your concern, but it's getting late and that sky looks ominous. I'll just poke around a little more, but I think it's useless."

Shelby glanced at her watch. "You're right, gotta run. Good luck. Let me know if you find anything, okay?"

Matthew gave her an odd look.

"What can I say, you've got my curiosity piqued." She gave him a quick wave and followed the path back to the main walkway up to the castle, reaching the doors just as the heavens opened. She glanced back at the rain and made a face.

So much for a busy day.

She'd just gotten the coffee started when the phone rang. It was Taylor, calling from the main store.

"I'm working in town today, in case you didn't know, and you'll never guess who's here," she said in a hushed voice.

"Who?"

"It's that number-one fan of Savannah Page, you know, the one who says she's also a true-crime writer. She was talking to you the other day, she says."

"Rachel Michaels."

"That's right. She seems a bit shifty to me, but maybe that's how it goes when that's your topic. She asked if you were in today, and I said you were at the castle location. And she said she just thought you might alternate stores. I mean, who even stops to think about that? Then she started asking me about Matthew and also asked if we had any books about or by him. What's up with her? Like I said, she's acting, I don't know, kind of covert."

"Covert? Define covert."

Taylor almost whispered, "She keeps glancing at the front door, the whole time she's been here. Strange, you know?"

Shelby thought about it for a few moments before answering. "First off, I think she was making sure I wasn't coming in before asking you about the books. When she was in here the other day, she asked me to do something, and right now I'm probably the last person she wants to run into."

"Why's that?"

"She asked if I could line up an introduction to Matthew. She wanted to pick his brain, I guess. I checked with him first, and he said no way. When I told her that, she wasn't too happy. I guess she thought I was her ticket to meeting him. And then she said that she wants to write about his wife's death. I told her it wasn't likely he'd talk about that either. Can you imagine?"

"Huh. Well, maybe she's doing an end run, going directly to his books first, which we don't have any of anyway. I did suggest she try the library."

"What's she doing now?"

"She's gone through our small section of true crime and is now thumbing through cookbooks."

"Hope she at least buys one of those. I'm glad she's added some intrigue to your day, anyway. Is it busy there, by any chance?"

"Nope, but that's not a surprise on a day like today."

"So true. Would you keep me posted about our shopper? Gotta go. I've finally got my own customers coming in."

When she was once again able to think about Rachel and her appearance at the bookstore, a couple of hours later after a surprisingly busy time, she figured Rachel must not have bought a cookbook or she would surely have heard back. Perhaps she'd taken Taylor's advice instead and headed to the library. She was certainly determined, but Shelby guessed you had to be to make it as an author.

The question was, had Rachel been determined enough to break into Matthew's house?

That thought came out of the blue but seemed so logical, she knew she needed to find Matthew and talk it over with him.

The ringing telephone put a hold on that for now. She saw it was the main store. Maybe Taylor had been too busy to call until now.

But it was Edie on the line. "Are you sitting down?"

"Yes, but why are you in the store?"

"Because Taylor called me right after calling her husband. She's in the hospital."

"What happened? Is she okay? Have you heard anything?"

"Not yet, but Chuck has promised to call when there's news. She told me she had some pains, almost like contractions, but it's way too early for that. She probably shouldn't have come in today. I hope that doctor gives her strict orders about what she can and cannot do. She can be quite determined, as you know."

"I do know that. This is upsetting, but we'll hope for the best. I think her earlier miscarriage was at only a couple of months in. Like I said, we'll hope for the best. But how are you? Are you up to doing a shift today? Can Trudy spell you?"

"No, she can't. Trudy has gone to Syracuse for a day's shopping trip, but I'm fine. I won't do any shelving or the like. I promise to just sit here and talk to customers, and take their money of course," she added with a chuckle.

"I like the sound of that. Well, keep me posted if you hear any news, and be sure to let me know if it gets too tiring. I can always close early here and relieve you."

Shelby kept her hand on the receiver after hanging up, trying to gather her thoughts. She hoped and prayed everything would be okay for Taylor, but she also had to look at the schedules and make certain they were prepared. Of course, Taylor had been off the active roster for a couple of weeks now, but Shelby acknowledged that she'd liked the idea of having Taylor as a possible backup, especially with Edie's knee. It seemed like they definitely needed to hire that part-timer, sooner rather than later. Once she had the baby, Taylor certainly wouldn't be available again for some months, maybe even years. They'd talked about it, but she knew Taylor was being optimistic when she said she'd find a way to still pull a shift here and there.

Shelby did in fact close up an hour early and headed straight for the main store when she got off the boat. Edie looked exhausted.

"It was so slow after a short blip of activity, I was sure I'd fall asleep," Shelby explained. "Why don't you head home, and I'll finish up here."

Edie didn't object, which proved to Shelby just how tired her aunt was. "I'm going to call you a cab," she said.

"I guess so."

Again, no objection. Shelby took a close look at her aunt and was surprised to really see the aging woman in front of her.

Not that she was that old, only in her early sixties, but it was a reminder to Shelby that she needed to be more thoughtful around Edie. She hoped they would have many, many years ahead in which to make up for lost time.

What would she do without Edie, now that she'd found her?

Chapter
Twenty-Eight

Shelby checked her cell phone for any messages the next morning and, seeing none, gave Edie a quick call before leaving home.

"Nothing since Chuck's call last night to say he was taking Taylor home. I hope she had a restful night."

"So, you don't know anything more about what happened?"

"No, and I don't like to be too nosy. I'm sure Taylor will tell us what she wants us to know. I'm sure we would have heard right away if it was bad news. We'll keep each other posted, shall we?"

"Thanks, Edie. I hope Trudy is in today and you're staying at home."

"Yes, she is, and I know when I've hit my limit. Thanks for suggesting the cab yesterday. It was the smart thing to do."

"Something else we have to be smart about is hiring another part-time staffer."

Edie sighed. "I know, I know. What I don't know is why I'm dragging my feet. We've had some good résumés dropped off since summer. I'll ask Trudy to bring them all over after work today, and I'll go through them again. Then we can confer to choose who we want to interview. Hopefully, they're still available. Sound like a plan?"

"Perfect. I know that Taylor was hoping to continue with the odd shift, but I don't think we can rely on that."

"Uh-huh, I hear you. Now, I don't want to keep you too long and make you late. I will call you, I promise."

Shelby couldn't shake the feeling of being on edge, even after talking with Edie. She spent extra time brushing J.T.'s coat before filling his dish. She knew he would wolf down his food and then head off on his own, although he did choose to stay indoors again that day. What would she do with him over the winter? She realized she hadn't given that any thought. Surely Edie wouldn't mind having him in the house, but if she did, Shelby had to have a plan. She also realized she couldn't imagine finding him a new home. He'd really become a part of her life, even after such a short time. She just hoped he would be okay with the change of location and not decide to relocate on his own. She was at his mercy.

After they'd both eaten, she quickly washed the dishes, then headed for Chocomania. She'd missed not treating herself the day before. Besides, she wanted to see what was happening in Erica's life.

She waited in a short line until Erica took her order.

"A nice start to the morning for you," Shelby said, looking around the busy shop.

"Seeing you? Yes, it is." Erica looked over at the customers who were enjoying their orders in the store and then pulled off her scarf, shaking her head. Her short haircut seemed ideal for so many reasons. Not only did it frame her face perfectly; it also shook out and back into place so easily. Shelby tried not to be envious. Erica retied the scarf without need for a mirror, then folded her arms and smiled.

Shelby shook her head, laughing. "That is nice for me, too, but I meant the busyness."

"It's been steady, which is great. I missed seeing you yesterday. What's happening?"

"Well, Taylor went into the hospital briefly yesterday. She was working at the main store when she had some pains. She's home now, and I haven't heard an update except that she seems fine. For now."

"That is worrying. I'm glad to hear she's okay, though. Have a truffle on the house to calm your unease."

"You have the solution to everything." Shelby chose a salted caramel truffle and popped it into her mouth. "Mmm, so wonderful. Thank you, and a medium latte as a chaser, please. By the way, have you seen anything of Bryce?" she asked as Erica made her order

Erica glanced over and smiled. "Since you ask, we did go out to dinner on Wednesday evening."

The look on her face told Shelby all she needed to know. "Wow. It looks like it was a great evening. You didn't have any reservations, you know, with the chief talking to him and all?

"Sort of, but I figured she'd have locked him up if it had been anything serious, right? And I was curious about why she'd been questioning him again, but I didn't get up the nerve to ask him."

Shelby nodded but decided not to fill in any details. That was up to Bryce. "So, he hasn't left town?"

"Why?" Erica looked wary. "Are you still thinking of him as a suspect?"

Shelby realized she'd have to be careful how she answered. "That's not my first thought, but if he's having to stick around, it could be because the chief hasn't cleared him yet. Or it's totally because of you," she added, which brought a smile to Erica's face.

"He said he's able to do a lot of his work from here," Erica volunteered.

"Aha. That's handy."

"Isn't it? And what's happening in Coast Guard land?"

"It so happens that we're going to the Wine Festival tonight, following a light supper at my place. Just something easy, nothing special," she added quickly when she saw the glint in Erica's eyes.

"Right. Wine, a moonlit night, dancing. It sounds pretty romantic to me." Her smile was mischievous and contagious.

"I am ever hopeful. But, as much fun as this has been, I have to run yet again if I want to catch the shuttle. Thanks for the latte," she said as she slid a five-dollar bill across the counter. "Hope your day keeps busy."

"You, too. Let me know when you hear more about Taylor, okay?"

Shelby nodded and hurried through the door, wondering why she was always on the run for the shuttle. She could easily leave her home earlier if she didn't just meander about in the mornings, or she could even get up a bit earlier each day. She did like the mornings, especially those with a stunning sunrise.

The early morning turned out to be just a promise of what turned into a beautiful, sunny day. The temperatures rose in the afternoon so that Shelby actually removed her jacket while taking a short walk on her afternoon break. It had been a fairly busy morning and she'd skipped lunch, so she decided a treat was in order. A walk it was. As she walked past the Sugar Shack, she wished it were still open. An ice cream cone would really have hit the spot.

Taylor called just after Shelby reopened the store.

"How are you feeling? What happened? Wait, you don't have to answer that part if you don't want," Shelby said, trying to keep the worry out of her voice. She knew Taylor didn't like to be coddled.

"I'm fine, but the pains were a warning, according to the doctor. I had an early morning yesterday and then did some housework. I know. My mother-in-law was all over me about it, but I needed to be doing something; that's why I thought the store was the answer."

"Well, I hope you'll take his advice and start taking it easy."

"That will only raise my blood pressure, which is another problem in itself. He did relent and say I could go to the store for short stints as long as I didn't do anything physical. Just sit there and talk. Like Edie." She chuckled. "Now you have two of us."

"Well, I'm relieved to hear that, but unless you're so desperate you'll burst—although that might not be the best saying—I want you to stay home. We love having you in the store, but your baby is more important."

"I will be smart about this, don't worry. How's it going today?"

"It's been busy, thanks to the great weather. And that's even better for the Wine Festival tonight."

"Ah, you and Zack are going, I take it?"

"That's right. And I'm looking forward to it."

"That sounds promising. I wish we were going. We had a great time last year, but Chuck is working tonight, because of the festival. I hope you'll have a very enjoyable time. And I'd suggest that you don't talk about the murder tonight."

"What makes you think I'd do that? Wait, don't answer."

Another chuckle. "Well, just so you get the point. I'll let you go now, and thanks for worrying about me. But don't. I'll be okay. Bye for now."

Shelby hung up, feeling relieved. She quickly called Edie to bring her up to speed. After she'd hung up, she heard what sounded like some children near the indoor fountain. She wandered to the open door, hoping they weren't tossing things in like the noisy group the week before.

What she saw instead was Rachel Michaels heading purposefully upstairs. She had her hair pulled back and fastened into a short ponytail that stuck out above the back strap of a dark baseball cap. The collar on her brown windbreaker was turned up, but didn't cover much of her face. But Shelby had the distinct feeling Rachel didn't want to be recognized.

Shelby's curiosity meter hit the high mark, and she quickly turned the *Open* sign around to say *Back in 5*, then followed

247

Rachel, who was clearly trying to be as unobtrusive as possible by mixing in with a small group of tourists.

Shelby reached the top of the stairs just in time to see Rachel slip through a closed door to a room at the front of the castle. Shelby knew that room was off-limits to the public, being the former bedroom of Joe Cabana. She'd been allowed a quick peek in from the doorway when she'd first come to the castle, and as far as she knew, it remained fairly true to how it had been when Cabana was alive. The former owners hadn't ever gotten around to redecorating that part of the castle, or maybe they knew what an attraction it could turn out to be and so had left it alone.

What was Rachel doing in there, anyway?

Shelby walked over to the door and glanced around to make sure a security guard wouldn't come by and butt in. It seemed to be all clear, so she slowly turned the handle, trying for some stealth, and gradually pushed the door open wide enough to slip through an opening.

It took her eyes a few seconds to adjust to the darker room. No lights were on, but there was some daylight coming through the partially closed blinds. She looked for Rachel and spotted her at a desk, rifling through drawers. She watched for a few seconds, hoping Rachel might find what she was looking for before she surprised her. Finally, it looked like Rachel had given up as she straightened from being hunched over.

"What are you doing in here?" Shelby asked in a loud voice. She was pleased to see Rachel visibly jump and look totally surprised when she turned around. Shelby wanted her to be off her guard.

"I, uh, well, why do you want to know?" Rachel's look turned quickly from one of surprise to a glare. In her right hand was a small flashlight, but what Shelby noticed was the gloves on Rachel's hands. The thin white synthetic kind. In the movies, that's what the cops wore when searching for evidence.

"Because the public isn't allowed in here, as the sign outside the room so obviously states. So, I'll ask again, why are you in here?" She crossed her arms to show she meant business. She also stayed close to the door in case the talk didn't go so well.

Rachel let out a big sigh and her mouth slid into a lopsided smile. "Okay, I'll tell you, but I know you won't be pleased. You know I was hoping to write a true-crime novel, and since you're no help with Matthew Kessler, and now that Savannah won't be writing about Joe Cabana's life and death . . ."

Shelby interrupted her. "How did you know that's what she was working on?"

"She alluded to it on her website, and then when I heard she was staying overnight here, it added up. Joe Cabana would be the perfect story. And so I thought that maybe I could do it and tie in both deaths for a new twist on an old tale."

Shelby felt the distaste in her mouth. That sounded so heartless.

Rachel must have sensed she'd erred. "I mean, look at it this way. Maybe they are tied to each other, and what I find out could help solve Savannah's murder. I thought maybe I could find something in Cabana's desk from around the time when he was murdered, some papers, or maybe even some evidence that his spirit was still around. I see you're not a believer in those tales."

"No, I'm not. And even so, it seems very farfetched that after all this time there would be some personal papers hanging around to be found in this room."

"I know that, but you never know what a fresh pair of eyes might find. I had heard that nothing had been changed in his room. It would be a start, anyway."

Maybe, but unlikely. "And what did you find?"

"Well"—she swiped a finger over the desktop—"you notice there's no dust? So, someone is in here cleaning on a regular basis. And that person could already have taken anything important, or just shoved it in a drawer. Unless, of course, Savannah rummaged through the desk the night she was staying here and she wiped the desk clean to cover her tracks." Rachel looked so pleased with her theory that she was smiling.

Shelby refused to be taken in, although it was an interesting suggestion. Had that been part of Savannah's intention, that while staying overnight she could search the castle thoroughly, without anyone tagging along?

"How did you know about Joe Cabana, anyway?"

"Oh, come on now. I'm from the area and know most of the legends. And I've been reading up about him and the period lately."

That sounded logical, but Shelby wasn't sure what her next step should be. Something was telling her to be cautious. Was it gut instinct or Joe's spirit? She gritted her teeth. She would not be sucked in.

Whatever. Rachel did not belong in here, and there was no way she should have been so sneaky about doing it.

"That may or may not be the case, but I suggest you leave right now, or I will be forced to call security. Those rules apply to you, also."

What would Rachel do? Shelby told herself that Rachel was just an overly curious and willful writer, which could mean she'd be obstinate. Shelby had known many of those in her career. At least, she hoped she'd pegged her correctly.

Rachel kept smiling and took a quick look around the room before walking toward the door. "All right. I understand you have to stick to the rules. You look like a rule follower. So, I'll leave. But give some thought to what I've said. Maybe you could work it so that I could come back and take a closer look. You could join me, of course."

Shelby tried not to shudder, stepping aside and pulling the door open. "By the way, what happened about your idea to write about Matthew Kessler's wife?"

"As you well know, he won't see me. You told me that yourself. So, I decided to go back to my original idea. Maybe if you'd been a bit more helpful with him, I wouldn't have resorted to this. Oh, and there is one more thing." Rachel paused in front of Shelby and looked her straight in the eye. "I've heard you're dating Zack Griffin. Did he tell you that we used to date? In fact, I spent a lot of summers around here, and Zack was one of the perks. And guess what? I'm seeing him again on Sunday."

Chapter
Twenty-Nine

Z ack arrived a few minutes early that evening, a small cat-
nip plant in one hand and a bottle of wine tucked under
his arm.

"I hope you don't mind my being early?"

Shelby pretended to glance at the clock behind her. "You
mean five minutes? No, that should be okay." She smiled as
she relieved him of his offerings. "Thanks so much. This looks
interesting." She held up the plant. "I gather it's not for me."

"Only if you're into cat edibles. I thought J.T. should have
some recognition, too."

"You obviously know the way to his heart."

"His heart isn't the one I'm aiming for."

His look was suddenly serious and intense. Shelby felt her
heart flutter and wondered if she was about to have a heart attack
or something. The next instant, he smiled and she relaxed. She
still felt a bit shaken but resolved to put it out of her mind until
later. Just as she'd forced herself not to think about what Rachel

had said about the two of them dating. She was not about to become *that* jealous woman.

"I've made a Caesar salad, thinking it would be a light start to the evening. Would you like a glass of wine first? Or we could eat right away. I just have to add the dressing and croutons."

Zack looked at his watch. "Why don't I pour and we can start sipping while you dish it up?"

Shelby found a corkscrew and handed it to Zack. "Sounds like a plan."

They decided to take their plates up to the roof, since the sun was still shining. Shelby was glad she'd grabbed her jacket, though. She loved this time of day and this location for enjoying the slowly setting sun. She glanced at Zack and found he seemed as entranced by the view as she was.

"I'm assuming you've been to this Wine Festival before," she finally asked, taking a sip of her wine. She looked at the glass, held it out to him, and laughed. "Maybe we should have had water with our meal. I hadn't thought about that."

He chuckled. "It's all good. And yes, I've been to this almost every year since I moved here. There's quite an impressive array of wineries who come to this. And, of course, the selection of cheese and other accompaniments is impressive."

"Hmm. I've never gone to one. There weren't any that I was aware of, in Lenox, anyway."

"Really? Well, we'll have to make this special, then. You do like to dance, I hope?"

She nodded. "Love it. It sounds like you might, too." She was hopeful. In her short dating experience, the one thing she had found out was that few men liked to dance.

"I do."

"That's rare."

"I know, men have gotten a bad rap for that, but I've always enjoyed dancing. And it will be even more special tonight."

Shelby was still smiling after they'd done the dishes together, despite her protests about doing them later on her own. They walked hand in hand toward the Scenic View Park at the end of Fuller, right across the street from where Zack lived. She glanced at this place, her eyes drawn to the distinctive red door and trim. It really made the white of the clapboard house pop.

The covered pavilion was open on all sides and sat at the crest of a small hill leading down to the river and Casino Island. Tiny white lights had been strung around the edge of the roof, and a small band was tucked into the far corner where there was enough free space for couples to dance. The tables all had white cloths on them and large signs hovering behind them with the names of the different wineries.

It looked to be a big success, if the size of the crowd meant anything. Shelby felt the enchantment of the event as they wandered along the aisles, and she recognized many of the faces around her. Zack seemed to know most of them, and he'd stop frequently to chat or just share a small wave. Shelby felt proud to be introduced by him and noticed the speculative glances from several women around her age.

She was glad they'd had a light meal, as she attempted to try a taste of most food items. She went easier on the wine, though.

As they slow-danced to several romantic songs in a row, she knew this was the highlight of the evening. She felt an emotional closeness to Zack, one that she realized had snuck up on her. It was something she'd been avoiding for years. It made her feel jubilant, but it also scared her.

Zack had his arm resting across her shoulders as they walked back to her place, and she started wondering about what to expect when they got there.

"Did you enjoy it?" he asked.

"I loved it. All of it. I had such a good time."

"Good. So did I." He gave her left shoulder a squeeze.

Shelby chuckled to herself.

"What?" Zack had felt it.

"I was just thinking about what Taylor said. She warned me not to talk about murder tonight. As if."

"Definitely not a topic for tonight." He stopped under a streetlight and turned to face her. "I'm right, aren't I?"

"Of course," she answered, a little too quickly.

"Why do I get the feeling, then, that I'm not right?"

"Uh, I shouldn't have brought it up. I don't know why I did. It just floated into my mind. Next time I'll think before I speak."

He sighed. "Okay, better tell me what's on your mind." He started walking again, this time holding her hand.

"Are you sure?"

He nodded.

"Okay, well Matthew was certain someone had broken into his place, and I started wondering if it was an author who had asked me to set up a meeting with him. She wanted to ask him some questions about writing, but he said no. Then she told me she wanted to write a book about the murder of his wife. And I told her he wouldn't go for that either. The timing of the break-in seemed like quite the coincidence. So anyway, I spotted this author in the castle earlier today, and I followed her upstairs to where she snuck into Joe Cabana's bedroom, which is off-limits, by the way. When I confronted her about it, she said she had shifted the focus of her book to Cabana's death and was looking for information." She glanced at him before going on.

"Then, when I asked her to leave, she said you two used to date and she was seeing you tomorrow night." She hurried on before he could think she was merely jealous. "So, I thought maybe you could try and find out, in some way, if she was the one who broke into Matthew's."

Zack stopped walking. "You what? No, don't bother going through it all again. I gather you're talking about Rachel Michaels. We did have a date or two back in my high school days, when we were here for the summer. And she did call and tell me she wants to meet me for a drink tomorrow, but I said I'd have to get back to her."

"Oh. You hadn't mentioned knowing her when I first brought up her name."

"No, because it was so long ago and so insignificant, I'd actually forgotten. But I will tell you what I won't do, and that's interrogate her about a supposed break-in you think she might have committed. Do you have any idea how farfetched that all sounds?"

"Really? It adds up to me. But I can understand if you don't want to ruin a romantic reunion with something like that."

The minute it was out, she wished she could retract it. She started walking faster, wanting to leave the conversation behind.

Zack caught up to her, but they continued in silence until they reached the dock.

He paused and turned to face her, as if about to add something, but left instead.

Shelby tried not to cry as she climbed back aboard the houseboat.

* * *

The next morning, Shelby didn't feel too much better. She'd had a restless sleep, and she knew that was because her mind had kept working over last night's scenario, especially the ending. She really didn't want to be jealous. She didn't want to feel this way about Zack. But she had to admit to both emotions. She acknowledged that she'd grown very fond of him over a few short months, something she'd thought she'd never do. And now he was annoyed with her, but even worse, he was taking out someone else. How could such a wonderful evening have turned out so wrong? She could almost hear her dad's voice saying, "I told you so."

The worst part was that she'd shown him she was jealous. She shook her head all the way downstairs. *Oh, Shelby, you idiot.* Why couldn't she have kept her mouth shut?

Maybe it wasn't so bad, she thought while dishing out food for J.T. But she knew it was. She couldn't see a way to fix things, aside from time-traveling back about twenty-four hours. *Not going to happen.* Why did life have to get so complicated? Wasn't a murder enough?

She tried not to give it any more thought while she got ready for work. She so needed a truffle. That would help, but she wouldn't breathe a word about what had happened to Erica.

Shelby checked her watch as she left home. She had twenty-five minutes until the shuttle. Plenty of time.

Chocomania seemed surprisingly quiet for a weekend, Shelby thought as she walked in. Only two tables were in use, and Erica looked calm. At least some things were status quo, even if Shelby's life was on a tilt.

"Good morning. In need of a fix?" Erica asked as Shelby approached the counter.

"Two of your spiciest truffles and a latte, please, and thank you." Two sounded about right. For starters. And the more heat the better.

"Uh-oh. Either you had a very, very late night and require energy, which is what I'm hoping. Or . . ."

"It's the *or*, and that led to a restless sleep. So, both. A late night and an *or*," Shelby admitted, then wished she could take these words back also. She didn't want to get into it.

"I'm sorry to hear that. Do you want to talk?" Erica busied herself at the espresso maker as she spoke, giving Shelby some space, or so it seemed.

Shelby gave it some thought. She'd never really had a close girlfriend before, one to share all the really personal stuff with. Oh, sure, there had been friends, especially at work, but they never heard about her deepest feelings and fears. But this seemed right.

"Zack and I went to the Wine Festival last night, as you know, which was a lot of fun, but later . . . I think we had our first real argument."

"You mean aside from all the times he's told you to back off investigating, but you've continued, so he's come down hard on you?"

Shelby nodded as she gratefully accepted the latte Erica passed over.

Erica's eyebrows rose, inviting more information, but her smile was sympathetic.

"I'd had a bit of a run-in earlier in the day with Rachel Michaels, the out-of-town author who wanted me to introduce her to Matthew. That meeting didn't happen, so I think she had it in for me. Anyway, when I saw her again, she told me that she used to spend a lot of summers here as a kid, and that she and Zack had dated at one point, and that she was going out with him on Sunday. I asked him to question her for me, which he refused to do, so I confronted him, sort of, although I hadn't meant it to sound like that, and he said it was true."

"Oh, wow. I can't believe that of Zack. He was never one of those guys who played the field."

"Well, maybe he didn't say they were definitely going out. His version was that he'd told her he'd get back to her if he could get away for a drink."

"Okay. That's sort of different. It's not what I'd call a real date. She was just trying to wind you up. So, when did they last date?" Erica waved at a couple as they were leaving.

"One summer when he was in high school and she was visiting here."

"Really? I can't remember her. Of course, I haven't seen her yet. Maybe I should get a look and see if it jogs any memories or anything."

Shelby shrugged. "Oh, I don't know if I want to know anything else about her, especially her past, except if it's tied into the murder."

"Huh. I'll bet he also put two and two together and told you not to do any more sleuthing."

"He started with that."

"Well, you two have been down that path before, although not with the added ingredient of a Rachel. And he could be right. Don't do anything that puts you in danger again. Promise?"

Shelby stifled the unease she suddenly felt.

"Not intentionally, that's for sure."

Chapter Thirty

In the end, Shelby had no idea if Zack was going to follow through or not on plans to see Rachel. Although she did have the feeling that he wouldn't meddle, just as he'd said, so she guessed it was up to her. The questions was, where and when to find Rachel? But did she want to talk to the woman and give her even more of an opportunity to rub Shelby's face in the so-called date?

Shelby did know that she didn't want to try finding her that evening in case she actually ran into her and Zack out together. In fact, Shelby's plan was to lay low as soon as she got home. A nice quiet evening with J.T. on her Bose, and his namesake purring on her lap. Sounded good.

She had been right to dread that the slow start that morning would mean the whole day would be the same way. She was relieved when the phone rang and it was Trudy.

"How is it over there?" Trudy asked right off.

"Slow and slower. What about you?"

"Typical Sunday afternoon. You should consider keeping the same hours on the island—noon to four PM."

"I do like that idea, but I'd better check into it and make sure it's okay with the board. Now, what can I do for you?"

"I've got a glitch with the book club meeting this Thursday and I'm hoping you can help. You remember Mimi? Well, she's ended up in the hospital and probably won't be out by the meeting. Since it was her night to present her choice of book, she's asked if we could give her a spot another time. She'd hate to have all her reading and research go to waste."

"That sounds reasonable, doesn't it?" Shelby asked when Trudy stopped for a breath. She thought of dear, charming Mimi, one of the sisters, the one who loved gossip and ghosts. She hoped it wasn't too serious. Shelby thought Mimi was in her late eighties. At least, that's what she had assumed at an earlier meeting of the Bayside Book Babes Plus One. The club was officially sponsored by the store and organized by Trudy. Shelby had found the four women and one man—the Plus One—to be a delightful group, enjoying gossiping as much as talking about the book. "Why is she in the hospital?"

"Oh, you know what's going around these days—knee problems. She's been on the waiting list for a knee replacement for some time now, and she took a spill yesterday. Nothing else is hurt, but they've decided it's time to replace the knee. Sound familiar?"

"She and Aunt Edie should start a support group."

"Exactly. Anyway, I was thinking, since several of the members were at Savannah Page's signing and bought her book, maybe we could talk about it. And of course, since you had so much to do with her, I'd hoped you would come and tell all. I know the gang would like that. They so enjoyed having you with us last time you came."

"I remember. Knowing them, I'm sure there'll be some questions about her murder, too."

"You can count on it. Juliette and Leonard are going to Buffalo for the weekend and leaving Thursday afternoon, so I suggested we hold the meeting on Tuesday evening, which suits everyone. Would you come?"

Shelby thought about the upcoming week and its lack of evening activities, such as dates. "I'll be happy to. It's at your place again?"

"That's a relief, and yes, it's at my house. Thanks, Shelby. We'll talk before then. I've got a customer. Got to go."

Shelby wished she could say the same thing. But, in the meantime, she was fascinated by the relationship between Juliette and Leonard. It was none of her business, really. She'd have to ask Trudy at some point, just because she could. She liked the idea of there being another mature romance. Maybe that's what she had to look forward to. Just wait a few decades. It wasn't likely to be happening these days.

Matthew wandered in while she was starting to wrap things up for the day.

"How'd it go today?" he asked, leaning against the counter.

"It was really slow this morning and I thought the day would be wasted, but these last two hours have been busy. I think the weather clearing up helped. It seems people aren't quite ready yet to give up seeing the castle."

Matthew chuckled. "I'd bet we'd have visitors all year round if it stayed open. In fact, at one time the board even thought about doing just that and adding some outdoor winter activities. But saner heads prevailed, especially when they couldn't figure out how to get people over here if, and usually when, the river freezes. I'm just as pleased about that."

"How do you get on and off the island if that happens?" She'd never thought about it before. "I guess I never thought about what you do in the winter. You do stay here?"

"Someone has to keep an eye on the place, and I really do enjoy the isolation of it all. I get a lot of work done. And getting off the island isn't a problem once the ice gets to a certain thickness. I use a snowmobile or sometimes even walk."

"Wow, I can't imagine that."

"I'm in good shape, you know." He flexed an arm muscle.

"Oh, I don't doubt it." Shelby chuckled. "But it must take a long time."

He shrugged. "Some days it does. It depends on the ice. If you don't mind my saying, you don't seem your usual chipper self today."

"I'd never thought of myself as ever being chipper. I just hope I haven't driven any customers away before buying, if it's that obvious."

Matthew looked like he was waiting for an explanation.

"Okay, I am a bit down. Zack and I had an argument last night."

"About you snooping again?"

"No, not really." She looked at him a few moments and sighed. "Well, I guess in an oblique way. Rachel Michaels told me that they had dated a while ago, and they're going out this weekend. I think he was miffed when I mentioned it and asked if he'd question her."

"Oh, boy. You actually asked him to question her? Look, I'm not going to give advice to the lovelorn, but I will say that Zack's a stand-up guy. I highly doubt you have to worry about him. And as for trying to get him to do your investigating, you know how he feels about all that."

Oh boy, how did we get into this conversation?

"It's not like there's any commitment or anything," she felt she needed to explain. "He has a right to date whomever he wants, but she is a murder suspect."

"In your mind, maybe. And if the police are thinking the same way, well, you know what I'd say."

"Yes, I do, Matthew, and thank you. By the way, I did have a run-in with her yesterday, which is when she told me. I spotted her going upstairs here and followed her into Joe Cabana's bedroom."

Matthew looked surprised, then suspicious. "That girl doesn't know when to back off. What was she doing in there?"

"She went through his desk, looking for some sort of tie-in to Savannah's murder, or so she said. I suggested she leave, and that's when she enlightened me about her date with Zack."

"Sounds mean-spirited, and I'll bet she made more of it than it really was." He thought a moment. "Maybe I should agree to meet with her after all and try to figure out just what she knows. I might also be able to figure out if she's the one who broke into my place."

"I didn't tell you, but after you said you wouldn't talk to her, she came back and said she'd like to investigate what happened to your wife. I told her you wouldn't have any part of that."

She saw the look of anger flash across Matthew's face and the set of his jaw as he answered. "Did she now? That's definitely not going to happen."

"So, you see, if you try to talk to her and get information out of her, she'd be hammering away at you for what she's after. Besides, even though I like her for the break-in, it would take a lot of resources on her part to do that. Like a boat, for starters. Right?"

"That it would, but I can't think of anyone you've mentioned who's as persistent as she is. You just never know what she might accidently reveal if we met up."

She noted the speculative look in his eyes, even though his jaw seemed to have relaxed.

"Really? I don't know. I think she knows what she wants and goes after it. She's a good talker, after all. What if she keeps focusing on your wife?" Shelby couldn't bring herself to say *murder* to his face.

"In that case, I guess I'm going to have to up my game and be the better talker."

* * *

Shelby stopped by Chocomania as soon as the boat docked and bought a small box of truffles. That would cheer her up.

"You're all smiles," she said to Erica as she handed over some cash.

"I have a dinner date." Erica grinned as she said it.

"With Bryce?"

"Yes, sorry. I know you're feeling down. Do you think it's wise that I date him?"

"For sure. Enjoy, just don't get in too deep." *Sage words, Shelby.*
"I'll be sure to keep that in mind. It's really just for fun. It's nice to be going out for a change, rather than watching my best friend from the sidelines."

Shelby realized Erica was talking about her, and she wondered when she'd acquired that position. It pleased her, though.

She smiled. "Well, enjoy."

She made her escape when Erica was besieged by a group of teens. She waved goodbye as she left. She had been hoping Erica wouldn't ask how she was feeling that night. Not much had changed since the morning.

Going home wouldn't help her mood, but she wasn't sure what would. Maybe some talk about babies would be distracting. She glanced at her watch. Hopefully they wouldn't be eating. She tried giving a quick call to confirm it was okay, but the line was busy. She'd stop in anyway.

She hadn't been to Taylor's before, but had passed the house plenty of times on her walks around town. It took less than ten minutes to walk there. A warm glow from a lamp looked welcoming, even though it was just beginning to get dusky out. In fact, the entire house looked welcoming to Shelby. It was a typical two-story clapboard house from the early fifties, white with navy trim. The windows had been recently updated, most noticeably in the living room in the front of the house. It looked massive, inviting lots of light inside.

She knocked, and Chuck pulled open the door almost immediately. "Shelby, how nice to see you. Taylor will be pleased, but I should warn you, she gets tired easily."

"Okay, I won't stay long. I sure hope I'm not interrupting your meal."

"Not at all. My mom and I are just preparing it, but it's nowhere ready yet. Here, let me take your jacket. Taylor is in the living room, to the left."

Shelby walked in and found Taylor on the couch, feet up, a book resting on her lap. Her hair looked disheveled, like she'd just gotten up from a nap. She glanced up at Shelby and smiled. From the kitchen, Shelby could hear voices. She'd make this a quick visit.

"Sorry to just barge in, but I was at sort of loose ends and thought I'd just pop by and see how you're doing. It would have been just a quick hi if you were eating."

Taylor patted the seat next to her. "Sit. I'm so happy to see you. I'm sort of fed up with being made to feel the invalid. That's why I so want to get out of the house."

"Dare I say, but you are an invalid, sort of." Shelby smiled to soften her words.

Taylor made a face. "Okay, maybe I sort of am, but to me that means being left in peace so that I can indulge in some good books. Say, maybe I could do up some shelf-talkers for you here at home. You know, 'staff recommends' with a few sentences?"

"That sounds like a terrific idea. I don't know why we didn't think of it sooner. You can let me know when you're in need of books, and I can drop them over and pick up the shelf-talkers that are ready. How well stocked are you?"

Taylor pointed to the two books on the coffee table. "Down to my last three. And I'm a fast reader, so I'll be in need real soon. But I hope to be in to work before that point."

"Noted. I'll try to get some over to you." Shelby didn't add, *so you won't go down to the store.* She glanced toward the kitchen and lowered her voice. "How are things going, guest-wise?"

Taylor shrugged. "She's actually being quite helpful, when she isn't dispensing advice. Imagine what she'll be like when the baby is born. I try to tell her that things are different these days. The theories about child rearing have changed. I've been reading up on it. After all, it's been almost forty years since she had Chuck."

"And how is that going over?" Shelby wanted to reach out and give Taylor's hands a reassuring squeeze.

"She nods and looks like she's agreeing but then goes back to the advice giving. Chuck has said she's been asking how long she'll be needed, so that sounds like she's got somewhere else to be, which is hopeful. I had thought she might be gone by the weekend, but my trip to the hospital was really bad timing. Now she thinks she's needed."

"Which she probably is, right?"

Taylor nodded. "Okay, I'll admit, she is a big help, especially in small doses. How are things at the store?" Taylor looked around her, then lowered her voice again. "And with the hunt for the murderer?"

"It was busy today for a change, and as to the second part, nothing definite."

Taylor yawned. "I'm sorry, I am really interested, but it's just that . . ."

"You also get tired quickly. I get it, and I should be going. Oh, by the way," she said as she pulled the truffle box out of her purse, "I thought you deserved a treat. Playing invalid is hard work."

Taylor grinned. "Oh, man, I am looking forward to these. Thanks, Shelby, and please, come back soon."

"You can count on that."

Chapter
Thirty-One

S helby had just pulled open her fridge door to look for some-thing to eat when a knock at her front door startled her. She grabbed her smartphone and tiptoed to the door, keeping out of the line of sight through the windows, trying to covertly peer through the window before opening the door. Zack. Her heart raced and her tongue felt tied in knots. Not a good way to greet him. She took a deep breath, hoping to compose herself, and opened the door.

He stood there looking tentative, which made her feel better immediately. At least he didn't look angry or like he was about to do something drastic, like tell her he wanted to break up whatever it was they had.

"Come in. I didn't expect to see you tonight." She felt her hands shaking as she pulled the door wider.

He walked in and went straight to J.T., who sat on the chair nearest the door, and patted the cat's head. "I was just in the neighborhood, if you'll believe that."

"Uh, in your boat?" She played along and peered outdoors, as if she seriously believed that.

He chuckled. "No, on my feet, and I admit, I came here deliberately. I wasn't happy how we left things last night."

She sighed. "I wasn't either. I guess I overreacted to Rachel Michaels. Dumb, right?"

Zack put his hands on her shoulders. "I think it's flattering. In fact, I'm quite pleased to get some kind of signal from you as to how you feel about me."

"Seriously? We go out, we eat out, we do other things, in and out . . ." She let her voice trail off suggestively.

He gave her a quick kiss on the lips. "I know all that, but there's still this part of you that's holding back. Like I said last spring, when we first started to get to know each other, I got the distinct vibe that you wanted to take it slow. So, that's what I did, but I really have been hoping we're now up to speed and thinking along the same lines."

Please, let me get this right. "I hope we are, too, but sometimes I get nervous."

"Me, too." He took hold of her hand. "We'll work on it together, okay?"

She nodded and leaned into him, her head resting on his shoulder for a moment. "You have an incredible amount of patience," she said, straightening up.

"I also have the strong desire to keep you out of harm's way." He led her to the love seat, and they sat facing each other.

"I have something to tell you. You asked, so I asked. I met Rachel for a drink just before coming here. I tried every which way I could think of to get some information out of her, but she wouldn't go there. It was a very quick drink, because I'm sure I made her uncomfortable. I don't have a clue as to what she'd been hoping to gain by meeting with me, but whatever it was, it didn't happen. As I was walking over here, I remembered that Rachel had relatives in town. I can't remember who, maybe an aunt and uncle. But as I said, I hadn't been really interested in her at the time, so none of the details stuck. But I do remember she had use of a small power boat, so I wouldn't be surprised if she charmed her uncle or someone else she knew back then into lending her a boat for a couple of hours, or maybe she even borrowed it." He placed air quotes around that last bit.

"So, you think she's capable of getting over to the island on her own?"

"Most certainly. Now, I want you to tell me all about the thefts at the castle, and let's try to figure out if that's something she might be involved with."

"I doubt she had anything to do with the stuff that's gone missing from the castle, because none of it, except maybe the plans, seems to be anything more than items that can be hawked or kept. But I did catch her in Joe Cabana's bedroom that day, so she definitely goes right after what she wants."

She glanced at Zack but quickly looked away. "And she was so pushy about getting to meet Matthew, and then upset when he said no, I can definitely imagine her going over and sneaking into his place."

"But why? What would she be after?"

"She wanted to write about his wife's murder, so maybe she was looking for any notes he'd made when he did his investigation. Or maybe she hoped to find some old newspaper clippings, although I don't know if he has any. He's a very private man and I don't like to go prying."

"You've got him pegged. Did he say if anything was missing?"

"He didn't tell me, but maybe you could ask him. You've got a pretty good working relationship with him, don't you, after he helped keep an eye out for smuggling activity in the spring?"

"Yes, but the key there is the working part."

Shelby sighed. "Well, maybe I could ask Aunt Edie, but she might get upset with that."

"Does it even matter if Rachel succeeded? If you let him know she's a possible suspect, that should be enough. Let him take it from there."

"I said as much, and he said he should have a meeting with her after all, but I don't know if he'll do it. Like I said, he's such a private man. Even if he can deflect her questions, I'm sure it would be a real downer for him, bringing up the past."

Zack sat looking at her, but she couldn't read his expression. "What?"

"I like this non-nosy, deeply caring side of Shelby Cox. I like it a lot."

Chapter Thirty-Two

Monday morning Shelby was in a decidedly better mood. Yes, she had to admit to herself that she'd been, and probably still was, a little jealous of Rachel. Even though Zack had convinced her that there was not, nor had there ever been, anything going on and that, in fact, he had tried to get the information Shelby had wanted. Still, it frosted her that Rachel would see right through her feelings and play that low-down card.

But today . . . everything was going to be just great. The sun was shining and she had an upbeat feeling.

She hadn't heard back from Prissy Newmarket, so she assumed they were still on vacation. No brunch today; however, she did have a shopping list from Edie, and that would be her priority after the prerequisite Monday morning cleaning routine.

She managed to get it all done in record time, although she wasn't about to check too closely what kind of job she'd done, especially when it came to the floors. She hadn't given much thought to what having a cat would do to her home. Not the warm, welcoming soft ball of fur, but the shedding part of it. And then there were the sometimes-muddy paws. She glanced at the sleeping furball settled on his chair and smiled. He'd really managed to cuddle his way into her life.

She made a quick lunch of salad and a grilled cheese sandwich and had just finished washing the dishes when Taylor called.

"Hi, Taylor. How are you doing today?" As usual, she felt a bit of apprehension when asking.

"I had a marvelous sleep. No little feet kicking, so I feel rested and raring to go."

"Uh-oh."

Taylor laughed. "Don't worry. I'm still lying low. But there is one thing I want to tell you. I asked Chuck about how the murder investigation was proceeding."

"You didn't."

"Like I said, or maybe I didn't, I need distractions, and he seemed to accept that. So, I don't know how deeply you're involved or what you know, although I'd like to hear all about it one day soon, but I thought I'd fill you in on the latest, according to Chuck."

"Oh, tell me." Shelby caught her breath. What could be happening now?

"Well, you know Savannah's fiancé?"

"Liam Kennelly, yes."

"Chuck says they gave him the okay to leave town a couple of days ago. They'd actually meant to do that sooner, but since he wasn't complaining, they thought they'd double-check all his info. So, he's definitely in the clear. But they do know where to find him if anything changes. So, does this help you in any way?"

"Well, I'd sort of assumed that he was in the clear, since I knew he'd left. But I'm more curious these days about Bryce O'Connell, Savannah's agent. Did Chuck mention him at all?"

"According to Chuck, they're not so sure about him, although if he demanded to leave, they couldn't stop him."

"That's interesting. I wonder what part they're unsure about. Did he happen to say anything about Savannah's laptop?"

"Nada."

"Or did he mention any other suspects by name? Like maybe Jenna Dunlop?"

Taylor took a couple of seconds answering, during which Shelby could hear another voice growing louder, possibly the MIL entering the room. Taylor's voice was muffled, as if she were answering said visitor. Then she got back to Shelby. "No, but it sounds like that's something you want me to be pursuing."

"Perhaps not. He'd get annoyed or suspicious if you asked for too many details, don't you think?"

"I'll figure out a way," Taylor assured her. "Leave it to me. I'll call you if I have anything to report. Final thing, I'll need some reading material by the end of the week."

"I'll be sure to come by with books. We have a pile of new advanced reading copies that came in, so maybe you could cull them for us. Give us your opinion on what to actually buy. How does that sound?"

"Super. I'd love to do that. Can't wait. Thanks, Shelby."

"You're welcome, and it was good to hear from you. Take care."

"You also. Ciao."

Shelby hung up, but her hand remained on the receiver.

And then there was one less suspect. But should Liam really be off the hook?

Chapter Thirty-Three

Shelby had mentally prepared herself for the book club on Tuesday night, or at least she thought she had. Having been blindsided on her last visit by questions about her investigating the murder of Loreena Swan, Shelby had come up with a few noncommittal statements about this new murder. Or maybe she should tell all and see where it led. These people absolutely breathed mysteries, and last time Leonard had directed Shelby to his daughter, a local hairdresser who did have some useful information. It could happen again. She just didn't want them to get so invested in it that they might go out on their own and check on details. Of course, that wouldn't happen. Would it? Nobody did that. *Except me.*

She took a deep breath before she knocked on Trudy's door. It was opened almost immediately by Leonard.

"Oh, Shelby, my dear. We're so glad you could come tonight. Juliette and I just arrived a few minutes before you. Let me take your jacket."

Shelby slipped out of her lightweight Columbia jacket and handed it to him. "Thank you. I sure timed it right."

He gave her a full smile and then ushered her into the living room. Shelby did a quick mental count. Still missing one. Who was it? She tried to remember all the names and was just about to ask when it came to her.

"I see Patricia isn't here yet," she said, accepting a glass of fruit punch from Trudy.

"No, she's not. She phoned to say she's running late, so we'll just start with the snacks and hopefully she'll be here in time for the book talk."

Trudy looked a bit on the harried side, Shelby thought. Not quite as well put together as she usually was. The extra little flip of her gray hair on the left side might have been deliberate, after all. Or maybe it was just a bad hair day. But who was she to say? She thought of her own disordered mop of tangles. Trudy's home looked amazing, as usual, with lots of colorful flowers in various nooks and crannies.

Shelby chose a chair next to Dolly. Although Shelby pegged her to be in her late seventies, early eighties, she had a youthful glow that almost screamed healthy lifestyle gal. It also helped that she had a style of her own. Not the flamboyancy of Edie, but lots of floating tops in pastel colors and casual pants in beige and creams.

"How is your sister?" Shelby asked, raising her voice a little. She'd remembered from the last time that Dolly sometimes forgot to put in her hearing aids. "I understand she's in the hospital."

Dolly patted her hand. "Yes, dear. She has to have a new knee. I miss having her around each day, but I do manage to get over to see her on a daily basis. I hope she'll be home soon, but on the other hand, I'm sort of worried about having the responsibility of her recuperating at home with only me around, you know what I mean?"

"Absolutely. It could be hard on you both. Is there someone else, a family member, who could help out?" Shelby refrained from adding *someone younger*.

Dolly shook her head. "Sadly, we're the only ones left in Alexandria Bay. The younger ones have all moved away, but we do see my niece, our niece, and her husband at least once a year. They run a small business, a cleaning service, so are never able to stay too long. They live in Syracuse, you know."

Shelby saw the sadness in Dolly's eyes and felt at a loss for what to say next. It didn't seem right that as some people aged, they had to face it alone. They were no longer in the middle of the family network. Or so she imagined. She realized that would have applied to Edie, also, before Shelby arrived.

Trudy interrupted her thoughts by passing a dish of sweets to her, asking that she pass it around. Shelby stood and walked over to Juliette. "How about a cookie or a Danish to start the evening?"

"Oh, yes. I see that Trudy must have stopped at Trailbaker's today. My favorite pastries. Do you think I can be a piggy and take one of each?" She looked up at Shelby, a sly smile on her face.

"Definitely. And how are you this evening?" She noted that tonight Juliette wore a decidedly Christmasy green-and-red fascinator, with a sprig of holly poking out at the side. Shelby hoped it was artificial; otherwise it wouldn't survive until the holidays. She'd realized that last time they'd met, it had been obvious that Juliette enjoyed dressing up for any occasion and considered a fascinator to be a fashion must.

Juliette sighed. "I'm feeling stressed out about Christmas already."

That explained the holly. "Why? It's still September."

Leonard chimed in from his seat beside her. "Oh, she usually has all her shopping done by now, but we seem to have been sidetracked this year. Next, she'll be starting to look for new ornaments for the tree and around the house. Juliette loves Christmas, don't you?"

He glanced at Juliette before continuing. "That reminds me, Felicity Foxworth has some of those hand-painted ones with Christmas designs in stock. I saw them when I stopped in there yesterday."

"She does? Thanks for telling me." Juliette's eyes were bright. "That may be a help, having them out so early. You see, Shelby, as Leonard said, I'm a real nut for Christmas and everything that goes with it. I volunteer at the hospital mainly to help put up the decorations."

"That's great, but it doesn't help if you're getting overly stressed." Shelby didn't get it, but realized that this year she'd better get into the spirit of the season. Fortunately, that was a ways off, regardless of what Juliette was planning.

"Just have to start pacing myself, that's all. Of course, I'm involved in so many other activities. If I'd have known I'd be so busy, I would have retired much sooner." She started laughing and was soon joined by the others.

Leonard held his glass up in the air. "To retirement."

"You can see we're quite a feisty group," Dolly said, as Shelby offered her another pastry before setting the plate down on the coffee table.

"I can see that, and I'm totally impressed. You all rock."

That brought on a new round of laughter as Shelby sat back down.

"We're also very mentally astute, so if you need any help with investigating this latest murder, you just let us know," Leonard added.

Shelby almost choked on the sip of punch she'd just taken, although she should have been prepared for the comment. "And just what makes you think I'd interfere in a police investigation, once again?"

"Lucky guess." Dolly spoke first and was joined by the others in another round of laughter. Shelby remembered that book club for these folks was one-third book talk and two-thirds joviality.

When the doorbell rang, Trudy hurried to open it. In a few seconds, both she and Patricia appeared.

"So sorry I'm late, everyone," Patricia said. "Nice to see you again, Shelby. I'd love a glass of punch, Trudy, and oh my, are those Trailbaker treats?" She grabbed a Danish and took a bite. "Oh, yes, I'd recognize this taste anywhere."

She sat on the love seat next to Trudy. "Now, fill me in on what I've missed."

"Not much, really. We were waiting for you before we start in on the book."

"That's nice of you, but I meant, what's the gossip?" She brushed a wisp of hair back from her forehead—a move, Shelby guessed, to draw attention to the latest colors in her hair. This time, she had large swaths of copper and dark-brown streaks highlighting her basically completely gray hair.

Shelby tried to hide a smile. She remembered Patricia now. She was more than a hair model. Gossip must be her middle name. Maybe this was her retirement hobby.

Trudy tried to keep things on track. "Nothing, really. Now, who all has read *Lies and Deaths: The A.R. Smith Story*, written by Savannah Page?"

All hands went up. Patricia spoke first. "Of course we did. We wouldn't be able to set foot in your house again if we hadn't shown up for the signing. We all know that. And of course, never buy a book you don't intend on reading."

Shelby's eyes flew to Trudy, who was smiling.

"I'm glad you all realized that," Trudy said, chuckling. "Now, rather than do a presentation on the book, I've asked Shelby to tell us some things about both signings. She also had supper with Savannah and her fiancé on Friday night, so we'll get to find out a bit about an author at play as well as read her work." She paused. "Her death was a tragedy. Shelby?"

"Right. Again, thanks for inviting me. I really do enjoy your gatherings. So, now, on to Savannah Page. I met her for the first time at the Friday afternoon signing at the main store. As you would have noticed, since you all attended, it was a very busy couple of hours, with Savannah doing a short reading and signing." She took a moment for another sip of punch. As had been the case ever since the murder, Shelby found it unsettling to think back to meeting Savannah. It was much easier just to talk without thinking. She realized that feeling would probably be with her for many months to come.

"That reminds me, Shelby," Juliette interrupted, "how is your aunt? She couldn't be there because of a fall, right?"

Shelby was grateful for the diversion. "That's right, but she's recovering nicely. In fact, she's as keen as ever to get back to work."

"And that lovely Taylor?" Patricia asked. "Just how is she doing these days? I hear she ended up in the hospital. I hope everything is okay with the pregnancy. It would be such a shame if she lost another baby. Of course, she's carried this one much further, so it should be okay, shouldn't it? Not that I've had a baby, so I'm not speaking firsthand here. She's in my prayers. You can tell her that."

Shelby nodded and then spent the next ten minutes filling everyone in on what was happening with the staff and at both stores, not quite what she'd expected to be doing.

"Trudy, I'm told that your daughter Erica is dating the author's agent. Are they getting serious?" Patricia asked.

Trudy looked uncomfortable as she shifted a bit in her seat. "Erica is quite her own woman and doesn't always tell me things like that, but she did say they had been out to dinner."

"Isn't he one of the main suspects?" Patricia continued. "I'm sure you must be worried about her welfare."

"As I said, Erica is an adult and makes her own decisions. I don't, and never would, object to someone she chose to date. Now, as you were saying, Shelby."

Shelby picked up her cue and told them about her dinner out with Savannah and Liam, embellishing a bit on some of the details, nothing important and purely for entertainment. She wrapped up with a comment that almost brought tears to her eyes.

"Those two days of signings were, incredibly, the busiest for the stores in what looks like a long time. And it was such a pleasure meeting Savannah."

Nobody said anything for a few moments, but then Trudy asked for comments about the book itself.

"I have a question for Shelby," Patricia said.

Uh-oh.

"Why did the board allow her to stay overnight in the castle? And, I guess just as importantly, why would she want to? Okay, so that's two questions, but what do you think, Shelby?"

Not a question Trudy had asked for, but Shelby was prepared for this part. "As for why she was allowed, you'll have to ask someone on the board. She said she wanted to stay there for research purposes, to get a feel for the place. Her new book was to have been about Joe Cabana's stay on the island, and his death."

"Do you think she believed in ghosts?" Dolly asked, sounding the most excited Shelby had heard her all night. "I ask only because Mimi will want to know anything that has to do with them, not that I'm a believer."

Shelby hid her smile. "It sounded like she might have."

Patricia leaned forward, pushing her copper-colored bangs away from her eyes. "Your aunt is on the board. What does she say about it?"

"She hasn't been able to go to all the meetings, as you can imagine with her knee." Shelby knew that didn't really answer the question, but she hoped someone else would jump in.

Juliette did. "I heard that Jenna Dunlop was spitting nails at the signing. It had something to do with the new book she's writing. Someone said Savannah had stolen her idea. Is that right?"

Everyone turned to her.

"Where did you hear that?" Patricia demanded.

"Oh, I'm not sure. Someplace around town."

"Jenna Dunlop isn't a real author," Patricia replied. "I've heard she publishes her own books, isn't that right, Trudy?"

"That's not always the way to judge an author. She's just chosen another way to get her work into print. Have you read any of her books?"

"No, I haven't. I didn't realize they were actually available. Do you have them in the store?"

Trudy looked a bit flustered. "Well, no, we don't, but that's a distribution matter."

Shelby wondered what the story was there but thought it could wait for another time.

"I heard she isn't any good," Patricia continued, sounding a bit petulant. Shelby wondered if Patricia liked to be seen as an authority and always needed to be right.

"Consider your source, Patricia. Now, I'm going to put on the kettle. How many for tea or coffee?" Trudy did a quick count and exited into the kitchen.

"You see, Shelby." Patricia picked up without missing a beat. "Many years ago, little Jenna Dunlop was thought to have shoved her rival down the stairs."

"Oh, you're right, Patricia," Juliette jumped in. "I'd forgotten about that. Yes, Mandy Sharp had stolen Hank Knopple away from Jenna. Or so the story went. They were teenagers, in grade twelve, I think. Anyway, they were at a prom in Warren House. That was an old heritage home that was rented out for events, like dances. Jenna made a scene, accusing Mandy right there while the dance was going on. Then they were heard arguing upstairs again, a bit later. The next thing, Mandy apparently let out a blood-curdling scream, and she went tumbling down the stairs. And there were many of them. By the time anyone reached her, she was dead."

Shelby was shocked. "What happened? Did they arrest Jenna?"

"Oh, they took her in for questioning and all, but couldn't make it stick. You see, they were heard arguing, but nobody saw them together those last minutes on the landing at the top of the stairs when Mandy was supposedly pushed. That must have been about twelve years ago or so. Chief Stone did a thorough investigation, from what I remember."

"Or she just fell, right? She could have tripped or something as she was starting down the stairs? Her long dress, maybe, since it was a prom?" Shelby asked.

"Hmph," Patricia answered. "That's what Jenna claimed, and since there was no real proof, she was let off. But it took the town a long time to forget about it."

Apparently, some never did, thought Shelby.

The thought that Jenna might have been angry enough in the past to kill a rival stayed with Shelby all the way home. Of course, it was just as logical that she hadn't done it.

But had she? And would she have again?

Chapter Thirty-Four

It was too important a clue to ignore, Shelby decided as she got ready for work the next morning. She'd be having supper at the Brew House once again, and she'd be armed with more questions for Jenna. But now, she needed to get to the shuttle. She'd been more tired than she'd expected that morning and had allowed herself too much time in bed. When would she learn? What with working six days a week, and recently these extra events, she found it all too easy to give in to exhaustion. She couldn't imagine how Edie did it but was now totally sympathetic to her aunt's role in Bayside Books.

J.T. looked like he needed more sleep, too, and had in fact headed upstairs and back to bed after eating all of his canned food in one go. Shelby took a quick peek at him before leaving. He looked like he was settled for the long haul.

During the shuttle ride, her mind wandered back to what she'd learned about Jenna. Although Shelby had pretty well decided Jenna wasn't a likely killer, maybe she'd been too quick to make that determination. She'd liked her, and maybe that had colored her opinion. She'd have to take a closer look now at what she knew. If only she had some idea of what Chief Stone thought of the possibility of Jenna as the killer.

As she left the shuttle and started up the path to the castle, Shelby noticed Chief Stone crossing the lawn in front of the castle, seemingly checking the greenery along the side with the door leading to the underground entrance to the passageway. Shelby quickened her pace until she reached the corner of the castle's stone wall and took a hesitant look around it.

She was just in time to see the chief disappear down the stairs. She next heard the door being opened and then closed. Shelby was tempted to follow but knew she'd probably be in deep trouble for doing that. For once she would follow that little voice in her head telling her to not do something. The door swung back open almost immediately, and the chief popped her head out before Shelby had time to realize what was happening and hurry off.

"Shelby Cox. Should I even bother to ask what you're doing, or do I go with what I know?" the chief called out.

Shelby knew it was a rhetorical question but moved a step closer so it wouldn't appear like she'd been trying to escape discovery.

"The bigger question is, what are *you* doing?" There, Shelby had dared to ask.

Stone chuckled. "And do you think I'd tell you? Wait there." She secured the door with a lock and slowly walked toward Shelby.

When they were so close to each other that Shelby could hear the chief breathing, Stone said, "I guess I can tell you because it's not really a secret anymore. I was just double-checking the lay of the land inside the door, seeing if what the boys said made sense. And it does, so that means I do believe their latest statement." She paused, waiting. "Aren't you going to ask me what that is?"

Shelby wondered if this was a trap of some sort. Why would the chief be willing to tell her anything? Oh, well. "So, what are they saying happened?"

"Let's go into your store, and you can make me a cup of that delicious coffee."

The chief led the way, with Shelby following close behind. After she'd unlocked the door to the bookstore, Shelby went directly to the back and got the coffee going. She hung up her jacket while waiting for the coffee to brew, then poured them each a cup. She already knew the chief took hers black, the same as Shelby.

"Here you go." Shelby sat on a stool behind the counter while Stone leaned against it.

"They finally confessed. It seems they weren't really pulling a schoolboy prank. They had something more serious on their minds. Since there's a wine cellar at the end of one of the passageways and it's listed on the plan, that's what they were looking for. I'm not sure what put that foolishness in their head, but I guess they heard rumors about it and that some of the bottles must be vintage stock by now."

"You've got to be kidding. What were they going to do with it?"

"Sell it, if it was old enough, or else drink it." She shook her head. "It took one of the dads coming down hard on his kid to

get a confession. But they hadn't really thought it out and weren't smart enough to wonder if there was still some wine down there. Which there isn't. The cellar was cleared out a long time ago."

"So, what about Savannah's murder? Could they have been involved?"

"They hadn't yet put their plan into action, but they were intending to break in on Sunday night. I guess there's a rumor going around about all the valuable wine stored in the wine cellar at the castle, although that's the first I've heard of it. Anyway, they were going to steal some. Now they're not. It was a pretty foolish idea. She put her hat back on. "Your Cody actually said he had trouble believing them, which was why he didn't give up the plan. But they do admit that they broke into the store and took the plan. Charges are pending on that one. Thanks for the coffee, Shelby. I'll be seeing you."

Stone had just about reached the door when Shelby asked, "What about Jenna Dunlop, Chief? Is she still a suspect?"

Stone whirled around. "Now look, just because I shared some information with you, which was already known to others, I'm not giving you permission to keep getting involved in all this. Do we understand each other?"

"Yes, we do. Have a good day, Chief." She was so tempted to ask what had happened with Jenna at that dance, but she knew this wasn't the time to push. Shelby congratulated herself on her smarts.

And she uncrossed her fingers that she'd been holding behind her back.

* * *

Chrissie appeared toward the end of the day and spent a few minutes wandering around, glancing at titles rather than chatting right away. Shelby thought she seemed preoccupied.

"Hey, Chrissie. How was your day?"

Chrissie seemed almost surprised that Shelby had said something. "Oh, fine, I guess."

"It looks like you've got a lot on your mind. Did you find anything more that's gone missing?"

"What? Oh, no." She looked like she'd just come from outside, her hair tousled, her blazer buttoned up to her throat, her hands stuffed in her pockets.

Hmm. "So, is the board going to look into it all?"

"I don't know. I haven't brought it up yet. I've had a lot on my mind." Now she looked like she might burst into tears.

Shelby thought the missing items would be a lot on one's mind, but would that be enough to cause Chrissie to break down? Was there more? "Anything you want to talk about?"

Chrissie flopped into one of the wicker chairs and spoke so softly, Shelby had to walk over to hear. "What was it you said?"

"Carter and I split up."

That took Shelby totally by surprise. She hadn't given the couple a thought in so long. "I'm sorry to hear that. When did it happen?"

"Last weekend. We decided it just wasn't working out between us. We'd postponed the wedding until next year, thinking it didn't seem right so soon after Loreena's passing."

Shelby hadn't even realized a date had been set in the first place, let alone postponed. Of course, she hadn't really known either Chrissie or Carter before his aunt's death. And it was only recently that she and Chrissie had become friendlier. She still found Carter to be standoffish in that entitled way whenever she ran into him in town, which wasn't often. And he didn't seem to visit the castle anymore these days. Shelby thought back to how certain she'd been that he'd murdered his aunt. She realized that should serve as a cautionary tale as she continued to gather information this time around.

Chrissie continued before Shelby could say anything. "But really, the more we thought about it, we realized we were both relieved by the postponement. It was a mutual decision, but you know, I kind of feel a bit down." She looked up at Shelby, who hoped tears weren't about to flow.

"I can imagine it's a hard time for you, regardless of the reason or how it was done. Have you thought about taking a break, going away for a short trip? I don't even know where your family lives. Are they in town?"

"My mom lives in town with her newish husband, and my dad lives in California with his even newer wife."

"What about going out to see him? Are you on good terms with them? It should be good weather out there at this time of year."

"I guess we're on good terms, but I don't think it would help getting away." She sighed and then sat up straight, pushing herself out of the chair. "I have to bury myself in work. That's always been the trick before when something has bothered me."

Surely there hadn't been anything as shattering as this before, Shelby thought but didn't say.

"Would you like to join me for supper tonight? I thought I'd go to the Brew House for a quick bite," Shelby surprised herself by asking. She immediately hoped Chrissie would decline, because that would cramp Shelby's questioning-without-seemingly-questioning Jenna.

Chrissie looked a bit cheerier. "Thanks, Shelby. That's sweet of you, but I'm going to my mom's tonight. I'd like to do that sometime, though. Okay?"

"For sure." Shelby let out a little sigh of relief as Chrissie left.

Shelby debated about going home first but decided to go straight to the pub.

Fortunately, Jenna was working, but she had her back to the door as Shelby walked into the pub. When Jenna turned around holding a tray of drinks, Shelby stood just a couple of feet away.

"While it should be nice to see you, I now get this feeling in the pit of my stomach when you walk in," Jenna said. "No offense, but you do ask a lot of questions."

"I know I do, but this is really important. Can we talk when you're on break? I think you should hear me out, after what I found out last night."

Jenna's eyebrows flew up, and the tray tilted a fraction before she righted it without spilling a drop. "Sure, okay. I'm due one in about half an hour. Grab a table. What do you want to drink?" She looked pointedly at Shelby.

"A glass of tonic water with a lime, please." It was too early to eat, she decided. She'd do that at home.

Jenna nodded and walked around Shelby, who wandered over to a table in the corner. A nice, somewhat quiet spot. Her drink appeared shortly after, and she took her time sipping it until Jenna slid into the chair across from her some twenty minutes later.

"All right, what do you want to ask now?" Jenna asked. She sounded tired and looked even more so.

Shelby decided to go the nice but direct route. "I just wanted to be clear on one thing. Why did you feel it necessary to make a scene at the signing? Savannah was probably well on her way to writing the story. You must have realized that. I know you said you wanted to embarrass her, but you know the people in this town, and didn't you give any thought to the fact that they might be less sympathetic to you?"

Jenna shook her head. "You don't understand what it's like to be a writer. Every idea is your baby."

"Oh, I do understand, believe me. Remember, I was an editor, and I've worked with many authors over the years."

"Yeah, but you've never been a writer, right?"

"You're right, I haven't. And I haven't even done any editing in a while. I'm strictly a bookseller these days. But while I can empathize with you, I can't help but wonder just how far you'd go to get revenge."

"So you do think I killed her, after all I've told you." It wasn't a question. Jenna had crossed her arms across her chest, ready to do battle. Or so it appeared to Shelby.

"Well, somebody did, and Savannah was a stranger in town. So, there's a likelihood it was someone local who did it."

"Yeah, but her agent's here, isn't he? I know because I tried to get an appointment with him, but he turned me down."

That surprised Shelby. "It's not really the right time for that, is it?"

"If not now, when? He's here, I'm here, and that story won't be written at this point. But I could do it since it was my idea in the first place."

They'd gone full circle. Did Jenna have any idea how damning that sounded? Shelby didn't think she could push it any further, though. Now was the time to deal with the rumor.

"I also heard that you had some difficulty with a rival several years back."

Jenna's face went white. "Who told you? They never let you forget, do they? I should have just moved away from here, but this is my home. And I have some very good friends who have stuck by me all along. Without them, well . . ."

Shelby watched Jenna wringing her hands as she took a deep breath. "Nothing was ever proven, and it couldn't be, because I didn't push her. Sure, I was pretty steamed at her that night, but it was my boyfriend who I was really angry with. I didn't push her. I could never do something like that. I had hoped that, after time, the busybodies would stop talking about it. It hurts, you know."

Shelby didn't answer. Jenna's anguish seemed real enough, but could that be a guilty conscience at work all these years? But Chief Stone had believed her, and that would have been a tough sell. Shelby realized she needed to let it go. Jenna wasn't finished talking, though.

"So, tell me," Jenna continued, leaning forward on her arms, which were resting on the table, "since I'm such a skilled murderess, how did I manage to kill Savannah when she was in the castle? It was overnight. How did I get over there?"

"For the sake of argument, you've lived here, what, your whole life? So, you must know someone who would lend you a boat."

"But then I'd have to kill that person to keep him from talking." She smiled like she'd made the winning chess move.

"Or you could have borrowed it, without permission."

Jenna sat up straight in her chair and leaned forward, lowering her voice. "I didn't do it. I didn't take a boat. I didn't go over to the island. I didn't kill her." She looked around the room. "I want to know why you're bugging me about this. The police aren't."

She had a point there. "I guess I just can't let it go. Someone killed Savannah Page, and you had a motive. If you hadn't been so public about it, no one would have known."

And you could have killed her and possibly gotten away with it. That thought presented itself, crystal clear in her brain.

"Can't you try to see my side of this? I felt the only way I could retaliate was to confront her in public. I want to be a real published writer. I want to be someone writing books that people want to read. Ideas are what I need to start out with, and then I have to figure out how to best write the story. I was sure it was a good story; in fact, Savannah confirmed that by stealing it. I'd already invested some time and research into it, and then I had nothing. Can you imagine how that made me feel?"

Jenna was almost pleading by this point. She seemed sincere, and it did make a lot of sense.

Shelby sighed. "All right, I do understand what you're saying, and you're right, I will back off. I'm also sorry for digging up the past, but I had to hear your side. I won't bother you about it again." She stood up and grabbed her purse.

"That would be nice." Jenna reached out to touch Shelby's arm. "I do think it's good of you to try to find her killer, though."

Shelby nodded and walked away. As she reached the door, Jenna hurried over to her. "And I'd really love it if you could see your way to read one of my manuscripts sometime."

Chapter Thirty-Five

S helby was kneeling on the floor of the store on Thursday morning, straightening the bottom row of the mystery section, when the door swung open and Bryce walked in. She couldn't cover her surprise as she stood up and welcomed him.

"I just wanted to have a look at this location," he explained. "And, also, I thought I'd wander around the castle and see why Savannah was so enamored of it. She did seem swept up by the mystique of it all."

"How did you know what she felt about the castle?" Had he just made a slip-up?

"She texted me after the signing here." He walked over to the bay window and peered outside. "It's a dynamite location, that's for sure." He seemed lost in thought.

"As is the entire castle."

"What? Oh, I'm sure. I can see why she wanted to set a book here on the island. Although I have to admit, I wish she hadn't gotten this idea, and then maybe none of this would have happened." He suddenly looked at a bit of a loss. "Sorry, it still seems improbable."

"I totally agree. I didn't know her well or for very long, but she left an impression." Shelby eyed him a moment before continuing, "She wasn't the only author interested in the Joe Cabana story, you know."

"I didn't at the time, but I have heard something like that recently."

"Did you hear that, during the signing at the main store, a local writer made a scene and accused Savannah of stealing her plot?"

He nodded. "I know, Jenna something. She works at that pub. I had lunch there one day last week, and she asked if she could talk to me. She told me about her idea and what she claimed Savannah had done."

"Yes, apparently, according to Jenna, they were both at the same writers' festival several months ago, and, again according to Jenna, she mentioned she was thinking about writing a book about Joe Cabana's death, and then suddenly Savannah is researching the same book."

Bryce shook his head. "Savannah wouldn't have stolen an idea. No way. She had plenty of her own. And I told as much to Jenna."

"When did Savannah first mention this idea to you?"

"I can't remember offhand. I'd have to check my emails, but I won't because I simply don't believe it." He looked determined not to go down that road.

"And I heard you're not even interested in seeing a proposal from Jenna."

"She caught me off guard. Besides, it's too soon."

"All right. There is also another true-crime writer who's been a really loyal fan of Savannah's, who came to the Bay to meet Savannah, and apparently they were going to have coffee together on Friday. Rachel Michaels, the writer, wanted to ask some questions about writing and researching."

"And Savannah agreed?"

"According to Rachel."

"That's unusual for Savannah. She was usually too busy to offer advice or help to upcoming authors. I wonder what the trade-off was?"

"Pardon?"

"Oh, nothing. Forget I said that. What happened with this Rachel?"

"She's still in town doing research. Apparently, she now also wants to write a story about Joe Cabana's death and tie it in to Savannah's."

He shook his head. "Any opportunity. There are lots of authors like that around, unfortunately." He wandered around the store, taking a close look at the various shelves. Just before leaving, he asked, "Do you know where she's staying, by any chance?"

"Rachel? At one of the B and Bs, although she didn't mention the name. She did leave me her email and phone number, though. Why do you ask?"

"Just gathering information. Thanks for letting me look around. I really think you've got a wonderful store here. See you later."

After he'd gone, Shelby thought it was odd that he hadn't followed through and asked for Rachel's phone number after asking about her. She also found it odd that he'd left in a bit of a hurry, but maybe he just felt uncomfortable talking about Savannah.

Maybe.

*   *   *

Shelby saw Bryce again the next day after work, and he was having coffee with Rachel. She took note that they were not in Chocomania, possibly so that Erica wouldn't see them. So, why had the two gotten together? Did it have to do with the conversation she'd had with Bryce the day before? *Of course it does.*

She continued down the street to the convenience store on Market, and after picking up some toothpaste and dental floss, she stopped in at Chocomania. She was surprised to see Bryce inside leaning over the counter and saying something softly to Erica. He sure got around.

Bryce looked over at Shelby and smiled, picking up his mug of coffee and walking over to a table for two.

Shelby had planned on getting a truffle but added a latte to the order. She chatted with Erica for a few minutes, and after Erica had disappeared into the back room, she took her purchase and went over to talk to Bryce.

"Do you mind if I join you?" She didn't wait for an answer. "I notice that you met up with Rachel Michaels, but you turned down Jenna Dunlop." She took a sip of her latte and watched his face.

He nodded. "Guilty on both counts."

"Why Rachel?"

"Because after you'd mentioned her, I looked her up on the Internet and saw that she had some cred. Whereas, when I checked up on Jenna, she did not. I'm not really looking for another self-published author at this point."

Hmm. "So Rachel is good?"

"Oh, I have no idea yet. I tracked her down to where she's staying, at Munro's B&B, and I asked her to send me some pages. I'll make a decision after reading what she sends along. Cold case stories are hot right now, so it would be advantageous to find someone to replace Savannah, although no one could fully do that." He looked so down that Shelby forgave him for her thoughts about his two-timing Erica.

"I have a feeling that she won't be that easy to work with, though," he added with a shrug.

Should she warn him that Rachel, beyond being a challenging client, was also a very real suspect?

Chapter
Thirty-Six

After Bryce left, Shelby took her empty mug back to the counter. But the look on Erica's face surprised her.

"Yikes," Shelby said. "Has business been that slow today?"

Erica gave her a quizzical look.

"You appear to be in a deep funk."

"I guess I am, but it's not about business. In fact, most of the day there's been a lot of activity here. It's only just died down in the past half hour. And then there's been Bryce, and you. So, everything's good."

"No, it's not. I can easily see that. So what gives?"

Erica leaned on the counter, crossing her arms. "It's Bryce. I saw him having coffee with that Rachel person yesterday and then again today."

"How do you know it was her?"

"I asked him, just before you came in." She shrugged. "I guess that's pretty dumb to worry about, since I've only gone out with him a couple of times. It's not like we're dating or anything. After all, it's not like he's going to stick around after the police are through with him."

Shelby stared at her friend. She hadn't realized how far gone her friend was, and with Bryce still a suspect. Not good. "If it helps, he's thinking of taking her on as a client. She's writing true crime, and now that Savannah is gone, I guess he has a spot open, more or less. Don't worry, she's nowhere near his type."

That brought a smile to Erica's face. "Nowhere near? How do you know what his type is?"

"The evidence stands before me. Take a look at yourself. Also, you're the one he's been so intense about, and I'll bet you're the reason he's staying here longer."

"What do you mean by that?"

"I was told he was free to leave town whenever he wanted."

"Seriously? You think he's staying because of me?" Her face beamed.

Shelby nodded, although she suddenly had the thought that it might be because he wanted to keep an eye on the investigation and try to deflect any suspicion from himself. She desperately hoped it wasn't that.

"All right then." Erica finished wiping the counter. "Do you have time for supper at the Mango Lagoon? I just can't stand facing making a meal, and unfortunately, I don't have any plans."

Shelby wondered where Bryce was headed after his coffee but knew it best not to mention that. She already knew that Zack had a stakeout that night, although he wouldn't share any information other than that. She wasn't sure how much longer she could contain her curiosity whenever he fed her tidbits of information about his work. She knew she'd have to work long and hard on that, if the relationship was going someplace serious. But for tonight, she wouldn't think about it.

"Sure, that sounds like fun." She waited while Erica closed up shop; then they walked arm in arm to the popular bistro at the corner.

So, this was where everyone gathered after the stores closed. The place was packed, with only two small tables still empty. They grabbed the one in the far corner and scanned their menus before talking.

"So, tell me, what's new with you and Zack?" Erica asked, pushing her menu to the edge of the table.

"Nothing's new. I haven't seen much of him this week, he's been so busy."

"No new arguments?"

Shelby glanced quickly at Erica, just in time to see the teasing smile on her face, before answering. "None that I know of. I've been very friendly and noncombative whenever we've talked on the phone."

They gave their orders to the server, who appeared fairly quickly, and then got back to the conversation.

"Good girl. You're coming up on your first Christmas in the Bay." Erica rubbed her hands together. "It's always my favorite time of year."

"I like Christmas too, but isn't it a bit early to be thinking about it? Mind you, Juliette at book club had the same thing on her mind. She'd even gone so far as to wear some holly in her fascinator."

"Oh, Juliette and her fascinators. She's a real character, isn't she? And quite the gossip. But it's not early if you're going to get into the spirit of it all. I've been looking at Pinterest and Instagram, trying to find new ideas for decorating Chocomania. You know, the town has a contest every year for the most festive store, and the prize is usually well worth the effort."

"Oh, yeah? Like what?"

"Well, an overnight stay and breakfast for two in one of the jacuzzi suites at the Bonnie Castle Resort." She wiggled her eyebrows. "Know anyone who might enjoy that? And a couple of stores have gift packages. Some passes to some of the summer festivals. Of course, there's my favorite, a specialty coffee a week from Chocomania."

Shelby clapped her hands. "I'd love to win that one. That's very generous of you."

"Not really. The chamber of commerce pays for the prizes and it's great for business, so I'm happy to be involved each year."

"So, I guess you can't win that one, but it's got my name on it, just saying."

"All right, as if I have anything to do with it. I'm actually holding out for the big one. Maybe, if I put in enough planning, it will happen. It wouldn't hurt for you to get started on it, too. I think I know someone who might appreciate some pampering at that hotel."

"Yes, you're right, I would," Shelby answered, refusing to rise to the bait. "But then again, so would Edie."

"Oh, right. Edie. Hmm. I guess being partners, you'd either have to go together . . . or arm wrestle for it." Erica grinned at the thought, while Shelby looked stricken.

Their orders arrived quickly, and they both concentrated on eating for a few minutes. Finally, Erica spoke. "Do you really think it's purely business between Bryce and Rachel?"

Shelby tried to think of something to say that would set Erica's mind at rest once and for all. Nothing came to her. "Yes, I truly do. Rachel is very ambitious, and having an agent has got to be up there on her to-do list. Now, will you get your mind back on track about Christmas?" *Or, she might even try to seduce him to get to that end*, Shelby thought, but quickly tried to erase it from her mind.

Erica grinned and went back to eating. They lingered as long as they could after finishing their meals but decided it wouldn't be right to stay any longer, with a line forming.

As they stepped out onto the sidewalk, Erica unexpectedly handed Shelby a small white paper bag with the Chocomania logo on it.

"What's this?"

"This is for your dessert, and to thank you for making me feel better earlier, and once again just now."

Shelby peered inside, although it was getting darker. "My favorite. Truffles. How did you ever guess?" She gave Erica a quick hug before they parted ways, Erica scooting across the street while Shelby continued straight ahead.

She ate one of the truffles—ginger lime—on the way home while watching the streetlights beaming along the way. She hadn't realized how late it had gotten. She tucked the remaining truffles in her purse and searched for her key, finding it and transferring it to her pocket.

She'd enjoyed having dinner with her best friend. That was a comforting thought. Far better than another evening thinking about murder.

Chapter Thirty-Seven

A s Shelby stepped onto her dock, she heard the sound of footsteps crunching across the parking lot behind her. *Oh, no. Not again.*

She spun around to check who was there, surprised to see Rachel. Again.

"We have to stop meeting like this," she joked, although her heart pounded in her chest. She didn't like to be surprised, especially at night.

"Oh, I agree," Rachel said, moving closer but without any similar playfulness in her voice. She sounded deadly serious.

"What can I do for you, Rachel?" She took a couple of small steps backward.

"Believe me, I only wanted to have another talk with you, but I think we're way past that at this point."

The tone of her voice didn't give any hints as to what was coming next, but Shelby didn't like where this was going. She squared her shoulders and tried to look like she was driving the conversation. "What does that mean?"

"I've tried to avoid this, believe me, Shelby. I like you. I like all booksellers, especially now, when I'll have a publishing contract soon. I had hoped you'd support me, hold a book signing or even the launch, talk me up to all your customers."

"I can do that. You just have to let us know when it's out." Shelby felt unnerved, and the thought crossed her mind that maybe she should call someone. Where was her phone? Why didn't she have Chief Stone on speed dial?

"Oh, I will, and it won't be long now. You know, Bryce O'Connell as good as offered to represent my new book, the one about Matthew Kessler's wife. You see, he wants to help authors."

She obviously didn't know that Shelby had talked to Bryce.

Rachel's smile turned into something more sinister. "But you don't really want to help me, do you? You've made that fairly obvious. Of course, you're only half of Bayside Books, aren't you? Maybe your aunt can help me, if you're not around." She planted her feet, then continued.

"And, to top all that, you wouldn't even connect me with Matthew Kessler. I asked you nicely, but it didn't work, did it? He could have been a big help to my career. What bugs me is that he could even have provided me with the research for this book. I'm sure he has a lot of research and newspaper articles filed away, although I couldn't find it. But now, since you didn't do your bit, I have to rely on my own methods to get that information, and I can. Just as soon as I sign with Bryce O'Connell, I'll be all set."

"You've found an agent. That's great news, Rachel. That should do the trick." Shelby tried to inject as much enthusiasm into her voice as possible rather than giving way to the ominous feeling that had started to grow in the pit of her stomach. "But you know, I did warn you about Matthew, how he guards his privacy."

"That's your story, but I know I can convince him otherwise. But that won't happen with you standing between us. I need him. I need this story. My books haven't been selling too great, but this one would be a big thing. And do you know why? Think of it. Best-selling author, accused of murdering his wife, drops off the radar and then turns up as a caretaker. What's happened over those years with the case? Do the police have any more information? Is Kessler back in the frame, or was he never out of it? And most importantly, why is he hiding out on a small island?"

"He's not hiding out, Rachel. He just doesn't like the attention. Not everyone does." She doubted Rachel could relate to that.

"The word according to Shelby."

The tone of her voice sent shivers down Shelby's back.

"And do you know what else, Shelby? I also know you've been asking questions about me. Do you think I would kill someone, Shelby?" She moved a step closer. "Do you really think that I would kill Savannah, even though she deserved it."

Deserved it? "I don't think that, Rachel. I just want to find out what happened, but I don't know enough about anyone to suggest she or he is a killer."

Shelby noticed a small movement behind Rachel and to the left. It sort of looked like Erica was ducking into the boat shed.

Was it her? At least someone was in there. Could that person tell what was going on? And did he or she have a cell phone to call for help?

"What are you afraid of, Rachel?" Shelby asked a little more loudly. She wanted to signal Erica, or whoever was there, that things were not right here.

"Is this the part where you question me and start recording on your phone? Pull out your cell phone, Shelby."

Shelby realized she might have underestimated Rachel—not her determination but her sanity. She pulled the phone out of her purse and held it up for her to see.

"Good. Now throw it in the water."

Shelby groaned. "Not really? It will get ruined." *And worse might happen to me.*

Rachel pulled her hand out of her pocket and waved a small gun at Shelby. "I'm not kidding."

Shelby felt all the blood drain out of her face. She struggled to keep her voice steady. "No, okay, take it easy. I can see that you have a gun." Could she be heard? She tossed the phone into the river. "There, now what do you want?"

"I wasn't really sure what I would say to you, but I guess things have sort of accelerated now, haven't they? How can I stop at this point? I've said more than I should, and I know you'll be sure to call the police if I let you go. I don't have time for that, and for sure, I'm not going to jail. I have a book to write. This time, no one will take it from me. It's my turn, isn't it? I've already paid my dues."

"What do you mean by that?"

"You think you're so smart, but you don't know anything. Savannah Page may have been a good writer, but she was a fraud. She used other people's ideas and hard work."

"What makes you say that?" Had she been talking to Jenna?

"I know because we were part of the same online critiquing group at one time, and so I reached out to her with a story idea. She was encouraging about it and even offered to read what I had written. I was a fool to send it to her, of course, but she was a famous author. Who would think she'd do something like steal it?"

"What are you saying? Which book are we talking about?" Not another writer wanting to set a story in Blye Castle.

"I hadn't finished it—in fact, I'd written only a few chapters—but I sent my outline and everything. I'd been working really hard researching the story for over a year. I had great hopes for it. And then, there it is, published under Savannah's name."

"Do you mean *Lies and Deaths*? That's the book you were working on? What happened after you sent it to her?"

Rachel nodded. "Oh, she eventually got back to me, all right, but she said it needed a lot more work. She even suggested that I spend more time developing another angle. I trusted her, so that's what I was doing when I saw on Twitter that she'd written the same book and it had just been published. Hindsight is weird, right? I should just have finished it and sent it out to a publisher."

The conversation was beginning to feel very weird to Shelby. She hoped to keep it continuing for a while, at least until she could figure out what to do, or until help arrived. If it actually would.

"What were you planning to do about it?" she asked. "As you said, the book's already been written."

"She agreed to have coffee with me after the signing, which I knew was just a ploy on her part. She must have had some excuse ready. Or maybe a payoff. Money would have been nice."

Rachel waved the gun in Shelby's direction and continued. "Depending on how it went, I planned to either break the story in the *New York Times* or take her to court. Or take the money and run."

Shelby nodded, trying desperately to think of how to distract Rachel and maybe get that gun out of her hand. Hopefully, Erica, if it had been Erica, had phoned Chief Stone by now and she'd be arriving any minute.

"So, since you missed the coffee date, you went to the island to talk to her, right? How did you get into the castle? How did you even get over to the island?"

"As I've already told you, I know this area. When I was a kid, my family would often bring visitors to this area for tours of the castles. I knew about the passages and about the outside entrance. I also knew which room she'd be staying in that night. The volunteers around there like to talk. So, I came in through the underground passages, hoping to sneak into her room and grab her laptop. It would have my chapters and emails, the proof I needed. But she wasn't in her room sleeping. She was wandering around. When I came up the staircase, she was there, and she sure was surprised. Shocked, actually." Rachel allowed a small smile. "We argued, of course, when I accused her. She lost her balance and fell backwards down the stairs. That was it."

Or you pushed her. Chief Stone wondered about the bruising on the body. Did you check to see if she was alive? How could you just step around her body and leave?

"It sounds like an accident," Shelby said instead. "In that case, you should explain everything to the police."

"I'm not that dumb. Why would they believe me? I'm better off just getting away from here."

"You haven't really planned this through."

Shelby saw the puzzled expression on Rachel's face, which disappeared as fast as it had appeared, so she jumped in. "Where would you go, for starters? The police are pretty smart, and they have a lot of resources. They're sure to eventually find out the truth and track you."

"I'm sure I'll figure it out once I tie up the loose ends." The look of confidence was back.

"What do you plan to do with me?" It had to be asked.

Rachel looked at the gun in her hand. "I'm sorry to do this. I hadn't started out to be a murderer." She looked back at Shelby, a smile on her face. "But, in fact, this could be good research."

Shelby started shivering uncontrollably but noticed motion again. It was indeed Erica. She now was moving cautiously from the shed towards the dock, a plank of wood in her hands.

If she hit a crunchy part of the parking lot . . . Shelby started to sing, loudly. She wasn't aware what she was singing, but she kept on going, to cover up any noise.

Rachel stopped advancing and stared at her like she'd gone mad.

That gave Erica a chance to run. Rachel turned toward the noise and Shelby launched at her.

She landed on Rachel as the gun fired. Shelby stayed on top of Rachel, but looked for Erica. *Please let her be okay.* She let out the breath she'd been holding when she saw Erica get to her feet from where she'd ducked, several feet away.

Shelby looked for the gun. It wasn't in Rachel's hand. She spotted it laying on the dock, just a foot or so away.

Rachel saw it too and elbowed Shelby, jostling to push her off. Shelby rolled to her right, stopping herself before she slid off the dock. She hit Rachel in the chest with her bent knee, sending her off-balance and into the river. The splash sounded colossal.

Shelby crawled over to the edge, trying to see if Rachel had stayed afloat and if she'd managed to grab the gun as she fell.

Erica reached Shelby, the plank in one hand and her cell phone in the other. She switched on the flashlight and shone it on the water, finding Rachel, who sputtered while thrashing about. Shelby couldn't see a gun in her hand, but it wasn't on the dock any longer either. Rachel had started swimming toward the shore.

"We can't let her escape," Shelby shouted, pushing herself up and stumbling to the end of the dock. Erica almost bumped into her when she stopped abruptly. "Where did she go?"

Erica shone the light back over the surface of the water and then along the shore. No sign of Rachel. After a second scanning, they saw her pulling herself onto the next dock just as a police car pulled into the lot, siren on and lights flashing. Chief Stone jumped out of the SUV and pointed her gun toward them. Erica directed the light in Rachel's direction, and she watched with Shelby as the chief strode quickly toward the dripping Rachel. When she had the handcuffs securely in place, Stone looked at them and gave a little wave.

Shelby hugged Erica, and they stood like that for several minutes, breathing heavily.

They heard the door of the SUV being opened and shut; then Chief Stone walked their way. "That was a close call, I'd say. Nice work calling me, Erica. And you, Missy Shelby, can't you stay out of trouble?"

"Believe me, Chief, I'll try even harder from now on."

"Huh. Somehow I doubt it. So, what have you got to tell me about this person?"

Erica waved her phone. "I taped it after calling you, Chief. Rachel as good as admitted to killing Savannah. You can take this, but I want it back as soon as possible, okay?"

Shelby asked, "Can I borrow it first?" She peered into the water, shining the beam where she thought her phone might have landed, but it was too murky. Her hands were shaking so hard she had to use them both. With a deep sigh, she finally passed it back to Erica.

"Darn. I'll miss that phone."

Chapter Thirty-Eight

S helby woke to the sound of someone pounding on her front door. She glanced at the bedside clock. Six thirty AM, usually a good time to be getting up, but not so much after the night she'd had. J.T. leaped out of her way as she swung her legs out of bed and grabbed her robe. In bare feet, she hurried downstairs and over to the door, glancing out before opening it. *Zack! Uh-oh.* She'd been hoping to fill him in before he heard about her standoff with Rachel.

He was in the room before she'd finished pulling the door completely open.

"Why didn't you call me last night? I would have come over. What do you think you were doing, anyway? Do you realize that you could have been killed?" He placed his hands on her shoulders and leaned his forehead against hers. "Do you?"

"Yes, I do realize it. I was there." The realization still scared her, and she felt the need to act tough.

He wrapped his arms around her and then quickly released her. "I don't get it, Shelby," he said, pacing around the small room. He also sounded argumentative. "I warned you not to get involved. We've been through this before. You were almost killed a few months ago. Do you have a death wish?"

"Now, just a minute," she said, hugging herself. She missed the brief warmth of his arms. "I tried to not get involved. I really did, but it just kept snowballing. And I wish you wouldn't yell at me."

"I know, I shouldn't. But how else can I get through to you?" He walked back to her and pulled her into his arms again. "I worry about you, you know?"

"I do know, and believe me, I appreciate it," she mumbled into his jacket. She pulled away and started her own pacing. "You worry about me, and Aunt Edie worries about me. That's a lot of responsibility for me." She tried to make light of it. She wasn't sure how to handle it other than to burst into tears, and that wouldn't do. "And I haven't even had my coffee."

She marched over to the counter, pulled out the coffeemaker, and got it started. She grabbed two mugs out of the cupboard while she waited, unwilling to turn around and face Zack. He didn't say anything, but she could hear him sit down at the counter behind her. When the coffee was ready, she turned and slid a mug toward him, then took a slow sip from her own before settling on the stool next to him.

"I am sorry, you know," she finally said after a couple more sips.

"I know, and I am, too. I shouldn't have barged in and gone at you like that. It's just that when Chief Stone called to tell me, I went a bit . . ."

"Out of control?"

The smile of his that she liked so much was back. "Yeah, that about covers it."

"Why would the chief call you, anyway? You told me you weren't involved in the investigation."

"Seriously? You don't think people know how I feel about you, even if you aren't ready to accept it yourself?"

She didn't know how to respond to that, but it was as good an opening as any.

"So, just how do you feel about me?" She was almost afraid to look at him, but she needed to see those eyes.

He put his mug down, reached for hers and also set it on the counter, then took her hands in his.

"I'm nuts about you, Shelby Cox. I probably should have come right out and said it before this, but I know you've been hesitant, so I didn't want to push you. So I won't ask how you feel about me. Not at this moment. But maybe we can discuss it some more over dinner tonight, at my place?"

She nodded, not sure she could speak.

"Good. Now, I'm sorry to run out on you like this, but I have to be in court first thing this morning, so I need to get going. I'll see you at six?"

"I'll be there."

He leaned over and kissed her. She could tell he wanted to say and do more, but he pulled himself away. She was smiling as she got ready for work.

*   *   *

Shelby's day was divided between being interviewed by Chief Stone, who had agreed to do it at the bookstore, and talking on the phone with Edie, reassuring her that she'd not been injured, nor even gotten wet. Then she had to stop at Edie's after work and let her see for herself.

"I don't think my heart can take much more of this, Shelby, you getting yourself in danger." She stood with her hand over her heart, the jangling of her bracelet getting softer.

Shelby smiled and patted Edie's arm. "Your heart is fine, Aunt Edie. It's your knee we're worried about."

"Nice try, but not reassuring." She sighed. "I just wish you wouldn't get mixed up in these things."

After leaving Edie, Shelby hurried home, freshened up, and changed before walking over to Zack's house. She felt a bit anxious as she knocked on the door, but that disappeared as soon as he opened it. He gave her a quick kiss.

"I'm sorry, I'm at the critical stirring-without-stopping spot in the recipe. I've poured a glass of wine for you," he said, pointing to the table.

"Thanks." She shrugged out of her jacket and draped it over a chair. "That smells delicious, whatever it is."

"It's my top-secret sauce, yet another of my specialties."

"I'm even more impressed, although you don't have to do anything more to convince me."

"No?" He turned around and looked at her, suddenly serious.

"No."

He grinned and went back to stirring.

"Can I help?"

"Just make yourself comfortable while I grill you some more about what happened last night."

She groaned, but knew it had to happen. She sat at a stool at the counter. She loved the open kitchen design, much like her own.

"So, what tipped you off to Rachel?" He glanced at her. "Aside from what you've already said about her."

"Huh. I'll admit that, at first, I just found her a bit pushy and annoying, especially after finding her in the castle. But I hadn't connected the dots to accusing her of murder."

"Which didn't really matter, because you stirred things up enough that she felt she had to make a move, namely, to eliminate you."

"True. What I didn't know anything about was Rachel's claim that Savannah had stolen the idea for her latest book. It seems that Savannah had a recent history of stealing ideas. I find it hard to believe, but there it is."

"Who thought crime writing could be so deadly?"

Shelby looked at Zack, but his back was to her. "Anyway, after Savannah's death, Rachel started asking all about Matthew and was so upset when he wouldn't meet her. If you'll remember, I did wonder if she'd been the one who had broken into his house."

"I never forget things, Shelby." He had finished plating the white fish with sauce and roasted potatoes he'd made and set her plate in front of her, pausing to squeeze her shoulder.

Her shoulder tingled where he had touched it. "What surprised me," she went on, "was learning from the chief that Rachel is Frank White's niece."

"She is, and that gave her access to information about the castle, and to a boat."

"How did you know? Have you already heard the story?"

"Chief Stone did share some details with me," he admitted as he sat down across from her.

"Ha. I thought you said you weren't on really good terms with her."

"I can be persuasive." He had come around the counter, taken her hand, and led her over to the table.

"Hmm, I know. So what else did she tell you?"

"Frank White didn't know that Rachel had used his boat to get over to the island, but he did start wondering after the murder, especially since Rachel had asked a lot of questions about where he'd be staying that night, and which room was for the author. Anyway, Frank didn't do anything because she's his sister's daughter." Zack slipped a forkful of the fish into his mouth and seemed pleased with the taste. "What I haven't heard is her motive."

"Rachel said she wanted to steal Savannah's laptop, because she figured the proof that Savannah had stolen her plot was on it, but I don't think she was being rational. Surely Savannah would have erased any emails or information that Rachel had sent. Anyway, they struggled at the top of the stairs, and the fall was an accident."

"Or so she says. You do know she stole the plans from the castle?"

"Why would she do that? According to Rachel, she's seen them before, and also she knows the castle fairly well after all those years of visiting it."

"According to Chief Stone," Zack said, "Rachel found the plans in the suite while she was searching for the laptop and decided they might come in handy."

"Savannah took them to start with? Wow, I didn't see that coming. Why? Maybe to help with her research? But I also find it hard to believe that Savannah might have stolen plots for her books, not once but twice. What are the chances of two writers accusing her of the same thing if it wasn't true?"

Zack shrugged. "Do you really want to know if it's true?"

Shelby thought a moment. "No, I guess not. She's still dead, regardless of what she may or may not have done. The penalty sure wasn't appropriate to the crime."

"And you sang? Seriously?" His face eased from looking grim to amused.

"Who told you that?"

"Chief Stone. It was recorded on Erica's phone, you know. Not a bad voice, but you suck at lyrics." He watched her face like he was memorizing it, then leaned across the table and kissed her.

Later, after coffee and a truffle, Zack led her over to the sofa.

"I know this won't make much difference," he said. "But I hope you've realized how dangerous it can be, trying to investigate a murder. You really do have to give up this sideline of yours."

"Uh-huh." She was finding it hard to concentrate with his hand massaging the back of her neck.

"Have you given any thought to what I said this morning?"

"Uh-huh." She hadn't been able to stop thinking about it all day. "And I have to admit that I'm nuts about you, too."

She'd meant to say more, like how she was still a bit hesitant, no, scared. But he kissed her for a long time, and that was just fine with Shelby.

After Zack had walked her home and they'd shared one final, lingering good-night kiss, she bundled up and went to the top deck, sitting on a chair and staring out toward the river. She felt happy. She felt loved. She felt safe.

This was her home now, and that made her happy, too.

She thought for a moment about what she'd said to Edie.

"Don't worry. This is sleepy Alexandria Bay. What else can happen?"

Acknowledgments

M y sincere thanks go out again to the wonderful crew that has been with me in this wild and wonderful process of writing! Most especially to my editor, Faith Black Ross, and to my agent, Kim Lionetti. I rely on them heavily and they pull me through, as do their various associates at Crooked Lane Books and BookEnds Literary Agency. They help make writing such a pleasurable and satisfying task.

Also, I once again thank my sister, Lee, for her eagle eye and thoughts on each writing project. Many thanks also to Mary Jane Maffini, who I'm following through the WWW—aka the Wonderful World of Writing. It's always such fun to kick around ideas and be an early reader of the books.

Thanks also to the great group of crime and mystery writers I work with every day—the fab gals at Mystery Lovers Kitchen and Killer Character blogs; the members of Capital Crime Writers, Crime Writers of Canada, Sisters in Crime, and Mystery Writers of America; and the lovely, smart, and supportive

Acknowledgements

booksellers on both sides of the border. That goes for librarians, too!

And then there's you, dear reader, who makes this all possible. Thank you for allowing me into your personal libraries, for the reviews, for the recommendations to your friends and reading groups, and for your comments. Let's enjoy the journey!